Even Goats Need Closure

D1636708

Also by the Authors

Esme Dooley

Esme Dooley & the Kirkkomaki Circus

Galileo! Galileo!

Even Goats Need Closure

Jane Donovan and Holly Trechter

Sky Candle Press

Zumbro Falls, Minnesota

EVEN GOATS NEED CLOSURE

Copyright © 2020 by Jane Donovan and Holly Trechter

All Rights Reserved. Published 2020 by Sky Candle Press.
Printed in the United States of America.

This book is a work of fiction. Any resemblance to actual events
or locales or persons, living or dead, is entirely coincidental.
No part of this book may be used or reproduced in any manner
whatsoever without written permission except in the case of
brief quotations embodied in critical articles and reviews.

For information, please address:
Sky Candle Press; Zumbro Falls, MN 55991.

First Edition
ISBN 978-1-939360-10-6
Library of Congress Control Number: 2020915734

To Peggy Gresham

who always pulls herself up
by her bootstraps

Apple Blossoms

Of all the lovely blossoms
That decorate the trees,
And shower down their petals
With every breath of breeze,
There is nothing so sweet or fair to me
As the delicate blooms of the apple tree.

— Hattie Howard

Somewhere in northern Minnesota…

Theo

> i was holding the restroom door open for her because she was using a walker - and she really was a sweet old lady - we'd been talking as we washed our hands. She was the first old person i've been in close contact with in, like, forever! The first since the virus has been over - anyway, as she walked away, i noticed she had toilet paper stuck to the bottom of her shoe. so i stepped on it to try to get it off and i slipped and cut my lip and got blood all over my David Bowie t-shirt !!!!

Lexi

> bummer!! you love that shirt!

Theo

> i know - but the funny thing was the old lady never even saw what happened, she just hobbled away - so i washed the blood off the best i could but it soaked into my shirt and even my bra - and now my lip is swollen as big as a grape

Lexi

> oh no! can you still eat? trying to imagine you not eating

Theo

> very funny - so when i get to the counter where mom was paying for gas, she was sobbing to the clerk, a complete stranger

Theo

> mom didn't even notice my lip because she was crying about how she just lost her husband. why does she keep breaking down to strangers?

Lexi

> not again! Didn't you tell her about that trick to stop crying?

Lexi was talking about this trick I'd found on the internet, which was supposed to cut off the flow of a person's tears. According to this method, if you squeeze your butt-cheeks together while simultaneously rolling your eyeballs towards the ceiling, your tears will stop.

Theo

> OMG Lex, she did try that but she looked like she had Tourette's or was going into a seizure so i had to tell her to stop

Lexi

> your poor Mom

Theo

> i know, she's a mess. she's been having a pretty good day though - actually she hasn't cried since we picked up aunt gally from the airport this morning. i don't want to sound mean but it makes me sooo frustrated when she says she's "lost" dad. she makes it sound like he's some sock in the laundry or that he died - but in reality she knows exactly where he is.

Lexi

> but does she really?

A jumble of thoughts and feelings hit me. I didn't want to think about Dad. Why had I even mentioned him?

Theo

> so i put my arm around Mom and shuffled her back to the car and when aunt gally saw us she thought we'd been attacked in some gas station hold-up. btw, what was your answer to that last question on the quiz?

We were taking this online quiz about how well you know your best friend. But Lexi is not just my best friend—she's also my first cousin. She's like a sister. Anyway, the last question was "Name four things about your BFF that most people don't know."

Lexi

> 1) you describe everyone by comparing them to a movie star
> 2) you're the future steven spielberg - filmmaker extraordinaire
> 3) you got a perfect score on your SAT
> 4) you're sweet 16 and you've never been kissed

Theo

> HA! very funny

I looked at a picture on my phone of Lexi and me. Mom had taken it this morning, right before we left. Lexi had said it was a terrible picture of her, but I didn't think so. You could tell we were related, and people usually thought we were sisters. We share the same dark hair, pretty much the same nose, and the same olive complexion. The only big difference is our eyes. Hers are chocolate brown, and mine are green.

BOOM! A peal of thunder went off so close it made our car shake. I cuddled Poppy, stroking her head. She wasn't one of those dogs that would freak out during a storm, but she did whimper.

The storm was the perfect cover for my loud munching of Cheetos. Though I have to say, eating was a bit painful with my injured lip. Mom didn't know (and would never approve) of the stash of junk food in my backpack. It was a parting-gift from Lexi who believed I was embarking on a new life in a backwoods, redneck wilderness, where old-fashioned general stores would only sell raisins and apples for treats. For the past two weeks, Lexi had been humming the "Dueling Banjos" song from the movie "Deliverance." She was convinced that moving to Minnesota was the *worst* thing imaginable.

Theo

> hey - they had plenty of junk food in that last gas station - so maybe it won't be as bad as you think

Lexi

> don't get your hopes up

Lexi

> btw i just googled the #1 pastime for teenagers in minnesota and it is...wait for it...FISHING! - which is the most redneck thing ever - but think of all the boys you'll meet at your family's fishing resort

Theo

> stop it

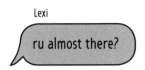

ru almost there?

"Mom, how much longer?" I called from the back seat. Mom and Aunt Gally stopped chatting.

"Maybe five minutes," Mom said, without taking her eyes off the road.

The lights from the car dash dimly lit her face, making her cheekbones look dramatically prominent and accentuating the circles under her eyes. I'd always been secretly proud of how pretty Mom was. I'd thought she looked just like Nicole Kidman, but at the moment, I was having a hard time seeing it. Her blonde hair had a lot more gray, and her blue eyes just didn't have their usual sparkle. Plus, she'd lost so much weight recently.

A wave of protectiveness washed over me. This wasn't the first time I'd felt a reversal of our roles, as if I were the mom, and she was the daughter. It had happened, like, all the time in the past five months. But now that Aunt Gally was here, I was hoping things would get better. Because the thing I'd discovered about being a mom was that it's exhausting.

I was starting to text Lexi back when I realized my phone had died. Shit. I searched through my bags to find my video camera—my pride and joy, the lovely Canon XF400. I wanted to try to get some shots of our first moments in town, although I doubted if I'd get anything good with this weather.

I slouched back against my seat. Well, more like *wedged* back. There was so much stuff in the car I had to fold myself like some origami stork to fit between the mounds of luggage, masses of bags, pillows, backpacks, and even a tent.

And my legs were just killing me. I tried to stretch them, but that was impossible. I'd grown seven inches in the last six months. At this point, I was all elbows and knees, and my hip bones stuck out so far they could be registered as lethal weapons. I felt like Alice in Wonderland, right after she took the bite that made her grow taller and taller and taller.

I watched the rain pummel the windshield. Our wipers scraped back and forth, their cadence matching the rhythm of Mom and Aunt Gally's conversation.

Ever since we'd picked up my aunt from O'Hare this morning, they'd been talking. Aunt Gally was cool. She could be pretty hilarious at times. She looked like Parker Posey, but then again, I compared everyone to movie stars, just like Lexi had teased. Aunt Gally had cut off her brunette dreadlocks since the last time I'd seen her. They were now replaced with a smart bob.

I noticed that Aunt Gally never once mentioned Dad. Instead she and Mom reminisced about childhood memories, plans for our family resort, and pretty much everything Black Beaver Bay. They made their hometown sound like something straight out of a Norman Rockwell painting.

Suddenly, Mom slammed on the brakes.

"Oh, my God!" Aunt Gally cried.

I turned on my camera.

A looming, illuminated billboard stopped us in our tracks.

The sign read, "Welcome to Black Beaver Bay!" Underneath those words, a cartoon cowboy was riding a giant beaver with big buck teeth. Strangely enough, both the cowboy and the orthodontically-challenged beaver had sausage links trailing from their mouths. Across the bottom of the sign was a flowing, red banner that read, "Home of the World-Famous Banger Sausage!"

"Mrs. Banger," Aunt Gally moaned. "How could I have forgotten her?"

"Where's Hank the Beaver? Remember Hank and his welcome sign?" Mom asked her sister.

"That's on the other end of town," said Gally.

"Oh, yeah," Mom recalled. "You're right."

BEEEEEEP! A horn blared, making all of us jump. Poppy barked furiously. A heavy pickup truck aggressively roared by, and a lanky kid leaned out the truck window and threw a beer can. It smashed against our windshield, exploding into white foam that was instantly swept away by the rain and wipers.

We sat in stunned silence.

Finally, Mom said, "Somehow, that wasn't the homecoming I was anticipating."

"How rude!" I said indignantly.

"Well, I *am* stopped in the middle of the road." Mom sounded almost apologetic. She began driving again, and we entered the town.

The first building we passed was a rundown metal shack posing as a bait and tackle shop. The one, lonely street lamp cast a blurry light over a huge pile of wrecked boats. It looked like a junkyard—not the best first impression.

Mom slammed on her brakes again.

"What the…" Aunt Gally began. Her green eyes widened with surprise.

"I, I…" Mom stammered.

I peered out the rain-streaked window. All my images of a Norman Rockwellesque town were completely shattered.

Bathed in pink neon, the lights to "The Eager Beaver Strip Club" pulsated on and off. The windows were covered with silhouettes of nude women. A steady stream of men poured through the front door, where a burly bouncer stood sentinel.

This was absolutely epic! I put my camera right next to the window, hoping the rain wouldn't obliterate everything.

"Theo, don't film this," Mom groaned. "I don't want your Aunt Penelope to see this!"

Well, of course not, I thought. Mom and Aunt Penelope were both professors in Women's Studies. A place like this would be the *last* thing Mom would want her sister-in-law to see.

Aunt Penelope—Lexi's mom—had tried her best to talk us out of moving. She thought Mom should take more time to decide what to do. If Aunty Pen heard about "The Eager Beaver," it would only confirm her belief that we never should have left Oak Park.

"My childhood memories have been vandalized," Aunt Gally said, although she seemed amused. "That used to be the farm implement dealership, Theo. Your mom and I would ride our bikes there to buy strawberry soda."

"Well, *this* certainly wasn't on the Chamber of Commerce site." Now Mom sounded indignant.

"If the resort goes belly-up, we know where we can find some work," Aunt Gally joked.

"That's not funny." Mom sounded annoyed.

"Maybe somebody's lost her sense of humor," my aunt teased.

"Maybe somebody isn't very funny!" Mom replied.

Aunt Gally wasn't ruffled. In fact, she sounded excited when she said, "I wonder what other surprises we'll find."

"Hmph," Mom grumbled, pulling slowly away from the strip club.

We drove down Main Street at a snail's pace. Aunt Gally chattered away, once in a while eliciting a laugh or comment from Mom. We passed a restaurant, some bars, and a gas station—all of them a blur of lights in the rain.

"Stop!" Aunt Gally cried suddenly.

Mom obeyed.

"That's where Mr. Hendrickson used to live." Aunt Gally pointed to a nondescript house nestled between an antique store and a tire shop.

"Who's Mr. Hendrickson?" I asked.

"Please don't tell me he had anything to do with your decision to move back here," said Mom.

"No. Oh, my God, are you kidding me?" Gally sounded a little insulted. "I'm here to resurrect the Cove."

Poppy whined.

"I think she needs to pee," I told them. "Are we there yet?"

"Almost," said Mom. She left Main Street and headed out of town.

"There's Hank the Beaver." Gally pointed to a ten-foot beaver statue that looked like he was carved out of wood. He held a small welcome sign to greet people who arrived in town. "Remember when we used to try to climb to the top of him?" Gally laughed.

As the streetlights faded behind us, Mom turned on her blinker, and we exited the highway onto a narrow, gravel road that was lined on both sides by pine trees. The dark trees crowded right up to the edge of the gravel, as if the forest were trying to reclaim its rightful land.

Finally, our headlights hit an old Arts & Crafts house. Mom stopped. It looked familiar, but then again, I'd seen photographs of this place many times.

"It looks rundown," Aunt Gally said sadly.

I turned my camera to the right, where a weathered sign read "Gillman's Cove." A wooden arrow with the word "Cabins" painted on it hung loose, pointing straight to the ground.

I turned back to the house. A trellised screened-in porch took up much of the front. In the yard, a faded whirligig of a man paddling a canoe whirled furiously in the wind and rain, but the poor man never got anywhere. The only thing I could think of that spun faster than those man's arms were my mom's emotions.

So *this* was the family fishing resort that we were going to turn into a flourishing business.

"Let's hope the electric company turned on the power," Mom said faintly. Slowly, we drove around to the rear of the house, stopping by a wide back porch. Mom turned off the car but kept the headlights on.

Poppy whined urgently.

"We're here!" I told her excitedly. Tucking my video camera inside my coat, I snapped on her leash and excavated myself from the mountains of bags. As I opened the car door, I whacked my head. *"Ouch!"*

The rain was shockingly cold, like freezing needles slashing my cheeks. I could smell the lake's watery, slightly fishy scent. Poppy quickly did her business, and we all hurried to the back porch, shaking the rain off, as best we could.

I wrapped Poppy's leash around my left wrist, and then I pulled my video camera out from my jacket and turned on its light. I was ready to capture our first steps into our new home.

I opened the screen door and reached for the knob of the solid pine door behind it. "You'll need the keys," Mom said, tucking her blonde hair behind her ears before rummaging around in her purse.

But I didn't.

The door practically opened on its own, with a creaking moan.

"Uh-oh," Mom whispered.

Aunt Gally whispered back, "If this were a horror movie, this is the part where everyone in the audience yells, 'don't go in there!'"

"Maybe the electric company forgot to lock up," I said.

"No, they do it all by computer. They don't drive out to the location anymore," said Mom.

"Well, we have Poppy. She can protect us." They peered down at my little Russell Terrier and looked doubtful.

"Let's at least see if the lights work," I said.

"Okay," Mom agreed, "but we'll only go in the kitchen, so if there *is* an intruder, we'll be right by the door…"

Impatient, I went inside.

"Theo," Mom hissed. But a second later, they both followed.

"Hello!" I called out.

Poppy barked.

There was only silence.

Mom found the light switch, flicking it a few times.

But everything remained dark.

Hmm, I thought, the electric company had *really* been hard at work.

As I panned my camera around, the room revealed itself. Dust sheets covered everything except the cupboards and the sink. I sniffed the air, which was laden with dust. Right away, I sneezed.

"Oh, my God!" Aunt Gally cried.

"What?" Mom clutched me, making my camera shake.

"This hasn't changed since Grandma Fay's funeral. It's exactly the same as we left it, twenty-five years ago! He must have never come in here!"

The "he" she was referring to was my great-uncle Dickie. In his will, he had left all his property to Mom and Gally.

Mom mumbled, "We don't know that."

"Let's come back in the morning," said Gally. "We can stay in one of the cabins tonight—at least we could build a fire—and I'll call the power company first thing tomorrow."

Poppy sniffed the air and began to pull me into the adjoining room.

"Theo…" Mom trailed off, sounding exhausted. But Poppy was unstoppable. Growling, she led me into the dining room.

I scanned its interior with my camera. Just like in the kitchen, the furniture was draped in white sheets. Poppy's growl became more sinister.

And then I saw him.

Hanging from the dining room chandelier was a man—a very dead man. My hand shook, as I zoomed in on his face. He was an old white man with white hair and a drooping mustache. His skin gathered in bunches over the rope around his neck. He wore a look of pure exhaustion, with purple smudges beneath his closed eyes. It was as if death had been just too much for him.

Grabbing my shoulder, Mom let out a pitiful, frightened scream.

Then Aunt Gally screamed too. Her green eyes flew wide open with shock. "Oh, my God!" she gasped. "Mr. Hendrickson?"

❀ 3 ❀

"So who is Mr. Hendrickson?" I asked for the third time. But my mouth was full of a Hostess Ho Ho, so maybe they couldn't understand me. I couldn't stop eating! I was absolutely ravenous, and even with my sore lip, I was plowing through my ninth Ho.

We were back in our car, with the heater and headlights on, watching the police, the EMT's, and I don't know who else slip back and forth between the house, and the ambulance, and their squad cars—and I do mean slip. A man in a rain poncho just fell right on his butt, probably because the lawn had turned into a slippery slide. I should be filming this, I thought, but I was too busy nervously eating.

Watching the men in white suits reminded me of the coronavirus, and how we'd been deluged with nightly news reports that showed people in white suits dealing with the deadly infection. It was *not* a good memory. Mom interrupted my morbid thoughts.

"I don't think it looked like Mr. Hendrickson," she murmured. She sat staring straight ahead, watching two men in white suits on the porch. She was compulsively eating Cheetos, one right after another, like she was chain-smoking, except with Cheetos—and honestly, seeing her like this was surreal. I'd never seen her eat junk food. Not in my entire life. So now, witnessing her annihilation of not one, but *four* snack-sized bags was as shocking to me as seeing the corpse—who might (or might not) be named Mr. Hendrickson.

"Oh, it's him alright." Aunt Gally's voice rang with conviction. She took another bite of her Twinkie. We were eating the junk food that Lexi had given me.

I swallowed, cleared my throat, and asked for the fourth time, rather loudly, so I couldn't be ignored, *"Who* is Mr. Hendrickson?"

"He was our high school history teacher," said Mom. "Gally had a mad crush on him. She was absolutely smitten!" Mom pursed her lips together like she always did before she smiled.

13

"We all did!" Aunt Gally's voice sounded nostalgic. "He was a gorgeous man. Roman nose, chiseled cheekbones—just beautiful." She took another bite of her Twinkie before adding, "The single most embarrassing moment of my life happened with him." She burst out laughing.

Mom actually began giggling. Now *that* was a sound I hadn't heard in months. This piqued my curiosity, to say the least.

"Tell me," I begged.

Aunt Gally groaned but then started her story. "Well, it was the night of our Senior Awards banquet, and I had won the Art Scholarship. When I walked across the stage to receive it from Mr. Hendrickson, I tripped—I *knew* I shouldn't have worn those stupid high heels—and Mr. H gallantly held out his arms to save me. Somehow—don't ask me how—my braces got stuck on the zipper of his pants!"

Now, we were all laughing. "Oh, my God, it was horrible!" Gally continued. "I mean, if you could die from shame, well, I would have perished right then and there." She took another bite of her Twinkie and then held it out in front of her, examining it suspiciously. "I thought these things were outlawed."

"They were going to stop making them, but they didn't," said Mom. "What am I doing? Why am I eating these?"

"We're in shock," Gally pronounced. "Why do you think they always have huge spreads at funerals? People need food to fortify themselves through times like these." She took two more *really* big bites.

Mom shuddered. "Why would he hang himself in our house? Why would he—or whoever it is—go through the trouble of breaking into our house to hang himself? Did he know we were coming back?"

No one answered. We watched as two men in white suits wheeled out a gurney with the dead man on top. He was now zipped up in a body bag. This isn't going to be good, I thought. It was way too slippery. And just as I'd half-expected, the man at the foot of the gurney fell, and the body bag tumbled into a mud puddle.

The three of us groaned simultaneously, as if we were spectators at a football game.

Then, to make matters worse, the other man slipped and fell directly on the body bag.

We all groaned again.

As the men in now-muddy suits fought to stand up, they lost their balance again, and then *both* of them came crashing down on the poor, deceased man.

"Please, someone make this stop!" Aunt Gally cried.

"At least he can't feel anything," I said, realizing too late that it probably wasn't appropriate.

"Hey, here comes somebody," I pointed out eagerly. It was a man carrying a flashlight.

"Oh, my God, this night just keeps getting stranger and stranger. Isn't that Pete Hicks?" Aunt Gally said under her breath.

Mom rolled down her window partway. A burst of wind blew in, spitting rain.

"Good evening," he said with a nod. He was a bull-chested man of average height. His hat was covered in plastic that looked like a shower cap. He was a cop.

Poppy exploded with high-pitched barking.

"My name is Deputy Hi…" But he didn't get to finish.

"Pete? I knew it was you!" Aunt Gally cooed, leaning over Mom, and peering up at his face. "It's Gally. Gally Gillman." She stretched her arm as far as she could, managing to get it out the window, so he could shake it.

"Hey there, Gally." He grinned. "And Ana." He nodded, smiling easily at Mom.

"Good to see you," Mom replied. Her voice sounded sincere.

"When I got the news that a Gillman had reported trouble at Gillman's Cove—well, I knew it had to be you. My cousin works for the electric company, and he told me they got a request from you, Ana, to turn on the power out here."

I studied his face. I could see how someone might find him attractive—in that movie-star, Luke-Wilson kind of way. I wondered how he knew my mom.

"I'm afraid I need to get a formal statement from you girls," Deputy Hicks went on.

Hmm, I'd never heard anyone call my mom a girl before.

"Come on in and get out of this rain," Aunt Gally offered.

"There's no room in here!" I blurted.

Deputy Pete panned his light into the back seat. I jerked my hands up in front of my face, to ward off his Gestapo-like searchlight.

"Pete, this is my daughter Theo," Mom introduced me.

"Ah, the next Miss Apple Blossom." He grinned mischievously. I had *no* idea what he was talking about. He turned his attention back to Mom and continued, "I'm afraid it's against protocol for me to take a statement in your car."

"Would you like us to go in the house?" Mom asked.

"Technically, that's a crime scene, so you'll have to stay out—for the time being."

"We were going to stay in one of the cabins anyway. What if we did it there?" Aunt Gally offered.

"That sounds fine. I can sweep it for you and make sure it's safe. Cabin A?"

"Sounds good," said Mom.

"Follow me." Deputy Hicks tapped the hood of our car.

"Pete, wait!" Aunt Gally called out. The deputy swung back to the window. "Was the dead man Mr. Hendrickson?"

His face clouded with uneasiness before he told her, "Yes."

Aunt Gally whispered under her breath, "I knew it."

"But why would Mr. Hendrickson hang himself in our old house?" Mom blurted out.

"He didn't." Deputy Pete's response totally startled me. "Mr. Hendrickson died a week ago. I went to his funeral."

Lexi

did you get any shots with your camera?

Theo

yes! i got at least a couple of seconds that were good - but when mom screamed and grabbed me, she accidentally shook the camera

Lexi

so how did this old teacher really die?

Theo

i guess he died in a car accident - anyway after we gave our statement to deputy pete we had a family powwow in the cabin. mom is having serious doubts about staying. she's like totally freaked out. aunt gally is adamant about staying, and i'm kinda leaning towards staying - it's WAY more interesting here than i thought it would be

It was super early the next morning, and I was back in our car, texting Lexi as my phone charged. Thank God I had found my charger! And before texting Lexi, I had sent a long message to Grandma, telling her everything about our arrival last night. As far as I was concerned, she was the boss of the family. I had no doubt she would know exactly what to do.

Grandma had replied with a cryptic text, telling me to beware of sour apples. I wondered if she had me confused with somebody else. Maybe it was some kind of advice for a recipe.

I glanced over at the cop car that was parked beside our cabin. Deputy Pete had ordered a patrol car and an officer to stay outside for the night, just as a "precaution." I studied the sleeping officer. Some precaution, I thought.

Lexi

besides, if you left, where would you go?

Theo

i know, right!?! going back to oak park won't solve anything. i mean dad is gone, our house is gone, mom's job is gone - at the end of summer you'll be gone. it's like we really have no 'home' to go home to

I opened another Pop Tart, throwing the wrapper on the floor. Our car looked like a hangover at a junk food festival. There had been too much going on last night to clean up after ourselves. With my foot, I pushed the wrappers underneath the seat. Thank God my lip felt much better. Even the swelling was completely gone.

As I texted Lexi, I was also reviewing the footage I'd filmed last night. I kept rewinding to the frames of Mr. Hendrickson's body. I would have to describe his face as "ghoulish."

Lexi

WOW! i've had a lot of crazy thoughts about you moving out to the middle of nowhere, where people's knuckles scrape the ground - and everyone is everyone else's first cousin - but not in my wildest dreams could i have imagined this

Theo

oh - i forgot to tell you about this strip club in town called 'the eager beaver' - i thought mom was going to have a coronary when she saw it last night

Lexi

LOL

Theo

of course my mom doesn't want YOUR mom to know about the strip club - misogynistic treatment of women and all

Lexi

i never tell my mom anything - you know that - besides, i think my mom has become like the most judgmental person EVER!

Theo

i fear my mom has become delusional. she said last night that she imagined coming back here would make everything better - the pain of 'losing' dad would somehow be erased and she'd be giving me the chance to make memories in this idyllic place - i wanted to say excuse me? i may be only 16 but i know what idyllic is and THIS is not idyllic! more like the walking dead !!!!

Poppy started whining. I'd taken her out to pee earlier, but she obviously had to go again. Or maybe she just wanted to get out of the car.

Theo

dog duty - ttyl

Be careful Sally!

Ha! Sally was her nickname for me because when we were little, she thought I looked just like the heroine from "The Nightmare Before Christmas." Ironically, since I've had my growth spurt, I looked even *more* like Sally now.

With my video camera in hand, I snapped the leash on Poppy and carefully unfolded myself from the car, taking care not to bump my head. The problem with going through such a rapid growth spurt is that you forget your true size. Not wanting to wake up the snoozing policeman, I quietly closed our car door.

I filmed a few seconds of the sleeping cop. "This is how your hard-earned tax dollars are put to use," I whispered into the microphone, before I headed into the nearby woods.

The strong smell of pine was awesome—kind of like the Christmas tree lot back home, only so much better. In the pre-dawn light, I could make out a path on the forest floor. I let Poppy lead the way. She sniffed the ground as we went down a natural incline, which shortly opened up to a beautiful vista. This was my first glimpse of the lake.

I had to stop.

The sun was just breaking over the horizon. Orange, pink, and gold streaks smeared the water, looking exactly like an Impressionist painting. A squirrel above me jumped from a pine bough, making tiny droplets of last night's rain spray down in a glittery mist. It was stunning. Ironically, the only word that came to my mind was "idyllic."

I stood there, trying to imagine what Mom and Aunt Gally's childhood had been like. It must have been, like, pretty cool. How could it have been any other way? And why would anyone ever want to leave? A feeling of pride swelled inside of me. This was my family's land—which technically made it my land too. But even as I felt this, I knew it wasn't really mine. Only an audacious person would think one can "own" Mother Nature.

I turned on my camera to catch the sunrise. This place would be a great opening shot for a movie. Actually, this spot would be an incredibly romantic place for sweethearts to kiss. Again, I thought of Lexi. She was totally convinced that once we had the resort up and running, there would be a perpetual revolving door of boys from hearty Nordic stock—tall, strapping young lads—coming and going with their fishing poles, checking into the Cove, and checking *me* out. She predicted I'd be the best-kissed girl in Minnesota by the end of the summer.

The ridiculousness of Lexi's idea made me smile. Her dream of being a writer made her concoct twisted plots and storylines about my life. I wondered what she was imagining now—after I'd told her about the dead body we'd found. No doubt she had me starring in my very own horror story.

Thinking of Mr. Hendrickson's body, I shivered. I picked up Poppy and hugged her to my chest, but that didn't get rid of my goosebumps. Even though it was the beginning of April, it was freezing—although that's not why I was shivering. I kept envisioning the purple smudges under Mr. Hendrickson's eyes. He had looked so sad—almost like he knew someone had dug him up and rudely hung him in our house.

Just then, I heard a mournful cry. It sounded like an animal. Was it a goat? A sheep? A lamb? I didn't know my barnyard animal calls well enough to distinguish between a goat and a lamb. But I thought it might be a goat. It was bleating, and it sounded close.

Suddenly, something touched my shoulder.

❊ 5 ❊

"AAAAIIIIYYYEEEE!" I screamed, whipping around to see who or what had so softly touched me.

It was Aunt Gally. "Jeez Louise." Her mouth twitched with amusement. "I'm sorry, kiddo. I didn't mean to scare you."

My heart was thumping so hard I thought it would burst right out of my chest. I panted, trying to catch my breath.

"Your mom is convinced you've been abducted." She laughed gently. "I told her I'd look for you. We're getting ready to go eat breakfast. Are you hungry?"

"Always."

Twenty minutes later, we were sitting in a slightly sticky booth at the back of Mabel's Cafe, a Black Beaver Bay landmark. Aromas of bacon, pancakes, hash browns, and syrup swirled in the air, and they smelled fabulous! A country-western song was playing in the background. "You never even called me by my name…" floated from the direction of the kitchen.

I couldn't stop staring at the strange decor. Covering the walls were glass boxes that contained real taxidermy beavers, which were dressed in clothes and posed in different scenes. I pulled out my phone and took a picture of the diorama above our booth. It boasted a beaver in a dentist's chair having his front teeth filed by a beaver that was dressed like a dentist. I sent it to Lexi. Then I began filming with my video camera.

"Theo, could we please have one meal without that camera in our faces?" Mom sighed.

I shut it off. Some people just didn't appreciate creative genius. Never mind, I thought. I was already plotting a short documentary with these beavers serving as the narrators. I loved doing voice-overs.

I pried my eyes away from the bizarre taxidermy displays and looked at the plastic menu, wondering if I could order everything. I was ravenous.

"Ready to order?"

I looked up from the menu and did a double take.

Our waitress was a broad-shouldered girl, about my age, wearing an orange waitress outfit with fishnet stockings and oversized work boots. Her white crew cut was heavily spiked, and it somehow complemented the dog collar around her neck. Her tattoos, multiple piercings, and thick eyeliner made her look real badass. Her name tag read, "This place SUCKS."

She was the first teenager I'd seen in Minnesota. I wanted to film her and send it to Lexi to prove that not *everyone* here was a Laura Ingalls clone. In fact, I thought our waitress slightly resembled Kristin Stewart—post "Twilight."

After she took our order and disappeared, Mom started talking business. "Hopefully we can get it up and running by Memorial Day. That gives us almost eight weeks to revamp the cottages…"

"Whoa!" I cut in. "Last night you were, like, ready to bolt! And now you're all gung-ho…"

Aunt Gally interrupted, "She just needed a good night's sleep. Nothing a little sleeping pill couldn't take care of…"

Mom interrupted, "You didn't!!!!!…"

Aunt Gally interrupted in turn, "Well, you were so freaked out last night…"

Mom interrupted again, "We were *all* freaked out last night…"

Aunt Gally interrupted yet again, "And I told her if she didn't try this business, she'd always regret it…"

Mom interrupted yet another time, "I was never going to walk away from this."

I felt like I was watching tennis stars slamming a ball back and forth across a net, and I was glad to see this change of attitude in Mom. There was a tiny glimmer of her old self.

The waitress came with their tea. "Careful, it's hot," she said, setting it perfectly on the red, linoleum-covered table. "Your food will be right up." And then she left.

"Jeez, fast service," Aunt Gally said, impressed.

"Well, they're not exactly crawling with customers." I glanced around the cafe. The only other patron I could see was an old man sitting at the counter, drinking coffee. He wore a furry aviator's hat with flaps over his ears. As I watched him, he took a flask from his pocket and generously poured something into his coffee cup.

"That's because we're so late," said Aunt Gally.

"Late? What do you mean?" I was perplexed. It wasn't even eight o'clock.

"I used to waitress here, and let me tell you, there's quite the morning rush around six o'clock."

Just like that, our food appeared, and my "Trucker's Special" looked incredible—two pieces of country-fried steak with sausage gravy, two eggs, two sausage links, cheesy hash browns, and toast. Mom and Aunt Gally's oatmeal looked anemic in comparison.

"This place SUCKS" made small talk as she refilled our water glasses and placed ketchup in front of me. "Are you guys just passing through town?"

Aunt Gally gave her a friendly smile. "No, we actually grew up here. We've moved back to reopen Gillman's Cove."

"The new and improved Gillman's Cove," added Mom.

The waitress came to life. "Oh, wow," she said enthusiastically. "Then you're the guys that found Mr. Hendrickson's body!"

Mom let out a soft moan.

"I've forgotten how fast news spreads around here." Gally's eyes twinkled, as she stirred her oatmeal.

"Yeah, it was like all over town last night," our waitress confided. "I heard about it at the gas station. The woman that works there, her son is an EMT."

The waitress's gossip seemed to only encourage my aunt, who said, "You seem to know the lay of the land around here. Have you heard anything about who did this?" If my aunt ever tired of being an acclaimed interior decorator, she'd make a bang-up detective.

The waitress leaned in closer to us, her voice very hush-hush. "There's actually been some crazy shit talk about the occult being involved because Archie Brewer's black cat, Mr. Whiskers, went missing last night. And Mrs. O'Shannon's shrine of Mother Mary was destroyed. But some people think that was just because of the storm instead of a group of wandering devil worshipers. I mean, we all know that old bathtub she had propped up around poor Mary has been leaning like the tower of Pisa for years now."

The old man at the counter called out, "Jigger, I need a refill."

"Coming Wally." Our waitress waltzed away.

I dug into my plate of food, relishing every greasy forkful. It was heaven! As I plowed my way through this culinary wonder, I kept examining the strange decor. The opposite wall held a beaver in a martial arts costume, with his leg in a high kick position above his head. Next to him, a beaver in overalls sat at a table, eating a plate of spaghetti. The long noodles swirled around his fork and his prominent front teeth.

Aunt Gally teased me, "Good thing you're young, Theo. That meal is a heart attack on a plate." She tucked a strand of her dark hair behind her ear.

Suddenly, my phone rang. I peeked inside my vest pocket.

"Theo, please…" Mom began.

"It's Grandma," I told her.

Mom and Aunt Gally looked at each other with raised eyebrows.

Mom wondered, "Why would she be calling at *this* time of day?"

Grandma was in Kashmir. I couldn't tell you for sure what the time difference was, but I'm guessing it was a big one.

"Because I texted her this morning, telling her you were having second thoughts." I figured I might as well come clean.

"You did what?" Mom's voice went up an octave, which happened when she got upset. A flush spread across her high cheekbones.

Quickly, I gulped my milk, wiped my mouth on my sleeve, and answered my phone.

"Hey, Grandma!"

"Darling…static…static…static…"

The phone reception was terrible—as if she were halfway around the world. But then again, she was. Finally, I could make out a few words.

"Is Galangal there?" It sounded like she was shouting.

"Galangal, she wants to speak to you." I handed the phone to my aunt. I noticed that both Mom and Aunt Gally rolled their eyes.

(Grandma, who is kind of a big deal in the cooking world, had named both her daughters after spices—Anardana and Galangal. Neither one of them has ever forgiven her.)

"Hi," Aunt Gally said, and then, "What?…I can't hear you… What?…What?" Gally's dark eyebrows bunched together. After a long pause, she said, "Hello? Hello?"

Gally handed me my phone.

"The connection was terrible." She looked a bit puzzled. "I could barely make out what she was saying. I only heard a couple words."

"What?" Mom asked (sounding like her sister).

"Plan that damn funeral."

❄ 6 ❄

"Whose funeral?" I wondered out loud. Were we somehow responsible for planning Mr. Hendrickson's funeral?

We sat at the table, deep in thought.

"Oh, I bet she means Uncle Dickie," Mom guessed.

"I forgot all about him," I said, ashamed. But in my defense, I'd never met the man, and he didn't seem real to me. And now that he was dead—well, technically he wasn't real anymore. I hardly knew anything about him. Except this:

Uncle Dickie was Grandma's brother. The two had some huge, blowout fight years ago, when Dickie had inherited the family resort. Because of this fight, we hadn't been back to Black Beaver Bay in twenty-five years. Grandma had absolutely forbidden it.

I also knew that, strangely enough, she'd paid a man at her brother's poker parties to spy on Uncle Dickie and report back to her. For someone who didn't want anything to do with her brother, she sure wanted to know everything her brother was doing!

When Uncle Dickie died six weeks ago, Grandma—his next of kin—had requested that his body be held until spring, when she'd be back in the country. She told me she wanted to see him one last time, and that she planned to bury him in a bright green Gumby costume.

Aunt Gally took another sip of tea. "I'm sure we would have remembered our sacred duty of burial if we hadn't found Mr. Hendrickson hanging around last night."

"Or if we had *known* Uncle Dickie," Mom added. "Remember, we only met him once, at Grandma Fay's funeral."

"What?" I asked. Somehow I'd imagined he was an ever-present fixture in their childhood.

"He joined the Navy right after he graduated from high school, and he was stationed all over the world. We never saw him," my aunt answered.

Well, that explains a lot, I thought. No wonder they'd forgotten about his funeral. From the sound of it, they didn't know him any better than I did.

As if reading my mind, Mom said, "The only things we know about him are tidbits we heard from your grandmother."

Right then, "This place SUCKS" slipped us our bill. "Thanks a lot you guys, and good luck!" she said cheerfully.

As we rose to leave the booth, I slammed my knees into the table. *"Ouch!"*

While Mom and Aunt Gally went to the bathroom, I moved around the empty restaurant, filming every beaver box. Then I made my way to the front door where a bulletin board hung, covered in flyers. I studied them.

Auction bills dominated most of the space, and there were a number of benefits for people with illnesses. A bright pink poster caught my eye. It was an advertisement for the "Miss Apple Blossom" pageant. Anyone under the age of eighteen qualified. The deadline to sign up was over a month ago.

This jiggled something in my memory. What was it? Oh, yes. Deputy Pete had mentioned this last night. I felt myself blushing, as I realized he must have been making fun of me. I definitely did not fit the profile for a Miss Apple Blossom—not with my mixed heritage. The poster had a photo of a blonde girl—a Barbie look-alike—in a tiara. Someone had taken a black magic marker and drawn horns, crossed eyes, and a mustache on her.

I walked outside. The aroma of Mabel's cafe evaporated as I stepped onto the stick-strewn sidewalk—remnants from last night's storm. I turned and saw our waitress leaning against the cafe wall, eating a carrot and flipping through her phone. I noticed that her cell phone was a newer version than my own.

Again, I felt like filming her. I wanted Lexi to see that communication up here was *not* done by smoke signals or tin cans connected by strings. The waitress lifted her head, and I quickly looked away. I didn't want her to think I was creeping on her, so I went to our car and let out Poppy.

"What a cute dog," the waitress said in a friendly voice.

This was obviously an invitation, so I walked over to her. She bent down to pet Poppy, rubbing her vigorously. "She's a Russell Terrier, isn't she? My grandpa had one of these. They're like the best dogs in the whole world."

Instantly, I liked her. You can tell a lot about a person by the way they treat dogs.

She stood up and flashed me a smile. I noticed her eyes were an interesting shade of blue-green. "So where you guys from?"

"Oak Park." Her quizzical look made me realize that not everyone was aware that Oak Park was the center of the universe. I clarified, "Illinois. By Chicago."

"Oh." She nodded. "Cool. Will you be going to school here?"

"No," I said, kind of sheepishly. "I graduated."

She couldn't hide her surprise. "Really? How old are you?"

"Sixteen. But I was homeschooled, and it can go a lot faster than regular school." I tried my best to downplay the fact that I had already graduated. I didn't want her to think I was some freakishly nerdy book kid who didn't have a life. Even though I kind of am.

"You're so lucky! School here is pretty lame. I have a whole year left." She pulled another carrot from her apron pocket. "Want one?" She offered me a carrot.

I shook my head no.

"I'm starving!" she said emphatically. "You have no idea how hard it is to serve that food and not be able to eat it! I used to love the Trucker's Special! It took everything I *had* not to snitch a sausage link from your plate." She chomped on her carrot more vigorously.

"But I've been on this diet," she explained. "And I can't eat the Special anymore because I've got to lose weight!" She said it so dramatically that I couldn't help but smile. There was something endearing about her forthrightness.

Truthfully, I told her, "I don't think you need to lose weight."

"You should have seen me twenty-five pounds ago," she said with a laugh. She finished her carrot. "I only have seven more pounds to go to reach my goal weight!"

A voice from inside yelled, "Jigger!"

"I gotta go." She smiled at me, and I wished I could have kept talking to her. My thoughts must have shown on my face. "Hey, do you have your phone on you?" she asked affably. "I should give you my number. I can show you around town."

"That would be cool!" I told her. We exchanged phones and typed in our contact info.

She chuckled. "I forgot to ask you your name."

"I'm Theo."

"Well, Theo, I'm Jigger. I'll give you a call." She hurried back inside Mabel's.

After leaving the cafe, we drove all around town. It looked so different than it had last night during the storm. I kept telling Mom to stop, so I could get some clear shots with my camera. Mom and Aunt Gally seemed mostly critical of the changes that had taken place during their absence, and they really got excited if a house or building was exactly as they'd remembered. I noticed that Mom did *not* drive by the strip club.

Their memories didn't seem to match, though. Mom recalled things one way, and Gally another. The only thing they totally agreed on was that Hank the Beaver looked exactly the same.

They were perplexed when they discovered an entirely new housing development with brown, vinyl-sided houses littered everywhere. I wondered how anyone could tell which house was theirs because they all looked identical. I felt a stab of homesickness, thinking about our Queen Anne house that we'd just sold in Oak Park.

When we came upon the place that used to be their beloved pizza hangout, I thought they would absolutely start wailing. It had been replaced by a Subway. Just then, my phone rang. "It's Grandma again. Maybe she found a spot with better reception."

"She probably galloped up to the top of a mountain on a yak," muttered Gally. In her next breath, she asked, "Can yaks gallop?"

"Hey, Grandma!" I greeted her.

"Darling, what's wrong with your mother and aunt?" There were many things I could say to that, but I knew she was just asking a rhetorical question. "Why in the hell don't they carry their phones? Put your mother on immediately!"

I handed my phone to Mom.

"She's coming through loud and clear now." I smiled. Mom pulled over to the curb, and Gally and I listened curiously to one side of the conversation.

"Hi," she said, followed by *"What?* That's illegal......... What!.........No.........Wait.........Okay........."

Mom began rubbing her forehead before she even hung up the phone.

"What!?!" Aunt Gally and I asked.

"She just received a call from the coroner. Uncle Dickie didn't die of a heart attack." Mom shook her head in disbelief. "He was poisoned!"

❀ 7 ❀

Twenty minutes later, we were rummaging around cabin B (better known as Uncle Dickie's cabin). Grandma had ordered us to get there before the police arrived. She was sure that once the cops were informed of the autopsy results, they would be snooping around.

"What exactly are we supposed to be looking for?" Aunt Gally asked for the third time.

"Anything incriminating," Mom answered for the third time.

His cabin was much nicer than the one we'd slept in last night— and sooo much more interesting.

Photographs and newspaper clippings filled his walls, along with kitschy wooden plaques with sayings like, "Teach a man to fish, and he'll play with his fly all day." I zoomed in on a particular plaque that read, "If I'm missin' I'm probably fishin'" Unfortunately for him, this wasn't true.

A framed newspaper clipping of a plaid-clad man, beaming with joy, made me stop. He was being hugged by a human-sized creature in a beaver costume. The caption read, "Dickie Gillman wins again!" His resemblance to Grandma was mind-blowing. I'd always thought Grandma was a doppelganger for Judi Dench. Somehow her brother looked just like Judi too.

I zoomed in with my camera, studying his face. Suddenly, he became very real to me. I wished I had known him.

"Where did Uncle Dickie have his heart attack?" I asked, before correcting myself. "I mean, where did he die?" According to Grandma's rambling phone call, it was cyanide that had actually killed him.

Aunt Gally joined me, studying the wall of photos. "Your grandma said he died in town, during Beaver Days, while defending his wood chucking title." She leaned close to a photograph.

"He held that title for years," Mom said over her shoulder. She was searching through his closet.

32

"I remember that contest." Aunt Gally laughed. "It was called, 'How Much Wood Could A Woodchuck Chuck If A Woodchuck Were A Beaver!' People would throw logs, or 'chuck' as fast as they could. The person with the biggest woodpile would win."

"Like, seriously?" I winced. "He died chucking wood?"

Aunt Gally nodded.

I thought it seemed an ignoble way to go. How sad to die while imitating a beaver.

"Your grandma said, 'Thank God he died in public.' Otherwise the police would have snooped all over this cabin," Mom called from the kitchen.

"And why would that be so bad?" I wondered out loud.

Both Mom and Aunt Gally laughed.

"Surely you know about your grandma's inherent distrust of authority. After she was arrested in Bangkok—well, she claimed to have proof of police corruption." Mom was now looking under the sink. "This morning, she called the cops in this town a bunch of bumbling Barney Fifes."

"Who is Barney Fife?" I asked.

"Oh, he was this lovable but incompetent cop from an old TV show," Mom explained.

I thought of the snoozing policeman I had filmed earlier. Grandma could possibly have a very valid point.

"Anyway, she doesn't want anything incriminating or shady about Uncle Dickie's life to fall into the wrong hands and make us the talk of the town," Mom finished.

"Too late for that," said Aunt Gally. "Especially after last night and Mr. Hendrickson."

"She actually bribed the coroner to notify her before he gives the police his results." Mom shook her head in amazement. "She said it was as easy as taking candy from a baby, and that the coroner fell all over himself to please her because he was one of her old flames."

"And just how many old flames does she have?" Aunt Gally's eyes sparkled.

Hmm, I thought. Was Grandma trying to protect her deceased brother's reputation, or her own? From everything *I'd* seen, he looked like a really nice old man. What could Grandma be worried about?

A long workbench stood beneath a double window with a panoramic view of the lake. Bits of fur, feathers, pliers, scissors, string, and wax were strewn across the top of the bench. A coffee cup that read, "I'd rather be fishing" sat by a pair of spectacles. It looked as if he had just stepped out and would be back any second. Thinking about it made me sad.

"What did he make?" I asked.

Mom and Aunt Gally said simultaneously, "Fishing flies."

I continued to film his workbench, and then I began to open its drawers.

"Theo, could you put that camera down and help us look?" Mom sounded flustered.

"I *am* looking," I told her. "Through my lens."

"Your grandmother wants us to get to the bottom of his poisoning. She thinks we have a better chance of figuring it out than the cops." Now Mom was searching under the couch cushions.

As went through the workbench drawers, I wondered about Grandma's long-standing love-hate relationship with her brother. How did she feel when she found out he'd been murdered? Did any of her anger towards him disappear? Then I thought about my dad. How would I feel if I found out *he* had been murdered?

The last drawer I opened was shallower than the others. I'd seen *way* too many black-and-white noir movies to not know what *that* meant. Taking out all the contents, I found a half-circle cut into the edge of a layer that was a false bottom. I lifted the layer, revealing a large manila envelope! Peeking inside, I found dozens of small envelopes.

I dumped them out on the floor. The name "Dickie" was scrawled across their fronts, and none of them had postal markings. Cautiously, I opened one. It was a love letter!

"Hey, I might have found something here," I called out. Mom and Aunt Gally were immediately kneeling beside me.

After scanning a few lines, Aunt Gally exclaimed, "Wow!"

I skipped to the end of the letter to see the signature. It was simply signed "A." That didn't give us much to go on.

"We'll take them with us," Mom said, scooping them up and putting them back into the manila envelope. "They might be relevant. Good job, Theo!" She ruffled the top of my head, which she hadn't done in ages. It probably helped that I was kneeling. Now that I was taller than she was, she really *couldn't* do it anymore.

"I think we looked things over pretty well," Aunt Gally concluded.

"Let's just give it one more go." Mom seemed energized by this whole search. She'd swept her blondish hair into a ponytail and had rolled up her sleeves.

Stepping towards the mantle, I tripped on the oval, braided rug. I fell, hitting my knee on the coffee table and landing flat on the floor before the fireplace. *"Ouch!"*

But I saved my camera.

"You okay?" Mom asked absent-mindedly.

"Yeah," I mumbled. Everyone was so used to me tripping and falling and bumping into things that this was par for course. As I rose from the ground, I noticed burnt paper in the fireplace—paper with writing on it. Here again, my countless hours of watching old movies made me curious.

I grabbed the largest piece of paper from the long-dead fire. It looked like a remnant of a legal document.

"Hey, what's this?" I asked.

Mom and Aunt Gally were on me like flies on a half-eaten sucker. The word "Agreement" could clearly be made out.

"Is there more?" Aunt Gally asked. She got down on her hands and knees and sifted gently through the charred remains.

"Here's something," she said, excited. She had found a scrap with the date "January 21st."

That's when we heard the distinct crunch of gravel. A car had pulled up in front of the cabin. It was Deputy Pete. Poppy ran to the door, barking.

Looking guilty, Gally whispered, "Jeez, why does it feel like we're doing something illegal?"

Because we kind of were, I thought. We were removing potential evidence from a potential investigation.

"Quick, anything else in the fireplace?" Mom asked.

"No," Gally said, standing up. She brushed ashes off her hands.

Mom put the charred remains of the document in the manila envelope that held the love letters. Then she slipped the envelope inside my vest and said, "You two leave. Let me do the talking."

8

Dust motes swirled through the air, as Aunt Gally and I whipped the covers off the furniture and opened the curtains. Couches, tables, rocking chairs, ottomans, oil paintings, buffets, standing lamps, bookcases, and pretty much *everything* in the house had been meticulously covered with white sheets. The newly unearthed furniture was seeing sunshine for the first time in more than twenty-five years.

Aunt Gally's delight was obvious. Her laughter filled the house as she kept discovering treasures from her childhood. "Oh, I remember this," she joyfully repeated with every new find. She reminded me of a child on Christmas morning—albeit one who was opening presents from her past. And I was the dutiful parent, videotaping her happiness.

I wished Mom were here because I knew she would enjoy this. Could she still be talking to Deputy Pete? And if so, just *what* were they talking about? Uncle Dickie? Mr. Hendrickson? Something else?

When we'd left them at the cabin, the deputy had told us that the main house was no longer a crime scene, and we could go ahead and move in. He told us the grave robbers had only been in two rooms—the kitchen and the dining room. The forensics team could tell by the footprints left in the dust that all the other rooms had been undisturbed. Unfortunately, the perpetrators had worn some covering over their shoes, so no shoe treads were available.

Aunt Gally and I had left quickly, as Mom had asked us to do. But it had been *way* over an hour now, and I was experiencing one of those annoyingly nagging feelings.

"Did Mom and Pete ever date, like in high school?" I asked my aunt while we worked in the library. What if Mom *liked* him? Then I thought, OMG, what if she *married* him? The last thing I wanted was a stepfather.

"Oh, God, no." She blew some dust off a gilt-edged book. "He worked at the Cove, mowing lawns and helping with boats and stuff.

He followed her around like a lost puppy dog, but your mom never paid any attention to him. Poor Pete."

This news did not make me feel any better. I uncovered a fainting couch, and Poppy bit down on one end of the sheet, wanting to play tug of war. Throwing the whole sheet over her, I burst out laughing when she wriggled her way out.

The electricity had been turned on, and the furnace was working hard, churning out heat. The house was coming to life, and the more we uncovered, the more cheerful it became. You never would have guessed what we'd seen here last night. Even the light fixture in the dining room looked normal—not sagging or bent from the weight it had previously held.

When we went upstairs, the first door we opened led to an old-fashioned bedroom. Aunt Gally let out a small gasp and whispered, "Grandma Fay."

As she tenderly opened the floral curtains, tears came to her eyes. Gently, she removed the white sheet that covered the bed, revealing a colorful quilt below. Sitting down on the quilt, she ran her hand lovingly over the stitching, and then she smelled the embroidered pillowcase.

"I wish you could have known her," she said softly. "She was just a wonderful, wonderful person."

"That's what Mom always says." I turned off my camera.

"It's been decades, and I still miss her." She wiped her eyes.

Grandma Fay was Grandma's mom. Technically, this was Grandma Fay's house. But since Grandma had been raised here, and then Mom and Aunt Gally had been raised here, several generations had viewed it as their home. Maybe a house was like "The Velveteen Rabbit." It has to be truly loved before it turns into a real home.

Removing a sheet from the dresser uncovered framed photographs. Black-and-white pictures of children stood proudly on top of the bureau. I pointed at them. "Who are they?"

"That's Grandma and Uncle Dickie when they were little." Aunt Gally lifted a frame and studied it. Two little kids—wrapped to within one inch of their lives in scarves, hats, and mittens—sat on a wooden sled. Uncle Dickie's head rested lovingly on Grandma's shoulder.

"What ever happened between those two?" I asked.

"It's complicated." She continued to look at the photo. "When Grandma Fay died, our mother was on her third—no fourth—husband. That really rich Russian." She frowned. "I guess Grandma Fay thought her daughter was so wealthy she wouldn't have to worry about money. So she left everything to Uncle Dickie."

"And he never got married?"

"I think growing up with your grandma was enough to put him off women for the rest of his life." She laughed, which made me laugh too. Although it *did* make me even more curious to read those love letters we'd found in his cabin.

We left the bedroom and made our way into another one.

"Oh, my God!" Aunt Gally's mood changed immediately. "It's a time capsule!" I turned on my camera and filmed her reaction.

This bedroom was from a completely different era than Grandma Fay's. Posters of Prince, Billy Idol, Adam Ant, Bruce Springsteen, and more nearly covered all the lime-green walls. Beaded curtains hung at the windows. Gally pulled off the sheet that was draped over the bed, exposing a brightly flowered comforter. She plopped down, making the bedsprings squeak.

"This was my room," she said happily. Jumping up, she whipped a sheet off the bookcase, where a record player and records waited. "I bet these would be worth something now. Vintage vinyl is hot."

"Where is Mom's bedroom?" I asked.

She led me across the hall and opened a door. After removing the sheets and opening the curtains, we stood back and viewed the room. Bookcases took up much of the wall space, except for a narrow bed, which was covered in a brown comforter and tucked in the corner. A desk and chair stood beneath the window. The only thing that was on the wall was a framed photograph of Sandra Day O'Connor. It was, well, boring.

I sat at the desk, trying to imagine Mom as a teenager, quietly studying, being super earnest and all. She'd always tried so hard in life to do the right thing—to be the responsible daughter, wife, teacher, and mother. "Poor Mom." I sighed.

Aunt Gally sat on the bed. We looked at each other. "Your mom is going through a really hard time right now," she started. Oh, no, I didn't want this to turn into "the talk." Every well-meaning adult I knew had taken me aside this spring, placed their hands on my shoulders—well, some of them couldn't reach my shoulders—and told me that everything would be okay. It just takes time and blah, blah, blah.

"She's grieving," Gally said simply.

"I know," I answered, a bit too sharply. "I did the grocery shopping and the cooking, took the meals to her bed, got her more Kleenex, paid the online bills, hired the movers, did the laundry—you don't have to tell me. She had like a complete breakdown."

"Well, that totally sucks." Her bluntness made me laugh. Which was a good thing because I could feel a lump growing in my throat.

"I'm so sorry I was out of the country." She paused, looking out the window. "When bad things happen in life," she continued slowly, "it derails you. All your plans come to a screeching halt."

And she would know. Her husband died in a car crash three days after their wedding. But that was decades ago. It was clear that my aunt had figured out how to move on.

"When this happens," she said, "you need a little time to nurse the heartache. But it's not good to dwell too long. Eventually you have to pick yourself up, dust yourself off, put on your big girl panties, and keep going. Now that I'm here, hopefully I can help your mom get back on track."

I nodded.

"But you need closure too," she said gently. I wished she hadn't said that. I could feel tears beginning to burn my eyes. "So how can I help you?"

I wiped my eyes, mad at myself. "Well, I really want to get my driver's license. I have my permit, but like you said, everything came to a screeching halt."

"That's easy." She smiled. "And what about school? Have you decided where you want to go?"

I shook my head. "Mom talked me into taking a year off. She's become like overly clingy and doesn't even want to *think* about me leaving for college, because then she'll be all alone."

"She won't be alone." Gally smiled confidently. "What else can I do?"

"Can you make me stop growing?" I joked, wiping my nose.

"Are you kidding me? I'd kill to be as tall as you! You're so gorgeous! The prettiest Gillman yet!"

Her nice words (even if they weren't true) completely did me in, and I started crying. Aunt Gally came over and gave me a huge hug. All I thought was OMG I'm turning into Mom. I tried squeezing my butt-cheeks together and rolling my eyeballs towards the ceiling, but it didn't work.

Aunt Gally broke off the hug and pulled me up from the desk chair. "Come on," she said. "I have just the cure."

Holding me by my hand, she dragged me back into her bedroom. There, she flipped through her records and selected an album, which she put on her old turntable. "Let's hope this still works." She crossed her fingers and placed the needle onto the record. Scratchy static filled the room, as she cranked up the volume.

She hopped up on her bed, pretending she held a microphone. Suddenly, the room swelled with the opening notes of Prince's "Let's Go Crazy."

"Dearly beloved, we have gathered here today to get through this thing called life!"

I couldn't resist, so I hopped up to join her. I knew the words as well as she did. We sang our hearts out, jumping, dancing, and laughing—until the bedframe gave out and smashed to the floor, which made us laugh even harder.

Finally, she got up and turned the record player off. The house felt thick with silence. We panted, trying to catch our breath. That's when we heard the crunch of car tires on the gravel outside, so we hurried to the window. I thought I'd see Mom's car, but instead, a long stretch limousine gleamed below us.

The driver exited his side and came around to open the door. An extremely large woman, well over six feet tall, stepped out of the limo. She was dressed in a satin, flaming red cowboy suit, trimmed with white fringe. Donning a white Stetson hat that added a foot to her stature, she snapped her fingers at her driver. He ran to the trunk, where he retrieved a gigantic gift basket.

"Oh, my God," Aunt Gally whispered, "It's Mrs. Banger!"

❀ 9 ❀

"Who's Mrs. Banger?" Somehow, she looked familiar.

Then it hit me. She was dressed like the cowboy on that welcome sign we'd seen last night—the sign for the Banger Sausage Company.

"Someone I hoped I'd never see again," Aunt Gally groaned. "Let's not answer the door."

Frozen, we stood silently upstairs and listened. We heard her knock once.

"Why is she so bad?" I whispered.

"Remember that old TV show, "Bewitched"?

"Of course." I mean, who hasn't watched "Nick at Nite"?

We heard a second knock.

"Do you remember that snoopy neighbor, Mrs. Kravitz?"

"No."

We heard a third knock.

"Well, Mrs. Banger makes Gladys Kravitz look like Mother Teresa."

We heard a fourth knock, and then there was silence.

"Maybe she went away," my aunt whispered hopefully.

"Hello?" a voice boomed through the house.

"Let's get this over with," Gally said, resigned. We hurried down the stairs.

In the kitchen, the giant cowgirl stood shamelessly, acting as if she had all the right in the world to trespass. She'd placed the overflowing gift basket on the table and was snooping around.

Then she saw us.

"Welcome home!" she cried, lassoing Aunt Gally into an awkward embrace, squeezing her in a death grip before holding her at arm's length and looking her up and down.

43

"Praise the Lord, you haven't changed one iota since your Grandma Fay's funeral," she boomed. "And how is your love life? Any new husbands? I hear our Ana up and married herself a foreigner!"

At first this confused me. Mom married a foreigner? Then I realized Mrs. Banger was talking about Dad. I wondered how Dad would have taken this comment. Because even though he was born in India, an American couple had adopted him when he was two. Raised on Froot Loops, Bugs Bunny, and "The Dukes of Hazard," he felt he was as American as anyone else.

Without waiting for an answer, Mrs. Banger plowed on, "And who do we have here?" She turned her gaze on me. Her gray eyes held a hardness that couldn't be disguised by her jovial manner.

"This is Ana's daughter, Theo," Aunt Gally wheezed, recovering from the bear-like hug. "Theo, this is Mrs. Banger."

Mrs. Banger's mouth spread into a thin-lipped smile. She reminded me of Kathy Bates in "Misery"—if you added a foot to Kathy and maybe a hundred pounds.

"Welcome to Black Beaver Bay." Mrs. Banger spread her arms. I thought she was going to hug me too, so I took a few steps back. To my relief, she totally changed gears and asked "And where is Ana?"

Now that was a good question, I thought.

"At one of the cabins," said Gally.

"Oh," said Mrs. Banger, "I'm sure I'll catch up with her later." She looked around the antiquated kitchen, composing her face into a remorseful expression. "I'm here to express my condolences about your poor Uncle Dickie, God rest his soul. Such a fine man. I'm sure you are heartbroken about his passing."

"Umm, yes," Aunt Gally said after a moment. "It's very sad."

I felt sorry for my aunt, being put on the spot like this. I mean, what could she say? That she hardly knew the man?

"Have you made the funeral arrangements?" Mrs. Banger pried.

"We're waiting for our mother to get back in the country. It could still be a few months yet," Aunt Gally answered, without really answering.

"Well, of course," the cowgirl said smoothly. "How *is* Georgina doing these days? I mean I see her on TV every week—who doesn't follow that crazy cooking show of hers..."

"Great!" Aunt Gally interrupted. "She's fantastic. She's in Kashmir right now."

"So, a couple of months..." Mrs. Banger mused. "Well, I'll be sure to stop by and say hello when she's here."

Please don't, I thought.

"That gives you time for a nice, little visit then." She gave us a smile full of questions.

"Actually, we're planning on staying and fixing up the place. We'd like to reopen the Cove by Memorial Day weekend."

"Really!?!" Mrs. Banger's one-word response summed up her complete distaste in our plans. "You've taken on a mighty big task." She gritted her teeth but then instantly caught herself. "Well, if anyone can do it, I know you girls can!" She patted Gally's shoulder in a patronizing way.

"We're not going to do all the work ourselves," Aunt Gally said, unable to hide the irritation in her voice. "Of course we'll be hiring contractors."

"Yes, yes, of course," Mrs. Banger agreed. "I'm sure it will work out just fine." Poppy was smelling her boots, so Mrs. Banger gave her a swift kick to shoo her away. Poppy whined and scampered over to me. I picked her up and held her tight. The nerve of this woman! She's the one that needs a kicking, I thought.

"Oh, I heard there was a little excitement here last night." Her voice held a nasty tinge of delight, but maybe I only imagined that because I'd already decided I couldn't stand Mrs. Banger.

"Yes..." my aunt began but was cut short.

"It's disgusting!! Desecrating a grave is such an unholy act." Her voice and white curls shook with outrage. "Do they have any idea who did this?"

"They're working on it," Aunt Gally told her.

Leaning closer to us, she said in a conspiratorial voice, "It does make you wonder if the fact that Bert Hendrickson was an atheist had anything to do with it. Those nonbelievers," she said self-righteously. "Why, he was trying to teach evolution to our poor children. Can you imagine!"

Aunt Gally had had enough.

"It was so nice to see you again." She stuck out her hand to shake Mrs. Banger's massive paw. "And thank you so much for the lovely gift basket," she added in her best sugarcoated voice. "I wish we had more time to talk, but as you know, we have tons of work to do."

Mrs. Banger blinked. "Yes, I'm sure you do." She seemed taken aback at being dismissed. After pausing for a second, she cleared her throat and forced a smile. "Well, the good Lord knows I shouldn't dally. I have a promotional appearance down in the Twin Cities." She waved her hand over her costume, as if to explain why she was dressed the way she was.

I opened the door, hoping she'd get the hint. But the bumptious bigot would not be budged.

"Oh," she stalled in the doorway, letting all our heat escape, "in case you haven't heard, our neighbor Millie Kerkenbush, has gone missing. The poor dear has dementia. So sad. There are search parties out, but no one has found her yet. Be sure to keep her in your prayers."

Aunt Gally nodded.

"Well, God be with you, girls. Let's hope that last night's shenanigans won't cast a black cloud over your *plans*."

"Goodbye," said Gally. "Thanks again."

I shut the door so fast I almost caught some of her swinging fringe.

We stood in silence, waiting for her limo to leave. When she was good and gone, Aunt Gally collapsed on the kitchen chair, and I sat down next to her.

"She's gone. And praise the Lord for that!" Aunt Gally winked at me.

❀ 10 ❀

"Governor at Gillman's Cove for Fishing Opener," the headline read. The newspaper clipping was dated 1952. Beneath it was a grainy black-and-white photograph of a man and a woman shaking hands. The woman was holding a fish by its mouth. She looked as if she were sharing a joke with the man because both of them were laughing. It was a moment captured forever. I wished Grandma Fay were still alive, so I could ask her what they'd been chatting about.

The caption said, "Governor Anderson congratulates Fay Gillman, who caught the largest walleye on opening day, measuring 31 inches and weighing 6 pounds."

Munching an Oreo, I continued to look through Grandma Fay's scrapbooks. It was late at night, and Mom and Aunt Gally were asleep—each in their old bedrooms. I'd felt lucky to have Grandma Fay's bedroom, and after finding this treasure trove of family material, I felt even luckier.

Great-grandma Fay had saved everything! Looking through the letters, postcards, photographs, greeting cards, birth announcements, wedding invitations, newspaper clippings, and frilly valentines gave me a clear picture of what a full life she'd led. I had no doubt that I would have really liked her.

After examining a picture of her waterskiing, my hand brushed against a pressed corsage, crumbling the long, dried fern. I took more care as I turned the next page.

And then I stopped.

Hold the phone!

An 8x10 black-and-white beauty shot of Grandma made my mouth drop. Her hair was done up in a super big bouffant—not Marie Antoinette-worthy, but still huge. A small bow was clipped above her temple, and her black eyeliner would have done Cleopatra proud. A satiny, slinky evening gown hugged her curves. Draped across her chest was a sash that read, "Miss Apple Blossom 1960." OMG!

Yet a greater shock was about to come my way, because pages later, I found a very similar photo of my mom! Hers had been taken decades after Grandma's. In Mom's photo, she wore a gown with massively high shoulder pads, and her sash read, "Miss Apple Blossom 1984." Mom's blonde bangs were hairsprayed straight up in the air, and she was wearing makeup—which I had never seen her wear in my entire life.

This discovery was *huge!* I whipped out my phone, took a picture, and sent it to Lexi.

And just when I didn't think I could be any more surprised, I found Aunt Gally's formal picture from when she was "Miss Apple Blossom 1985." Her dress looked similar to Mom's—with high shoulder pads—but her hair was very short and slicked back on the sides.

The adjoining page showed a newspaper photo of Aunt Gally in her tiara and sash, standing on top of a float, waving to an unseen crowd. Behind her, girls dressed in gowns were also waving. The caption said, "Miss Apple Blossom, Gally Gillman, and her Court of Sour Apples." Hmm. I thought that was rather harsh, calling the girls that hadn't won the crown *sour* apples.

But, like seriously! How could they have kept this a secret from me? Didn't I have the right to know that I descended from a long line of Apple Blossom Queens? Why all the family secrets? This train of thought made me pull out the manila envelope from Uncle Dickie's cabin.

Earlier in the evening, as we ate pizza, Mom, Aunt Gally, and I looked over the love letters we'd found in Uncle Dickie's cabin. There had been nothing personal. In fact, most of them were stanzas of poems. I pulled one out again and reread it.

Sail your smile into the air; it will reach and enliven me!
Breathe your fragrance into the air; it will sustain me!
Where are you, me beloved?
Oh, how great is Love!
And how little am I!
—A

Mom had recognized it as the work of a poet named Kahlil Gibran, but that still didn't give us any clues as to who "A" was. The sole letter wasn't much to go on. We didn't know the age, gender, or location of the writer. Since none of the envelopes had postal markings, we thought "A" might be someone local—although the letters could have been written many years ago, before Uncle Dickie moved back to town. And then there was always the chance that these letters had absolutely nothing to do with him being poisoned.

We'd all agreed that the remnants of charred paper in the fireplace were pieces of a purchase agreement. And we'd guessed that the purchase agreement was for our property. Someone had wanted to buy it. The fact that Uncle Dickie had burned it made his intentions clear that he wasn't interested. But had someone been driven to murder him, just to get the Cove?

I hopped out of bed, making Poppy wag her tail, and hurried across the bedroom floor. I peeked out the curtain. True to his word, Deputy Pete had once again assigned a cop outside our house. I wondered about the deputy's true objective. Did he really believe we were in danger? Or was it a way for him to get close to my mom? Because I saw the way he smiled at her, and it was soooo obvious that he still liked her.

Thinking of Mom, I found it strange that she was more insistent than ever to stay and open the resort. One would think that after learning Uncle Dickie had been poisoned, she would want to leave. But instead of hightailing it out of town, she was digging in her heels. She said at supper, "No one is going to scare me off our land!" It was very Scarlett O'Hara-like, although maybe this was a normal reaction from a woman who had recently suffered loss. She refused to have anything *else* taken away from her.

Suddenly, I heard that animal noise again—the one I'd heard the other morning. Was it a goat? It sounded upset or bothered by something, or maybe I was just reading into it. I went to the window again. A black starry night greeted me. I could see no animal.

I looked up animal noises on YouTube. Yeah, I'd definitely been hearing a goat.

My phone *dinged.*

Grandma

> Are you awake? I heard that old battle-axe visited you today. We used to have quite the feud, Marcella and I. Gally texted me about her visit. Snooping as usual. Beware of Sour Apples, is all I've got to say.

Theo

> ??? Are you talking about Mrs. Banger?

Grandma

> Sending help, darling! XOXOXO

Theo

> ??????

❀ 11 ❀

The following afternoon, I was eating a plate of French fries with Jigger at Beaver Lanes. The bowling alley was empty except for two guys in the arcade room, the bartender, and a man sitting at the bar. Large-screen televisions hung around the abandoned restaurant area, all of them airing basketball games. Thankfully, Jigger liked basketball as much as I did—which was not at all.

I'd been happily surprised when she called me at noon, wondering if I'd like to hang with her. Mom gave me her blessing to go, so I got out of cleaning, which was a double bonus, as far as I was concerned.

When Jigger picked me up in her beat-up pickup truck, I wondered if she had a twin or a double. Because the person that came to my house was *not* the same girl I had talked with the day before. Gone were the piercings, tattoos, spiked hair, and eyeliner. Instead, a fresh-faced girl with short, blonde hair greeted me. She laughed when she saw my surprise.

"That is all a getup to piss off my mom," she said. "I've been trying to get fired for weeks, but she keeps telling me I have to work through high school. And she's threatened to cut off my phone if I leave. Having your mom for a boss can totally suck!"

"But the tattoos…" I started.

"Just rub-ons," she said matter-of-factly. "I actually hate needles."

She drove me around town, giving me valuable info about what was cool and what wasn't. Like nobody would be caught dead at the pizza place because an old perv owned it. But Subway was cool, as long as you didn't go there first thing in the morning, when the bitchy manager was working.

She told me a story about Hank the Beaver, and how someone had stuck a Kotex pad over his mouth during the coronavirus. A picture of it went viral on Facebook, and the town elders had a fit.

And she showed me the pharmacy—the only place in town that carried good makeup, but the grouchy ladies who worked there would follow you around, thinking all teenagers were shoplifters. By the time we'd gotten to the bowling alley, I felt like I knew what was what.

After demolishing a plate of fries, I ordered fried cheese curds and fried dill pickles—thanks to Jigger's suggestions. She sat munching on a salad, while I indulged in greasy gluttony. Then she left me briefly to go to the jukebox and play Rihanna's "Love on the Brain."

Scooting back into our booth, she sighed. "God, you make that look good. I have six and a half more pounds to go. I can't cave in now." Looking longingly at my plate, she moaned in frustration. "I wish I could eat like you and never gain weight. You have no frikin' idea how lucky you are!" Jigger shook her head.

"I wish I looked like *you*." I paused to take another bite. "You've got a great figure. I, on the other hand, look like some kind of gangling stork creature."

We both laughed.

The music ended, and the man sitting at the bar went to the jukebox and selected a song. Guitar chords filled the room, followed by Bobby Gentry's "It was the third of June, another sleepy, dusty delta day…"

Just then, the guys in the video arcade room started shouting.

"No way, man!" a guy with a shaved head yelled and then gave a high staccato laugh.

"Dude! I am the one!" cried the short guy with noticeable sores on his face.

Jigger shook her head. "Don't mind Dale and Doogie. They're methers," she said in disgust.

"Heifers?" I must have misheard. As far as I knew, a heifer was a cow, so I assumed she was using some kind of Minnesota slang that I didn't know.

"Meth heads," she said more slowly.

"What does that mean?" I felt stupid for not knowing.

"They're on methamphetamine," she explained. "They're like total losers. Last year they were caught robbing parking meters, so they could buy drugs.

"Wow," I said quietly. I had no personal knowledge of methamphetamine or anyone who had used it. Being homeschooled, I'd led a sheltered life—a true product of my parents, who were both in the "slightly out of touch" world of academia.

I looked at Dale and Doogie again, half curious, half scared. They both wore dark hoodies and baggy jeans—something that had gone out of style in Oak Park years ago. The one with the shaved head was rocking back and forth, with his eyes almost closed and a perpetual joker's grin glued to his face.

They shouted again, so the bartender went into the arcade room and kicked Dale and Doogie out. Surprisingly, neither one of them put up a fight. As they made their way to the front door, they shuffled by our table. I felt myself freeze, afraid of a confrontation.

"Hey, Jigger," the one with the sores said.

Jigger ignored them, continuing to eat her salad.

When they were out of the building, I relaxed. Jigger had noticed my reaction. "Don't worry, they're really harmless. And completely stupid," she scoffed. "I think they have, like, one brain cell between the two of them."

Our conversation continued. One thing led to another, and before you knew it, we were talking about boys. She said she didn't have a boyfriend, and she wasn't looking. When she found out that I'd *never* had a boyfriend and never even been kissed, she waved her hand dismissively.

"I can fix *that* pretty quickly. I have four brothers at home who would love to meet you."

"How old are they?" I probably sounded *too* enthusiastic.

"Hmm, Josh is my twin, so he's sixteen. Jason is seventeen, Jacob is eighteen, and Jessie is nineteen."

When I looked surprised, she smiled. "My mom was busy, as they say."

"How does she keep all your names straight?" I asked seriously.

"She doesn't!" Jigger said emphatically and then went into an imitation of her mom. "Josh, I mean Jacob, I mean Jessie, I mean just someone come and help me!"

"Aren't any of them in college?" I asked.

"No, we have a farm, and they all work with Dad. But I'm not going to stick around once I graduate."

"What do you want to do?" I mumbled. The cheese curds had come, and I couldn't stop eating. OMG they were good!

"I want to work for the DNR," she said without hesitation. "Hopefully in the Fish and Wildlife department, but Parks and Trails would be pretty sweet too."

"You like fishing?" I asked doubtfully.

"It's the best!" she said enthusiastically. "Why do you think my nickname is Jigger?"

Mystified, I shook my head.

"Like a jigger pole…"

I shook my head again.

"Haven't you ever been fishing?"

I shook my head yet again.

"Oh, my God, you've got to be kidding!" Clearly, she was stunned. "And you guys are opening up the Cove?"

I nodded, too busy with the golden goodness of the batter-fried cheese curds to speak.

"Well, you're in for a treat. On the first warm day, I'm going to take you out on the lake. There are some great honey holes right by your place."

"Honey holes?" I shook my head, not understanding.

"Really good biting places for fish."

"Will you bring one of your brothers?" I asked eagerly.

She laughed. "You're pretty funny. So now that you've graduated, what do you want to do?"

"Get into films." I patted my video camera that was sitting on the table. I'd been filming our entire afternoon. Thankfully, Jigger had been super cool about it. "I'm hoping to get into some kind of film school. There's a really interesting one in LA. I'd love to make movies."

"I should have guessed. Well, that's way cool! I can say I knew you when…" She stopped, as an old man bumped into our table.

Standing before us in a slightly weaving manner, he wore a dirty flannel shirt over another dirty flannel shirt over another dirty flannel shirt. It reminded me of one of those Russian nesting dolls. His stocking cap could not hide his matted, tangled hair. He harbored an unpleasant smell—which only became worse when he opened his mouth.

"Jigger, you should be out there searching." In a delayed slow motion, he waved his hand (which held a drink) towards the outdoors.

"Hey, Jack," Jigger said flatly, shaking her head slightly at me.

"All able bodies should be a lookin' for old lady Kerkenbush," he slurred.

Instantly, I remembered Mrs. Banger saying that a woman with dementia had gone missing. I felt a stab of guilt, wondering if I should be out there looking too.

"My brothers and I searched all morning. I didn't see *you* out there," Jigger shot back.

"I got bad knees," he said defensively, finishing his drink in one huge gulp. "They mighta called in the FBI to search for her. Talk is a caravan of fancy white trucks and trailers have congregated at Gillman's Cove."

Jigger and I looked at each other.

"We gotta go," I said.

❋ 12 ❋

So here's the thing about small town gossip, which I learned from Jigger as she drove me back to the Cove. Most of a rumor will be false (like 97%), but about 3% of that said rumor will be true. Sometimes the numbers can vary, but the false part always, *always* outweighs the truth.

She gave me an example of a woman, Mrs. Billings, who broke her ankle last year. The rumor in town was that her disgruntled ex-husband, the football coach, had wrapped her in a cocoon, using old nets from the high school tennis courts. He'd kidnapped her, thrown her in the trunk of his car, and taken her to the basement of the school. There, he held her hostage for three days, feeding her pickled beets and forcing her to watch old family movies, in hopes of convincing her to return to their happy times on the farm. She watched countless clips of herself cooking, chopping wood, fixing the car, mowing the lawn, cleaning the gutters, canning the vegetables, painting the house, shoveling the snow, planting the soybeans, feeding the livestock, milking the cows, and chopping down trees.

He truly couldn't understand why she had left him.

When Mrs. Billings tried to escape, people said Mr. Billings had taken a twenty-pound barbell and shattered one of her ankles, so she would never be able to leave him again.

What *really* happened was that Mrs. Billings had broken her ankle when she slipped off a stepladder.

I wondered if Jigger had only told me this story to make me feel better because I was kind of freaking out during our ride back to my house. My mind was coming up with all sorts of possibilities and horrors of someone else being murdered. So when we roared up our driveway, it was a huge relief to see Mom and Aunt Gally standing outside, talking with a group of men.

Thanking Jigger for a great time, and promising to text her later, I hopped out of her truck and into pandemonium.

There were white trailers and trucks parked all around, but they weren't the FBI, and they weren't looking for poor Mrs. Kerkenbush. They were the "help" that Grandma had texted about last night.

Painters, plumbers, cement men, carpenters, and general contractors filled the yard, talking with Mom, who looked totally overwhelmed. Aunt Gally, on the other hand, was having a marvelous time.

"I always thought a swimming pool would be nice, right about there," my aunt pointed, as the workmen nodded their heads in agreement. "Maybe an infinity pool, overlooking the lake. It's such an amazing view."

"Gally," Mom said, exasperated. "Stop."

"And while we're at it, maybe we should build some more cabins," Aunt Gally added.

Mom pulled me aside to explain the situation. Shortly after I had left with Jigger, this crew of workmen had shown up on our doorstep, courtesy of Grandma. If we wanted any renovations, Grandma would foot the bill. For some reason, my mom did not seem pleased with this arrangement.

"We need to rein in Gally. She's coming up with all these ludicrous projects that would cost an absolute fortune. We don't have unlimited funds," Mom moaned, her stress level showing.

"Umm, well Grandma does." I knew I shouldn't have said it. Mom's look reaffirmed that belief.

"I *don't* want your grandmother paying for all this. Then she'll think she has the final word on what goes on here," Mom huffed.

"Well, won't she anyway?" I tried to hide my smile.

"You're not helping," Mom grumbled. "I need to start supper." She stormed towards the house, and I followed.

Poppy greeted me enthusiastically as soon as I entered the kitchen. Mom went to the counter, apparently to chop vegetables. This surprised me because she hadn't cooked in months—like, since last year.

"What are you making?" I asked curiously.

"Lime stew."

58

Ahh, lime stew was my favorite. Just the thought of it put me in an excellent mood. Also, the fact that she was cooking anything at all made me think she might be getting back to her old self—and that was hopeful.

Gally entered the kitchen, letting in a blast of cold air. She stood there, saying nothing, looking at Mom. The tension between them was palpable.

"We are *not* going to do all these harebrained projects of yours." Mom pointed the butcher knife at her sister. "This is a collaboration. We're partners. Fifty-fifty."

"I know," Gally said contritely.

Mom returned to cutting up her jalapeño pepper. "I feel I was blindsided by all these workmen! I came back from the grocery store and what do I see? Chaos!" She chopped the remaining vegetables so forcefully that I worried about her fingers.

I thought of the episode of Grandma's cooking show where she'd warned her viewers, "Never cook when you're angry (unless, of course, you're cooking for your mother-in-law) because your meal will turn out to be dreadfully appalling."

"And then!" Mom raised the knife in the air, like the Statue of Liberty holding her torch. "You add fuel to the fire! A swimming pool? Seriously? We live on a lake! What are you thinking?"

I wondered if Mom's strong reaction had more to do with her recent lack of control in her life, like what had happened with Dad, than with the workmen.

After a few seconds of silence, Aunt Gally asked, "Sooo, no tennis courts?"

Mom looked at her in disbelief. Then in spite of herself, she laughed out loud. Instantly the mood lifted.

Placing a whole chicken in the pressure cooker, Mom added garlic and onion to the pot. Gally and I sat down at the table, watching her.

"They're not just workmen, you know," Aunt Gally announced, smiling mysteriously.

"What do you mean?" I asked.

Gally turned to Mom and confessed, "I had a long conversation with our dear mother while you were at the grocery store. Yes, she sent these guys to do the work, but two of them are actually private security detail."

Ah, that grandmother of mine is brilliant, I thought. So full of surprises.

"You have *got* to be kidding." Mom shook her head.

"You know how she doesn't trust the police. She compared Deputy Pete Hicks to Howdy Doody," Gally said, trying not to laugh.

"Who is Howdy Doody?" I asked.

"He was a ventriloquist's dummy on a kids' TV show. Your grandmother was making a derogatory comment." Mom didn't look amused. After a pause, she asked, "Which two are the real bodyguards?"

"The ones that will be sleeping right there." Gally pointed to the sleek R.V. parked outside the kitchen. "The real workers are staying in the cabins."

Mom asked, "And just when was I going to be told about this?"

"I was supposed to relay it to both of you, so she wouldn't have to repeat everything three times," Gally explained.

Grandma did have a point. I could see that Mom was processing all of this. We waited for her to say something.

"It's pretty clever, Mom," I piped up, defending Grandma's plan. "If she'd sent men in black suits with earbuds, it would have started a whirlwind of rumors in this town."

"And just what do you know about the rumor mill in this town?" Mom asked.

"More than you think," I said wisely.

As the pressure cooker jiggled away, Mom finally said, "Okay. Maybe we should take some soup out to the bodyguards' R.V. as a peace offering. I was pretty dismissive earlier."

"Are you kidding me?" Gally clapped her hands in excitement. "We can do a lot better than that!"

❃ 13 ❃

An hour later, we were giving a full-fledged dinner party. Since Gally had to work with what she had on hand, it might not have been exactly what my professional interior decorator of an aunt would have envisioned, but what more could she do?

The five of us sat around the dining room table, which was now covered in a vintage tablecloth and adorned with mason jars and candles. Gally had found chunky stoneware bowls for the soup, plus salad plates for our French bread.

Edvard Grieg's "In the Hall of the Mountain King" played on NPR in the background. I ate quietly, watching the bodyguards curiously. They looked very similar—both were middle-aged, both had short dark hair, both were around six feet tall and muscular, and both were extremely quiet. We couldn't even learn their names. What were we supposed to call them? As Edvard Grieg crescendoed on and on and on, I came up with the brilliant nicknames of "Thing 1" and "Thing 2."

Gally filled the conversational void with ramblings and stories of her travels. She was entertaining us all with her recent exploits in London. Even though the bodyguards remained quiet, I could tell they were captivated by her description of Madame Tussaud's Chamber of Horrors, and how Gally saw a wax casting of Marie Antoinette's head right after her date with the guillotine. She said Marie's face had a look of complete surprise. Her mouth was wide open… Mom immediately changed the subject, asking everyone if they wanted more bread.

She passed me the breadbasket, and I indulged. The stew was delicious! I dipped my bread smeared with homemade garlic butter into the golden, spicy broth.

Gally's stories of her travels reminded me of when I was in London four years ago. I had soooo wanted to go to Madame Tussaud's, but Dad refused. He didn't want to waste time on a tourist trap like that.

Instead, Mom, Dad, and I spent a full week at the Victoria and Albert Museum, studying history. I'm pretty sure Gally had more fun.

As I ate, I couldn't help but think back to the dinner parties Mom and Dad used to have in Oak Park. Uncle Eddie, Aunt Penelope, and Lexi were the main guests at our table, but UIC faculty members were frequent visitors because Mom and Dad taught there. Those were happy times, with many laughs.

I recalled one dinner from a couple of years ago, when Mom had invited her boss to a summer cookout. Everything had tasted fabulous. Mom had painstakingly gone overboard on every detail to prepare the meal. For dessert, she had scoops of homemade ice cream covered with chocolate syrup.

When Mom's boss took her first bite, she raved about the flavor and asked about that "wonderful little crunch" she'd never tasted before. Mom, who hadn't taken a bite yet, looked closely at the syrup she'd just poured. She stood stricken, as she found tiny ants mixed in with the gooey topping. It had been my fault. I hadn't placed the syrup lid on tightly, so a whole colony of ants had drowned inside the syrup can. Just thinking about it made me laugh, snorting soup out my nose.

"Are you okay?" Mom asked gently.

"I'm fine," I croaked. I took a gulp of milk, glancing up at the light fixture overhead. No one would have ever guessed that we found a dead man hanging there only two nights ago. I wondered if there was something wrong with me that it didn't creep me out more. Because it really was a creepy sort of thing!

A sharp knock on the door shattered my thoughts. Quickly, Things 1 and 2 pushed away from the table, reaching inside their jackets for their guns.

Whoa!

Thing 2 went to the window and peeked out furtively. "It's a cop," he said in a deep baritone voice. He'd probably used up his word allotment for the week. Thing 1 remained silent.

The realization that these two were actually bodyguards seemed to stun Mom and Gally—or it could have been the sight of the guns that stunned them. Either way, they sat immobilized.

So I rose to answer the door and banged my hip on the corner of the table. *"Ouch!"*

When I reached the door, I found Deputy Pete. He was holding his hat in his hand, looking hangdog.

"Sorry to interrupt," he apologized, "but is your mom available?" He craned his neck, trying to see what was going on in the dining room.

Mom came to the door to greet him. I watched their faces closely. I could tell he liked her, just by his eyes. He couldn't hide it. For some reason, this really annoyed me. "What can I do for you, Pete?" Mom asked.

"Sorry to interrupt," he repeated, "but I thought you'd want to know. I just got a call from the coroner. He said your Uncle Dickie's death is now considered a homicide."

"Oh, no!" Mom gasped. I thought she was doing a pretty good job of acting surprised.

Gally joined us at the door. "What happened?"

Mom looked at her sister with raised eyebrows. "Uncle Dickie's death is now considered a homicide!" Mom gave her sister the "look." I didn't know if Deputy Pete would pick up on it, but *I* certainly knew what she was conveying, and so did Gally. It meant "be good."

"So he didn't die of a heart attack?" Mom asked innocently.

"No, he was poisoned," Deputy Pete answered firmly.

Gally gasped—maybe a little *too* dramatically.

"We'll need to search his cabin for possible evidence. Which reminds me...you girls were in there the other day. You didn't happen to find anything fishy, did you?"

14

Lexi

what did you tell him?

Theo

gally said we found a LOT of fishy things in uncle dickie's cabin because the whole place is covered in fish decor - which made him laugh - but we didn't really answer - which, i know, is lying by omission

Lexi

what do the bodyguards look like?

Theo

they're older - short dark hair - actually they look kind of similar - they don't speak - gally asked them questions but she couldn't even find out where they're from - or their names

Lexi

give me a better description than that! - i'm trying to write about this - who do they look like?

Theo

well they don't look like tommy lee jones if that's what you're wondering. they kind of look like ron swanson on "parks and recreation" - if you stretch your imagination

Lexi

who?

Lexi

does your dad know about the murder?

I rubbed my forehead. I didn't want to think about Dad. I changed the subject.

Theo

hey i made a new friend - i met her at this bizarre cafe called mabel's - it has these dead beavers in dioramas, dressed up in clothes - did u get that picture i sent u?

Lexi

i've been replaced - that didn't take long !!!!

Theo

knock it off -

Theo

what did you think of my mom's miss apple blossom picture?

Lexi

awesome!! Hey - gotta go - ttyl!

I went downstairs, where Mom and Gally were sitting at the dining room table, having a power meeting. Papers with estimates and drawings were strewn everywhere.

"I want the cabins to keep their vintage feel," Gally said with bubbly confidence.

"Exactly," Mom agreed.

I was happy to see them getting along.

"Hey, I'm taking Poppy out for a walk," I said, as I leashed her up and checked the battery on my video camera.

"Okay," Mom said over her shoulder.

As soon as I stepped outside, I noticed Thing 1, who was standing by the R.V. "Good morning," I told him. He nodded. As I strolled away from the house, he followed me.

"I'm just going on a walk," I called over my shoulder. He nodded again but kept following me. So this is how it's going to be, I thought. I'd be followed around no matter what I did. I felt like some ancient, traditional Japanese man, with his dutiful wife taking minuscule steps, ten paces behind him.

The morning air felt frigid as Poppy pulled me towards the forest. While strolling, I kept an eye out for an old lady—not that I was searching for her, but I did keep vigilant. Soon I began daydreaming about finding the missing Millie Kerkenbush. Maybe I'd become the town hero. Maybe I'd have my picture in the local newspaper with the caption, "Newcomer Finds Lost Local and Safely Returns Her to Loved Ones." And then I could put the photo in a new scrapbook to carry on the Gillman family history—a continuation of Grandma Fay's scrapbooks.

But if I did find Millie, how would I know? I had no idea what she looked like. Would she seem strange? Delusional? Hmm, that could describe almost everyone I'd met in Black Beaver Bay.

Maybe she'd be wearing a babushka headscarf, wielding a cane like a rickety crone. Then I shook my head. Did I think I was in some

Grimm's fairy tale? Although the tall pines above *did* make me feel as if I were in some kind of enchanted forest.

Once again, I heard the animal call—the one I'd identified as being a goat. I turned around, looking everywhere, but I couldn't spot it. Poppy obviously hadn't heard it, for she made a beeline to the lakeshore.

The sand was hard, crunching beneath my boots. I turned around and saw Thing 1 standing guard at the edge of the forest. I paused and took out my video camera, filming the lake. It looked black under the clouded sky—black, cold, and inky. Bending down, I stuck my finger in the water. It was freezing.

I ambled along the shoreline, stopping occasionally to pick up a smooth shell or stone. A vivid memory of my dad sliced through me, making me wince. Years ago, on a beach in Spain, he'd scooped up a handful of sand and explained to me that our brains will try to find a pattern in something as random as the clump of grains of sand in his hand. That's how our brains are wired—to find patterns. I remember looking at him in awe.

I shut that memory out of my mind, much like I'd blocked him on my cell phone. I kept strolling.

My mind turned to Jigger. I liked her. She was so forthcoming and easy to talk to. And super funny. And really self-effacing. She reminded me of Lexi. They were both natural storytellers. I wondered when I'd see Jigger again. And would she really introduce me to her brothers? Would they be as cool as she was?

Poppy and I wandered the full length of the beach until we came to a thicket of scraggly bushes. "Come on, Pops." Our walk had ended. It was time to head back. I tried to steer her in my direction, but she pulled me harder towards the leafless shrubs.

"No." I gave the leash a little tug.

She started to growl.

"What is it?" I bent down to her level, stroking her head, expecting to find a dead fish.

I gasped.

Shrouded by the scrubby growth, there was a shoe in the water. I focused my camera. It was a solid black shoe, which was attached to a thick, muddied leg. The leg was covered in torn pantyhose.

Quickly, I turned away, not wanting to see more. Yet some morbid curiosity inside of me made me keep looking. Around the stout knee, I saw the hem of a dress that bobbed gently in the lake. The rest of the body was too covered by the shoreline overgrowth to see.

Taking my boot, I pushed back the dead vegetation and saw a bloated, swollen face staring up at me. Water, sand, and bracken slapped inside her mouth with the tide of the lake. My hand shook as I filmed.

She had one eye open, staring up at the sky, although her pupil looked clouded and lifeless. Her other eye had something sticking out of its eye socket—something that looked like a smooth, metal stick. A cord of tissue or muscle trailed from the empty eye socket, bobbing along gently in the ebb of the water.

Picking up Poppy, I ran.

❀ 15 ❀

The thing about daydreams is that they rarely come true. So yes, I had found Millie Kerkenbush. But no, I didn't get to be the town hero. And I didn't get to return her safely to her loved ones. And there was no photojournalist taking my picture for the front page of the newspaper. In fact, nobody seemed very happy with me because nobody *was* happy that I had found Millie Kerkenbush *dead*.

A handful of people were gathered on the beach, watching the emergency workers and eyeing us up from afar. Now that I knew how fast news traveled in this town, I wasn't surprised. Mom, Gally, and I stood apart from the locals, watching the men in white suits who were trying to remove Millie Kerkenbush from the freezing water. The scene looked all too familiar. One of the men slipped, completely immersing himself in the lake, as he muttered expletives.

"I can't watch this again," Gally said under her breath. Turning to leave, she saw Mrs. Banger striding down the beach.

Towards us.

"Oh, my God," Gally groaned. "I just can't."

Mom moaned. "I knew I was too lucky when I missed her the other day."

"Tag, you're it!" Gally said, striding in the opposite direction. Then she stopped. "Theo, I need your help back at the house."

That was cool of my aunt. It was like a "get out of jail free" card. I hurried to her side, and we left Mom alone to deal with the one and only Mrs. Banger.

But we hadn't escaped just yet.

"Yoo-hoo! Girls!" Mrs. Banger shouted, waving for us to stop. She'd replaced her gaudy cowgirl outfit with a purple parka and tall rubber galoshes.

"We have something........." Gally's voice went silent but her mouth kept moving, to make Mrs. Banger think she must not be hearing correctly. And all the while, Gally was waving back at Mrs. Banger cheerfully.

When we reached the house, the painters were erecting scaffolding. The sharp clangs of metal hitting metal echoed loudly through the cold air. We were happy to escape inside.

"Brrr," Gally rubbed her arms, keeping her coat on. She turned on the oven and opened its door. Then she pulled a chair up close to the oven and sat down.

"Poor Millie Kerkenbush." Gally sighed.

"Did you know her? I mean, when you lived here?"

"Oh, yes. Your mom and I used to pick blackberries over by her house. Our land butts up next to hers. She'd always invite us in for cookies and milk." Sadly, she added, "She was friends with Grandma Fay."

I pulled up a chair next to her, watching the oven element turn orange. "So she was pretty old," I deduced.

"Hmm, she must have been in her nineties." Gally spread her fingers out to warm them.

"I'm surprised she wasn't in a nursing home."

"Maybe she had someone living with her?" Gally wondered.

Just then, Mom barged through the kitchen door, slamming it behind her. She was visibly upset. "Thanks a lot, you two!"

Aunt Gally and I glanced at each other knowingly, biting our lips to keep from laughing.

Mom began pacing the kitchen floor. "That old snoop!" Back and forth, Mom paced, regaling the horrors of her conversation with Mrs. Banger.

"She asked me where my husband was! Why wasn't he here? When would he be joining us? She is the most ferreting, old busybody that ever lived!"

"What did you tell her?" I asked.

"I said he was working," Mom grouched, taking off her coat. "Honestly, the nerve of that woman. What gives her the right?!" She opened the refrigerator, whipped out a bag of baby carrots, and started to chomp one angrily.

"And then she wanted to know all about the workmen! Where did we find them? Did we have the right permits? How long would they be staying? How much were they charging?!"

Gally said, "Jeez, it sounds like you were talking for hours, but it couldn't have been more than…"

"Four minutes," Mom interjected.

"That's longer than I could stand her the other day," said Gally.

"Maybe we won't have to deal with her for a while," Mom said hopefully.

"Praise the Lord," I said, prompting Mom to take a playful swipe at me.

As Mom's frustration dissipated, the mood turned somber. She slowly put the carrots back in the 1950s refrigerator and ran water in the sink to do dishes.

"Poor Millie." She sighed, as she squeezed the detergent bottle.

"I know," Gally agreed. "Remember her oatmeal raisin cookies? And she had that old, black goat. I was so afraid of him," she reminisced.

Mom laughed. "Remember when that goat got loose and ate all the fish strung up by the last cabin? That fisherman was so mad he chased that goat, trying to whack him with his fishing pole."

Gally chuckled. "I remember that goat chasing us through the woods, and how we climbed up that pine tree to get away from him!"

"You pushed me off the branch," Mom said in mock despair.

"I did not!" Gally protested, but I couldn't say I believed her.

I loved hearing stories like this. I could clearly picture them being little. I imagined Gally getting into all sorts of trouble, and Mom always behaving.

After a few moments, Mom said softly, "We should go to her funeral."

"Yeah," Gally agreed.

"And I suppose we should start making some kind of funeral arrangements for Uncle Dickie."

"You'd be better at that than I would," Gally said, trying her best to get out of it.

"Oh, no, you don't," Mom said quickly. "You are definitely helping me."

I broke in with, "Hey, why didn't either one of you ever tell me you were Apple Blossom Queens?"

They stared at me, startled, and obviously caught off guard.

"How…" Mom started.

"I found Grandma Fay's scrapbook. Why would you keep that a secret from me?"

"Jeez, it was so long ago, I'd forgotten all about it," Gally sounded sincere.

"I, I…" Mom stammered, completely embarrassed—as only a Women's Studies professor could be, about once being a beauty queen.

Suddenly my phone *dinged*.

Jigger

i heard you found mrs. kerkenbush's body

Theo

yeah, this morning when I was walking Poppy. how did you know?

I realized that was a stupid question. By now, it would be the talk of the town. No doubt people were saying a crazy beanpole of a girl from Gillman's Cove—not a "real" Minnesotan—had killed Mrs. Kerkenbush, so she could use her goats in satanic worship. I'm sure my dating potential had plummeted to oblivion.

❀ 16 ❀

A few days later, I woke to an obnoxiously annoying engine sound. High pitched, it whined and whined until it dragged me out of slumber. What was that? The workmen? They were supposed to be scraping the house, not mowing it. But it really didn't sound like a mower either—more like a bumblebee on steroids. Why wasn't Poppy putting up a fuss? When I opened my eyes, I found that Poppy wasn't there. What time *was* it?

As I hopped out of bed, I stubbed my big toe on my suitcase. *"Ouch!"* If I had put my clothes away, like Mom had asked me, this wouldn't have happened. But we couldn't find the key to my closet, so it wasn't *totally* my fault. I limped to the window and peeked out the curtains. It was blinding! Everything was covered in a dazzling blanket of snow. The sheer whiteness hurt my sleepy eyes.

I grabbed my camera and filmed the winter wonderland. Snow clung to every branch, making a sharp inverse outline of the trees. This could be an opening shot for a Fellini movie, I thought. As I filmed the beauty, a crazy person driving a snowmobile zoomed up and started doing circles in our yard. Although I'd never actually seen a snowmobile in real life, I felt like I knew something about them. I mean, who hasn't seen the James Bond movie "Spectre?"

As I filmed, Thing 1 (or it might have been Thing 2) left the R.V. and strode towards the snowmobiler. The driver pulled off a helmet to reveal a shock of blonde hair. It was Jigger!

I got dressed as fast as I could. Running down the stairs, I slipped, landing on my tailbone. *"Ouch!"* I hurried to the kitchen, where Mom and Gally were drinking tea and talking to Jigger.

"Snow day!" Jigger greeted me. Bundled in a black snowmobile suit, she looked like the Michelin Man. Her cheeks glowed, and her eyes twinkled. She was completely jazzed.

"I brought an extra suit for you." She handed me a bundle.

I wasn't expecting this at all. "Really?" I glanced at Mom, who was smiling.

"It's fun—you'll like it," she encouraged me.

"Whoa. You mean you've never been snowmobiling?" Jigger sounded incredulous.

"Well, no, but I've seen it in the movies." As if that would somehow make up for my lack of experience.

Jigger shook her head in disbelief. "Then let me show you how to put this on." She began helping me into the suit.

A knock on the kitchen door made us pause. One of the bodyguards motioned for Mom to come outside. As Jigger zipped and snapped me up, I heard Mom say, "it's fine" and "it will be okay" and "let her be a kid." Clearly, Thing 1 (or Thing 2) didn't think it was wise for me to leave. I tried to talk louder than their conversation, so Jigger couldn't hear them, but at the same time, I kept trying to eavesdrop on them. It wasn't easy.

Ten minutes later, I was bundled up and sitting on the back of her "sled," as Jigger called it. My video camera was tucked safely inside my suit, and I hoped to get some cool shots.

"Hang on!" she yelled.

With a mighty, whiny roar, we were off. It felt exhilarating! My visibility through the helmet was better than I'd thought it would be, and a few times I had to close my eyes when it seemed like we would surely crash. Going over bumps and rounding trees at a breakneck speed made me think Jigger was one absolutely crazy daredevil. I didn't know until later that there were designated trails that snowmobiles were supposed to stay on—and we weren't on those trails.

There was no way possible for me to film anything!

We flew across the highway and then followed along it towards town. When we reached Hank the Beaver, who looked like he was wearing a white stocking cap because of the snow, Jigger turned and gunned it up a hill. We shot past Black Beaver Bay and kept flying.

After about half an hour, Jigger pulled up to a round, metal building. It was an abandoned corn crib, and she explained that it was a warming spot for sledders.

I removed my helmet as I entered the corn crib. It took a second for my eyes to adjust to the dim lighting. There was a shabby, checkered couch and a few tattered lazy boys. In the center stood a metal drum with a pile of chopped wood by its side. I took out my camera and began shooting. Jigger placed some wood in the drum, and I realized it was a makeshift wood-burning stove. "Cool," she said. "Someone's already been here this morning. I don't have to start the fire."

She went over to a shelf and took down a radio, winding it. It was the kind that didn't need batteries. After she fiddled with a knob, an announcer's voice came in loud and clear. "For all your classic rock and roll, keep your dial tuned to Jack FM." Then a song from The Cure started playing. "I don't care if Monday's blue. Tuesday's grey and Wednesday too…"

I panned my camera around the walls, which were covered in graffiti and sayings—some of them pretty lewd. The phrase "skin bin" was painted more than once. I wasn't quite sure what that meant, and I didn't think I wanted to know. Once again, I looked at the shabby couch, this time examining the stains.

"Did you like the ride?" Jigger smiled. She was warming her hands in front of the stove.

"Yeah." I smiled back. "How long have you been driving?"

"I don't know. Maybe eight years," she said nonchalantly.

I tried to remember what I was doing eight years ago. I think I was in the middle of my Lego phase.

"Hey!" she said, excited. "You never told me your grandmother is the one on that cooking show, 'The Psychedelic Sous Chef.' She's hilarious!"

"You have no idea," I told her. "But how did you find that out?"

"Your arrival in town has been a pretty big deal," she explained. "Especially after Mr. Hendrickson. And now Mrs. Kerkenbush."

I groaned. "What are people saying?"

"Don't worry about it. It's only gossip," she reassured me. "Something else will happen, and you'll be old news."

I didn't find her predictions very comforting.

Suddenly we heard the multiple whines of other snowmobiles. I looked at Jigger anxiously.

"That's probably my brothers. I told them I'd be taking you for a ride this morning. They want to meet the hot, new girl in town!"

OMG, I panicked. While I'd never considered myself to be a vain person, my hands flew to my hair. I hadn't even brushed it this morning. Nor my teeth. I'm sure I looked ridiculous. I shut off my camera and slipped it back inside my suit.

The door to the corn crib creaked open, and Jigger laughed as I jumped about a foot. "You're so funny," she said.

Two boys entered and threw their helmets onto the couch. They joined us at the stove, and Jigger introduced me to her brothers—Josh and Jacob.

Jacob was the older and taller of the two. He had the same blond hair as Jigger. A noticeable scar ran through one of his eyebrows. Jigger told me later that he'd had a piercing, and it had gotten ripped out in a fight.

Josh, Jigger's twin, didn't look like Jigger, but he was really cute in his own right. His light blue eyes, fringed with dark lashes, looked striking against his blond hair. And he had the cutest smile! I grew tongue-tied when I shook his hand. In my mind, I imagined a tiny Cupid had just shot an arrow into my heart.

"So how do you like Black Beaver Bay?" Jacob asked me.

"Um, it's different," I muttered. More like an alternate universe, I wanted to say, but didn't. I didn't know how to talk to them. I was sure anything I said would sound stupid.

"So you found Mr. Hendrickson *and* Millie Kerkenbush," Jacob said. "That's pretty righteous!"

"Oh, shut up, Jacob," Jigger scolded her brother. "There's nothing cool about finding dead bodies. It'd be horrible. I'd like to see how *you'd* act, if you found even one." She swatted his arm in a dismissive way.

"Sorry," he said, embarrassed. "I didn't mean..." His voice trailed off.

Josh spoke up. "Everyone is just curious, that's all," he said kindly.

"So, are you a Vikings fan?" Jacob asked.

"What?" What a bizarre question. Why would he care how I felt about ancient Scandinavian raiders and plunderers?

"The football team," Jigger explained.

"I don't really know anything about football." I looked down at my boots. This conversation was painstakingly miserable.

"Too bad you're too late to sign up for Miss Apple Blossom," Josh said.

Now they were just plain making fun of me. Even though I was not in possession of a mirror, I knew I looked like the furthest thing possible from a beauty queen.

"Why are you looking like *that?*" Jigger asked. "All the girls try out for it. I am. The scholarship money is *huge.*"

"Yeah, like $50,000 huge," said Jacob.

"Seriously?" I couldn't believe it.

"Like, why do you think I've been busting my butt to lose weight for the last four months? The prize money could pay for my college. If I didn't need the money, I'd be eating ice cream right now!"

"You should have seen her last Christmas. She was pretty tubby," Jacob teased her.

"Yeah, go ahead and yak it up," Jigger joked. "Laugh all you want. But I only have six more pounds to go 'til goal weight!" She pumped her arms in the air like a prizefighter. Her brothers laughed

"It's probably a good thing you're not entering the pageant," Josh told me. "That means you won't have to deal with the Apple Blossom curse." He sounded serious.

Just as I started to ask him what the heck he meant, my cell phone *dinged*.

Mom

> I found Poppy lethargic and unresponsive. Taking her to the vet. Meet me there if you can

"Um, I gotta go," I told everyone.

❀ 17 ❀

The vet's office had that vet's office smell—medicine and vitamins mixed with wet dog. All sorts of cute kitten and puppy posters covered the walls, reminding humans to vaccinate their pets.

We took up all the seats in the waiting area. Gally, Things 1 and 2, Jigger, and myself were the only people here, which was a good thing because there was no more room in the room.

Jigger had driven me directly to the vet's office on the snowmobile. To say the ride had been harrowing was an understatement. We'd arrived just minutes after everyone else.

Mom was inside the exam room with the vet and Poppy. I wanted to go in but didn't know if I was allowed. The waiting was driving me crazy.

"So tell me again, what happened?" I asked Gally.

She squeezed my shoulder, trying to be reassuring. "Your mom found Poppy in the library. There was a pool of vomit by her side, and her breathing was shallow. She was pretty lethargic."

I thought back to this morning. Poppy hadn't been in my bed when I was awakened by the sound of the snowmobile. Then I'd rushed out the door so quickly that I hadn't noticed her absence. I hadn't even had time to eat. Suddenly, my stomach let out a loud grumble. Jigger looked at me.

"Do you think it was something she ate?" I asked.

Gally paused. "There were some plastic wrappers. I brought in all the pieces I could find. We don't know if she ingested some plastic, or if she's having a reaction to what she ate."

"What *did* she eat?" I agonized.

"Mrs. Banger's summer sausage from the gift basket."

I put my head in my hands.

Jigger said, "Doc Vesper is really good. Whatever it is, your dog couldn't be in better hands."

I felt a terrible guilt. Why hadn't I checked on her this morning? Maybe I could have prevented this. She just *had* to be okay.

Gally piped up, "Did you say Doc Vesper? Would that be Ben Vesper?"

"Yeah." Jigger nodded. "He took over the practice from the old vet.

"Gee, I went to school with a Ben Vesper." Gally seemed intrigued.

The piped-in music in the background played, "You're just too good to be true. Can't take my eyes off of you…" My stomach growled so loudly that the bodyguards looked at me with raised eyebrows. How embarrassing!

I noticed that Jigger was texting someone on her phone. My phone *dinged.*

Jigger

> **wassup with the chatty cathys sittin next to u?**

I looked at the stoic and silent Thing 1 and Thing 2. How could I explain them without telling Jigger everything? And if I did tell her, would she tell anyone else? How well did I really know her? I thought it over before texting back.

Theo

> **it's complicated. i'll try to explain later**

The bell above the door jingled. A plump beagle waddled into the waiting room, followed by an elderly man who looked a whole lot like Burl Ives—right down to the white goatee. Stomping his boots on the rug, he removed his fogged-up glasses. He assessed us one by one.

"Hi Mr. Anderson," Jigger waved. The beagle came over to Jigger, and she rubbed the dog's head. "Hey, boy, how you doing?" she gushed. I looked sadly at the beagle, really missing Poppy.

"Jigger." The newcomer nodded. "Looks like there's a full house this morning." He glanced at everyone again.

Gally popped up and stuck out her hand. "Hi Mr. Anderson, it's Gally Gillman. Remember me?"

Recognition dawned across his face. "Gally Gillman." Smiling, he shook her hand heartily. "I most certainly *do* remember you. Why, in my forty years of teaching, you were the only student I ever had who cut down the ropes in my gym, so you could get out of rope climbing!" He chuckled.

Gally blushed. "You must be thinking of someone else."

"No, it was you alright." He nodded decisively. Then he paused and said, "Sorry to hear about your uncle." Mr. Anderson patted Gally's hand. "He's sorely missed at our poker nights."

Oh! I knew that someone at my uncle's poker parties had reported back to Grandma. Could this man be the spy? I watched him with renewed interest. If you thought of Burl Ives as the snowman narrator in "Rudolph the Red-Nosed Reindeer," it would be hard to imagine him as any kind of spy. But if you've seen Burl Ives in "Cat on a Hot Tin Roof," you might think he was *more* than capable.

Quickly, I sent off a text to Grandma, asking about Mr. Anderson.

After his condolences and small talk, Mr. Anderson stepped over to a display of dog treats, taking two small bags and stuffing them inside his long overcoat. "Jigger, would you mind writing the doc an IOU for two bags of treats? My arthritis is acting up."

He said his goodbyes and took his leave.

Moments later, the bell once again jingled above the door. In walked a tall, thin, middle-aged woman with dyed red hair. Her gray roots were a shocking contrast to the unnatural red. Despite her disastrous tresses and plain features, she had an air of calm and self-confidence.

"Miss Honeycutt!" Jigger exclaimed. Leaping up from her chair, Jigger rushed towards the woman.

"Hello, Jigger!" Miss Honeycutt responded with a trace of laughter in her voice. "Looks like you've been enjoying your snow day." She nodded towards Jigger's snowmobile suit.

Aunt Gally walked over to the woman and extended her hand. "Gretchen? It's Gally. Gally Gillman. Do you remember me?"

Miss Honeycutt's face broke into a smile. "Of course!" Reaching out her arms, she gave my aunt a hug. "I'll never forget when you turned on the sprinkler system in the cafeteria to protest our awful school lunches!"

"You must be thinking of someone else," Gally joked.

"I heard you've moved back to reopen the Cove," Miss Honeycutt rushed on. "That's marvelous! I've been meaning to stop out and catch up on old times."

"That would be great! I know Ana would enjoy that too." My aunt looked genuinely happy to reunite with this old classmate.

"I'd love to stay and chat, but I have dozens of stops to make. Thank goodness for snow days! They give me a chance to work on my never-ending 'To-do' list." Miss Honeycutt handed Jigger a rolled-up piece of poster board. "Would you mind asking Doc to hang this some-where in his office?"

Saying her farewells, Miss Honeycutt left.

As Gally excused herself to use the restroom, Jigger sat down next to me and unrolled the poster. We looked over the list of events sched-uled for Miss Apple Blossom Days.

"Who was that?" I asked.

Jigger slapped her forehead. "I should have introduced you. I'm sorry."

Jigger explained that Miss Honeycutt was one of the chairwomen for the pageant—but also so much more. Jigger raved about the very average-looking woman's above-average accomplishments.

Not only was Miss Honeycutt the town treasurer, but she was also the head of the drama department, the coach of the girls' cross country team, the manager of the Starlight Dance studio, the owner of an indie publishing company, and the minister of the Episcopalian Church. In her free time, she competed in clogging competitions.

Gally rejoined us as the door from the examination room opened. Mom came out holding Poppy, who wagged her tail weakly when she saw me. I leaped out of my chair and ran to hold her.

"She'll be fine." Mom smiled. "Dr. Vesper pumped her stomach, so she's a bit groggy, but she's out of danger."

"I think she had a little too much garlic, but I won't know for sure until the results come in," said a man in a white doctor's coat, shuffling behind Mom.

"Garlic?" I was puzzled. "How did she get into garlic?"

Mom explained, "The wrappers we brought in had 'Banger Sausage' stickers on them. It looks like Poppy ate an entire package of summer sausage from that gift basket of Mrs. Banger's. The ingredient label showed a high content of garlic."

"But as I said, I won't really know until I get the lab results back," the vet explained, as he typed on his laptop. He had an intelligent, dignified air. His chiseled cheekbones reminded me of Viggo Mortensen, whom I've had a secret crush on ever since "The Lord of the Rings." Although maybe my view of the veterinarian was skewed because I was so overwhelmingly grateful that he'd saved Poppy.

"What else could it be?" I asked.

"The full toxicology report will take a few days. It could be anything from too much garlic, to Listeria—or maybe Staphylococus, which causes food poisoning."

"Oh, my God." Gally slapped her hands over her mouth.

"What?" asked Mom.

"After taking out the summer sausage and a few beef sticks, I gave that whole basket to the workmen! What if I poisoned them?"

Lexi

> so were the workmen poisoned?

Theo

> their foreman said they weren't feeling well but he called it the 'bottle flu.' I guess they drank too much because it was a snow day and they figured they wouldn't have to work. In the next 24 hours we should know if any of them have food poisoning

Lexi

> and you seriously drove around in circles, in the freezing cold, not really doing anything? sorry theo but that sounds soooo redneck! i mean, what's the point of snowmobiling? What did you accomplish?

Theo

> it was fun

I was trying to explain snowmobiling to Lexi. You would think that as a writer she would *want* to know about things she hasn't experienced. I took another bite of potato chip and dip, brushing the crumbs off of Grandma Fay's bed, before changing my playlist to David Bowie.

Lexi

> i fear you've been brainwashed already! you're turning into one of those clueless morons i warned you to stay away from - next thing you'll tell me you're going fishing!

Theo

ummm, jigger is planning on taking me out on the lake on the first nice day

Lexi

OMG theo, what's happening to you?

I was beginning to wonder if my newfound friendship with Jigger was bothering Lexi. Was she jealous? Maybe something else was going on with her. Either way, texting with her lately had become uncomfortable.

Ding! A text from Grandma came in.

Theo

gotta go, lex. grandma just texted me - ttyl

Grandma

Yes, Mr. Anderson has been my informant - for at least 15 years now. So is Poppy okay?

Theo

She's fine. I'm petting her right now.

I heard the mournful bleating of that goat again. I hopped out of bed and looked out the window. Was it just my imagination? I went back to bed and kept texting.

Grandma

what's the vet's name?

Theo

Ben Vesper. He was in Gally's grade. They had a strange reunion when they recognized each other. He said he'd never forgotten how she put salt - instead of sugar - in the Tang drink in Home Economics class

Grandma

ha! I do remember that. Your Aunt Gally had mishaps on a daily basis. Did you see any sparks fly between the two of them?

Theo

The vet and Gally? No. well maybe a little. They DID smile a lot at each other

Grandma

You need to play the part of a matchmaker. Gally always does better when there is a man in her life

Theo

Gally is great, she doesn't need a guy to be happy. You're thinking of the wrong daughter

Grandma

I know exactly which daughter I'm referring to. Your mother can be quite hopeless with or without a man!

Theo

> Grandma! Be nice. Besides, I wouldn't know how to be a matchmaker.

Grandma

> Adopt a litter of sick kittens - that would give you the perfect excuse to drag Gally into the vet's office with you

Was she kidding? She couldn't be serious. I decided to change the subject.

Theo

> Did Mom or Gally tell you about Mrs. Kerkenbush?

Grandma

> Yes they did. I prayed for her soul at the Kheer Bhawani temple this morning. I spent two hours in deep meditation, repeating her name over and over, sending her peace in her crossing. Ida was such a wonderful person.

Theo

> Umm, I'm pretty sure her name was Mildred

Grandma

> Dammit, well what's in a name anyway. Any revelations as to who poisoned my dear, dimwitted brother?

Theo

> No

Grandma

Any news about who hung Mr. Hendrickson in our house?

Theo

Deputy Pete stopped by tonight - he is ALWAYS hanging around - I think he likes Mom - anyway he said forensics came up with zero leads in the house. No footprints, no hairs, no finger-prints. He said it looks like a professional job.

Grandma

Or the cops could be lying, covering up the facts. So no leads on Mr. H. No leads on Dickie. I wonder what the coroner will find out about Mrs. K

Theo

I'm sure you'll be the first to know. From the sound of it, you have a special relationship with the coroner. Was he your boyfriend? He's not an ex husband, is he? And if you don't mind me asking, how many times have you been married?

Grandma

A true lady never reveals how many husbands she's had, but I think I've had seven. I'm not sure if remarrying an ex-husband counts as once or twice. Speaking of exes - have you heard from your father lately?

Theo

I blocked him on my phone

Grandma

Your half-brother or sister should be born soon.

Theo

Grandma

Far be it from me to ever tell anyone what to do...

Theo

ha!

Grandma

But for your own sake, the sooner you let go of your anger, the better. It's only hurting you. With that in mind, I came across an article that I thought might help explain your father's behavior. would you read it?

Theo

What's the name of it

Grandma

How to Cope When Your Father is a Dope

Theo

No thank you. If it was titled 'How to Cope When You Catch Your Father Screwing Your Cousins 19 Year Old Peruvian Wife and Then He Takes His Pregnant Teenage Mistress Off to Peru, Leaving His Wife in a Complete and Utter Breakdown and his Daughter to Pick Up the Pieces of a Shattered Life,' then I might consider reading it.

Grandma

oh dear...

Theo

Sorry, that was a bit hostile. Really, I'm fine Grandma. And Mom seems better than she's been in months. I think all this murder stuff is distracting her. she hasn't cried in, like days.

Grandma

Well that IS something! I guess murder does have its benefits.

Darling, I have to go. Aditya just arrived.

I threw my phone on the bed and hugged Poppy. Stroking her belly, I kissed the top of her head. I was so, so thankful that she was alright. *Ding!*

Jigger

fyi, my cousin told me about the coroners report on mrs. kerkenbush. she had a knitting needle stuck deep in her eye socket - i mean like all the way to the back of her skull - and they found no water in her lungs so they're saying she was dead before she hit the water. she was murdered!

❊ 19 ❊

That night, I dreamed of our old house in Oak Park. I stood outside, under the stars, looking at our ornate Queen Anne's home. All the windows illuminated the interior, and each window showed a perfect snapshot from my previous life. The dining room window showed the table where I'd done all of my schooling, but it now stood bare. The living room window showed the television and the couch where we used to sit together, laughing over old movies, but it was now ominously silent. The bathroom window upstairs showed the purple William Morris wallpaper. In my dream, I could hear the dripping of the water from the bathroom faucet. That sound had always bugged me, but now it produced such a poignant homesickness that I began to cry.

I turned my gaze to the right, where Lexi's house stood. It was identical to our house—identical in every way. My tears stopped, and I began to smile, for the tale of our twin houses was my all-time favorite story from childhood. I must have driven my father crazy, asking him to repeat it, like, constantly.

For you see, the identical houses had been built for identical twin sisters—back in the day when carriages were still abundant on the streets of Oak Park. The Swallow Sisters had been fortunate enough to be born into a world of wealth, where all their needs were met. Their doting father had presented the houses to them on their twenty-first birthday. And to show that he held no preference for one daughter over the other, he had the houses built identically—down to the exact same number of nails.

The houses, set back from the street by sweeping lawns, were separated by a shared driveway. Beneath the driveway was an underground tunnel that connected the houses, so the sisters could visit each other when the weather was bad, without ever needing to step outside. In the spacious tunnel, there was a cookstove and a little kitchen area, where the Swallow Sisters would meet at night, in their nightgowns and slippers, to share cups of cocoa while blizzards raged outdoors.

The sisters never married, remaining spinsters for the rest of their lives. They became the grande dames of Oak Park society, hosting many events at our houses. The Swallows were great friends with Frank Lloyd Wright, who lived just a few doors down from them. It was claimed he was a regular in their parlor. And supposedly, the sisters punished Ernest Hemingway when he was a child because he broke one of their windows. The Swallows claimed Ernest was a surly child and did not seem sorry for his misdeed.

Maybe my father's tales held more fancy than fact, but I never grew tired of his Swallow Sister Stories. They lived to be a hundred years old, and they died on the same day. After their deaths, a couple purchased both their houses. This couple was unable to have children, so they adopted baby brothers from India. My father was one of those babies, and that's how he came to grow up in those fantastic old homes.

He had funny stories about his childhood and the pranks he used to play on his brother. The two houses had been the perfect place for children to knock about—full of secret hiding spots. Time passed, and on one tragic day, his beloved parents died suddenly in an accident. Dad was only twenty-three when the houses were passed on to him and his brother. Dad took one house, and my Uncle Eddie took the other.

But back to my dream—as I looked at Lexi's house, I could see her family inside. Her father was in his office, dutifully working, while her mother was setting the dining room table. I could see Lexi upstairs in her bedroom, talking on her phone. Everyone looked busy and happy.

I turned back to my house and was surprised that all the lights were off. It looked cold and uninviting. Even so, I felt I had to go inside. Something was urging me to enter. I wouldn't have been able to stop myself—even if I'd wanted.

So I crept to the front door. Behind it, I could hear the ticking of the grandfather clock that stood in the hallway inside. The clock was *much* louder than it had ever been in real life. In fact, when I opened the door, the ticking became as loud as a bass drum. I covered my ears and hurried towards the kitchen.

However, without any logical reason, instead of reaching the kitchen, I found myself in the cellar instead. The tunnel door was closed, which was very odd.

It always stood open.

A chill ran up my spine.

Lexi and I had traversed this tunnel almost every day of our lives. As I reached for the latch, I heard the sound of rushing water—and the sound kept growing stronger.

When I opened the door, water surged at me with such a force that it shoved me back, pinning me to the wall. I saw my father and his girl-friend struggling in the tunnel, desperately trying to keep their heads above the rushing water. Their bodies were completely immersed, and they each had knitting needles stuck in their eye sockets. I realized I had a needle in my eye too.

My father called to me, "Theo! Wait! Stop!"

But the deadly water carried me away.

❁ 20 ❁

I woke from the dream, gasping in terror. My heart raced. I felt water coming out of my mouth but quickly realized it was just drool. The dream hadn't been real, I reassured myself. I touched my eye, half believing I'd find a knitting needle. I shook my head and tried to go back to sleep.

But sleep wouldn't come.

I heard a faint bleating from far off in the distance. If I wasn't imagining this, and there really was a goat, maybe the goat was an insomniac. Or maybe he followed the old ways of first sleep, second sleep, which Dad and I had studied.

First sleep, second sleep was a sleeping pattern that our rural ancestors followed. They went to bed when it got dark, slept for several hours—their first sleep—and then they'd rise and get busy. They might prepare a midnight meal, or tend the fire, or nurse a child, or fight with their spouse. Some brave souls would wander the moors, checking in on neighbors who might be sickly. After a couple of hours, everyone would go back to bed and fall into their second sleep.

That's how humans lived for centuries—until the Industrial Revolution. Once people had lights in their dwellings, they could stay up longer in the evenings.

I thought back to the goat. He could be unaware that the world was now industrialized, and he was behind the times, still following the old ways. Or maybe he was lost. Or maybe he was sleepwalking. This last thought made me smile.

I tried my best to fall into my second sleep, but I couldn't. Instead, I found myself thinking of Oak Park and everything that had happened to lead us to Black Beaver Bay. And I blame a large part of that on the virus. I think Covid-19 ended my parents' marriage. Or should I say, it had a huge influence on the events that shaped my current situation.

When the coronavirus spread across our country and ultimately led to a shutdown, I remember thinking it would be kind of fun to have Mom and Dad at home, for they were both professors and had to do the distance learning thing with their students. And the first couple weeks had been great. We had a lot of family time, with board games and old movies.

But after a month, I could sense something different.

The first thing I noticed was the silence. My parents didn't talk as much. Then they began spending more time alone, in their home offices, as the semester wore on. Within two months, they were sleeping in separate bedrooms. Maybe too much time together had driven them apart. Or maybe there were deeper issues that I'd never been aware of. But by the time the government started lifting restrictions and opening up the economy, I could see they had grown apart.

Anyway, my parents went to great lengths to hide their problems and act as if everything was normal when we got together with Lexi's parents. We all quarantined together. Not even a pandemic could sever the bond between our twin houses.

And then on the Fourth of July, Lexi's oldest brother came home with a new bride. My cousin John had married a beautiful Peruvian girl. The young couple planned to move back into the family home while John finished his medical degree. Her name was Alessa, and I thought she was more stunning than any movie star I'd ever seen. Her brown eyes were radiant, and her laugh was magical. When I sent a picture of Alessa to Grandma, she said, "Now there is one juicy piece of fruit."

You can probably see where this is going.

But if you want the condensed, calendar version of my family's demise, here goes:

Alessa joined our twin families (and houses) on July 4th. On Halloween, I accidentally discovered her relationship with Dad.

Our two families held our annual—always hysterical—Halloween costume party. I went to bed but then got a text from Lexi, who said she had saved a bunch of Halloween candy for me. She hadn't given it to me at the party because she knew Mom would make a fuss. So I decided to sneak over to get my bag of sweets, thinking that Mom and Dad were fast asleep, and no one would be the wiser.

When I got to the tunnel and saw that the door was closed, I was really surprised. It was always open. Always.

Then I heard soft music coming from the tunnel. Slowly, I opened the door and saw Dad and Alessa on the couch. She was straddled around his waist. They were kissing passionately—still in their Halloween costumes. Dad was dressed as Dracula, and Alessa was a Tyrolean maiden with fake blonde braids.

It took me a few seconds to realize they were doing more than kissing.

Shock flew through me. I stood there, not moving. It felt as if the wind had been knocked out of me for the rest of my life.

That's when my dad saw me. "Theo! Wait! Stop!" he called, as I ran up the stairs, crying. And because I'm such a klutz, I tripped running up the stairs and hit my shinbone. I cried out in pain. Soon Mom was at my side, and so was Dad. Within twenty minutes, both houses were all lit up again. The next day, Dad and Alessa left.

By Thanksgiving, Dad and Mom had been in contact, and he informed Mom that he was now down in Peru. Somehow they made it back to Alessa's native country, even with the airline restrictions. He said he missed us, and he was sorry. I remember not eating much that Thanksgiving.

Then on Christmas Eve, he called and said he was more than likely going to be staying down in Peru. He said with the uptick of corona cases in America, the airlines were really cracking down. Nobody was allowing flights into the States at that time. Again, he was sorry, and he missed us. I wouldn't talk to him—I hadn't since Halloween.

Mom and I didn't have the heart to put up a tree last Christmas. I think we ate blueberries and watched "It's a Wonderful Life."

And then at New Year's, we heard from my father again, and he informed Mom that Alessa was three months pregnant, and he would be staying down in Peru. After that phone call, Mom retreated to her bed, and I couldn't rouse her from it, no matter how hard I tried. She barely ate. And I kept begging her to brush her teeth, while I carried on with the business of running the house. Suddenly, and really unexpectedly, I was in charge.

Mom stayed in bed for five weeks straight. Then miraculously, she peeked her matted head from her filthy comforter on Groundhog's Day. She'd taken a phone call from Gally that had altered her frame of mind. Gally had told her that their uncle had died and left them the old family fishing resort.

By Valentine's Day, we had our house on the market.

By St. Patrick's Day, it had sold.

By Easter, I was packing up all my belongings, donating my childhood toys to Goodwill.

By April Fools' Day, we had moved to Minnesota.

So you can see how the demise of my family is choreographed with the major holidays on the American calendar. And now, April Fool's day will forever be associated with finding Mr. Hendrickson's body, so I really didn't have much hope for May Day—or anything beyond that. It was enough to put a girl off holidays, like, forever.

❀ 21 ❀

I am not a knitter. I know so little about knitting that I confused it with crocheting. So I had to Google it. Knitting is done with pointy needles, and crocheting is done with a hook. I also learned that knitting has been around for a long time. They've found knitted socks in the Egyptian pyramids.

The most surprising thing I read was its health benefits. Knitting can actually change your brain chemistry, and produce more serotonin and dopamine, and lower your stress hormones. That didn't seem to be the case for poor Mrs. Kerkenbush. And nowhere did I read that a knitting needle had ever been used as a murder weapon.

Yet I was glad I had Googled this information because I felt more prepared for my interview the following morning. Since I was the person who had found the body of Mrs. Kerkenbush, and her death was considered a homicide, it was protocol for the cops to ask me questions. Unfortunately, my limited knowledge of handcrafts never came up. The interview took quite a different turn.

Sitting inside Deputy Pete's office at the police station, I couldn't help but fidget in my seat. We were waiting for him to return and start the questioning. Mom sat by my side, glued to her phone.

Finally, I hopped up and began filming his office. I'd brought my video camera along in hopes of taping the interrogation. It's not that Grandma's inherent distrust of the police was beginning to rub off on me, but that I thought it might be fun to add to my growing compilation of scenes of Black Beaver Bay.

"Theo, I don't know if you should be doing that," Mom said half-heartedly. She obviously wasn't paying any attention, being engrossed with whatever she was reading on her phone.

I filmed the view from the deputy's window. Across the street, I could see the public library. I made a note to myself to explore it later. The branches from a nearby tree were bare and black. On the ground lay dirty patches of snow, remnants from the storm we'd had a few days ago. There was no evidence of spring coming any time soon.

I crept over to a wide bulletin board that took up most of one wall. Flyers of missing children and the FBI's Most Wanted were abundant. One flyer was of a missing cow—I zoomed in on that one. The cow's name was Gladys, but she would also answer to GladBags. If found, the poster advised you to not approach her, for she was known to get aggressive when she felt her personal space was being invaded. Her distinguishing characteristics were her preference for the color turquoise and a brown birthmark on her tongue. This can't be for real, I thought.

I moved on to some certificates and diplomas that bore Pete's name. Last month he had been named Policeman of the Year. I wondered how many cows he had to find to achieve this honor. Of course, if all the cows were as touchy as Gladys, it might be harder than I imagined.

Next I filmed a colorful map of Black Beaver Bay and zoomed in on the Cove. From a bird's eye view, it looked different than I had expected. I realized how close the Cove was to the Banger Sausage Company. Mrs. Banger really *was* our neighbor. I wondered where Millie Kerkenbush's house was located.

Pete returned to his office, giving me a strange look—or more accurately, giving my video camera a strange look. Quickly, I sat down in the chair across from his desk. Deputy Pete asked me to please turn off the camera, so I acted like I did, although actually it was still taping. I set the camera on his desk, and when he asked about the red light, I told him it meant the battery was charging. He fell for it. Grandma would have been very proud.

Before he started, laughter erupted outside his office. Aunt Gally was in the hallway, talking to some old acquaintance, recalling funny memories. "Remember when you painted the principal's office red?" Someone chuckled.

"You must be thinking of someone else." I could hear Gally's light-hearted laughter.

Deputy Pete cleared his throat and apologized for making us wait. He pushed a button on the tape recorder on his desk. "This is Deputy Peter Hicks. It is Monday, April 11th, and I am questioning Miss Theo Gillman…"

"Theodora Chandalavada," I corrected him.

He looked at me. I couldn't tell if he was annoyed or confused. "Okay, you're going to have to spell that for me."

So I did.

"Whew, that's a mouthful," he tried to joke.

"Yes, I imagine it must be hard for you," I said in all seriousness. Mom kicked my ankle but only lightly. My snotty comment seemed to have flown right over his head anyway, so I don't know what Mom was getting all worked up about.

"Theodora Chandalavada," he continued, "regarding her discovery of the body of Mildred Kerkenbush on April 5th."

"Was it the fifth?" Mom interrupted. "Oh, yeah, I guess it would have been."

Pete turned off his tape recorder. "You can't interrupt," he told Mom. His words were terse, but he was looking at her with his big, brown, sappy eyes, obviously flirting. It made me want to vomit.

"If you can't keep quiet," he said, "I'm going to have to ask you to sit in the hallway."

"Sorry!" Mom said meekly. "I'll be good."

That's when Gally came in and pulled up a chair next to me.

"Shhh!" Mom conveyed to her sister. Gally nodded.

Pete started the recorder again. "This is an interview with Miss Theodora…."

"Theodorable!" Aunt Gally teased. "That's what I used to call her when she was little."

"Okay. You two have to leave." Pete stood up and escorted them to the hallway, shutting the door on his return. Sitting down at his desk, he started the recorder once again. Possibly due to practice, he got through the prologue quickly and said, "Could you please give me an outline of your activities on April 5th?"

"Ah." I thought about that day. "I helped my mom and Aunt Gally clean the house in the morning, and then a friend picked me up…"

"Your friend's name?"

"Jigger…" It dawned on me that I didn't know Jigger's last name. Or her first name for that matter. But Pete must have known because he clarified, "You mean Jessica Jones."

"No way, are you kidding me? Is that her real name? Jessica Jones is like my favorite Marvel character! That's so cool! Have you watched that show on Netflix?"

Pete turned off the recorder. He was obviously annoyed. "Listen Theo, you need to take this seriously. We can wrap this up quickly if you just answer the questions and don't go off script."

He held my eye until I nodded. Then he hit the button again.

"So what did you and Jigger do?"

"She took me to the bowling alley and they have *awesome* cheese curds, by the way…oh, wait—that was the day before. Okay. On the 5th, I was cleaning and unpacking stuff in the house, and I took a break mid-morning to take Poppy, my dog, on a walk. We ended up down at the beach, and that's when I found her."

"Were you alone? Was anyone with you, besides your dog?"

I wasn't sure how to answer this. Were the bodyguards supposed to be a secret? Why hadn't I thought about this before? I could have asked Mom what to say. But since Thing 1 was my witness that I hadn't jabbed Mrs. Kerkenbush in the eye with a knitting needle and then pushed her in the lake, I decided I *had* to tell the truth.

"No, I wasn't alone. One of our bodyguards was with me."

Pete turned off the recorder yet again. "Bodyguards? Your mom hired bodyguards?" A shadow of anger crossed his face.

"My mom didn't hire them, and she wasn't very happy when she found out about them." This seemed to appease him. His body visibly relaxed.

"So it was Gally?" He smiled, once again looking like the nice cop. I shook my head no.

"Someone had to hire them. They wouldn't show up on their own accord." He looked pleased with his deduction.

Well, no shit, Sherlock, I thought.

"Actually it was my grandmother who hired them. She said…"

I paused, thinking about my next words carefully. I wondered if I could get in trouble for insulting a cop. Then I thought about the way Pete would look at my mom so lovingly, and how it was soooo annoying. Maybe I had no idea how to be a matchmaker, but I felt pretty sure I could be an excellent *anti*-matchmaker.

"Grandma said your police force is a bunch of bumbling Barney Fifes."

His eyes conveyed the fury inside him. If I'd wanted to make him mad, I'd succeeded in spades.

I should have stopped there.

But I didn't.

"And she called you a Howdy Doody sort of cop."

For a brief second, his brown eyes turned black. He actually scared me! As I watched him struggle to rein in his anger, I hoped my video camera was catching every bit of it.

He cleared his throat and sat taller in his chair. "Let's wrap this up." He hit the recorder button for the last time. He asked a few more questions and finished by thanking me for my time.

I whisked my camera off the desk and beat him to the door. I opened it, and Gally fell in on me. Obviously, her ear had been glued to the door, eavesdropping.

Gally could see by the expression on my face that something was up. We hurried outside while Deputy Pete asked Mom to stay. No doubt I was going to catch heck for my smart aleck behavior, but I didn't care. Seeing his anger, I now understood Grandma's misgivings about cops—and I fully agreed with her.

He was not to be trusted.

❀ 22 ❀

"Was your mom pissed?" Jigger asked, as she daubed foundation around my mouth.

"Oh, yeah," I mumbled. It was difficult to talk as she spread make-up all over my face. She'd ask me questions, but if I moved, she'd reprimand me and tell me to sit still.

We were in my room—well, Grandma Fay's room—and I was telling her about my visit to the police station. Earlier, we'd watched my video of Deputy Pete and his transformation into a mutant evil being. My film had even caught his eyes turning black, which had made Jigger say, "Whoa!"

But my mom had been mad, just like I'd expected. She said I knew better than to repeat things that Grandma said, and that I'd purposely tried to embarrass Pete, which wasn't a nice thing to do. I didn't tell her that my real objective was to be an anti-matchmaker. And it hadn't worked anyway, because he's been to our house, like, four times since my interview.

Just then, I heard the bleating of that goat again.

"Did you hear that?" I asked Jigger.

"Hear what?" she asked. But at that moment, she was playing a voicemail from her mom, so maybe that took up all her listening attention.

I shook my head. I must be imagining it. Poppy hadn't heard the bleating the other day, and now Jigger couldn't. Was I having auditory hallucinations?

"Don't move," she ordered, as she dusted my entire face with powder. I sneezed.

I had begged Jigger to do this. I wanted to see what I would look like with the kind of makeup she'd been wearing on the first morning we met.

"Just wait, I'm not done yet," she warned. She paused and found "Dance Monkey" by Tones and I on her playlist.

She told me, "Now tilt your head back and close your eyes." I could feel her brushing something on my eyelids. "The eyeliner is the trickiest part."

"It tickles."

She bossed me, "Let *me* do the talking." But in the next breath, she asked me, "Have you heard back from Doc Vesper yet?"

I held up my hand, so she would stop working for just a minute. "He said it must have been the garlic that made Poppy sick. And all the workmen ended up being fine. They just had hangovers."

Jigger grinned but then quickly grew serious. "You know, I've been thinking about all of this. Do you suppose Mrs. K's murder is somehow related to Mr. Hendrickson getting dug up?"

"There's more to it than that."

"Like what?" Her curiosity and concern were apparent—so much so that I told her about Uncle Dickie and made her swear to keep it a secret. The news hit her harder than I had expected. She'd heard nothing about this, and had believed that Uncle Dickie died of a heart attack—which told me that not *everything* in Black Beaver Bay went through the rumor mill.

"Wow," she said softly. "Like there could be a real serial killer here. Seriously, this is freaking me out. I'm glad your grandma hired those bodyguards."

"Thing 1 and Thing 2," I said, sharing my nicknames for them. "Yeah, a bodyguard can come in handy, especially if you need a witness when you find a dead body."

She sat down on the edge of my bed, thinking this over. "It has to be all related. But how?"

"That's what we think, although we can't connect the dots."

"When I was in the eighth grade, I used to love reading murder mysteries. And then I got hooked on all those cold case crime shows.

At one point, I thought I was going to go into law enforcement, because I wanted to be a detective."

"Well, let's put your knowledge to use, then," I joked. "Maybe we can figure this out."

She smiled, revealing her dimples. "*Maybe* we could be like the Scooby-Doo gang—you know, teenage sleuths."

"Well, I'd be Velma," I joked.

"And I'd be Fred."

Puzzled, I glanced at her.

"I have his hair color!" she explained, before rushing on cheerfully, "Okay, tell me everything you know!"

"You swear to keep this a secret?"

She held out her pinkie.

It was official.

So I told her everything I knew. She listened intently, nodding. She was so wrapped up in my story that she completely forgot she was supposed to be giving me a makeover.

"Are we done here, then?" I asked.

"Oh, no." She jumped up and started working on my face again. "What kind of tattoos do you want?"

I picked out a skull and bones.

Twenty minutes later, she moved on to my hair. It felt like she was putting it in pigtails, high on my head. She said, "Remember Abby on 'NCIS'? I'm channeling her."

"I need to stretch…"

"I'm almost done. Hang on…Okay. *Done!*" she cried. "Now keep your eyes closed." She took my hand and dragged me over to the mirror on the back of my door. "Okay, open."

I opened my eyes and jumped. Then I squealed. I didn't recognize the person staring back at me. This was so bizarre!

I looked like some badass, Japanese anime character. The eyeliner and false lashes made my eyes look huge! The tattoo on my cheekbone was totally cool. But the most shocking thing of all was the black lip-stick. It reminded me of something from an old Dracula movie.

Poppy looked up at me and whined.

"Do you like it?" asked Jigger.

"This is insane." I kept looking at myself, turning my head at different angles. Jigger took some pictures, so I could send them to Lexi because this would make her freak!

My door opened. It was Mom holding a bowl of dip and sliced vegetables. "What was all the noise? Is everything…" Then she screamed. She stared at me in astonishment. I worried she was going to embarrass me and start crying, but instead, she bit her lip and broke into a smile.

She confessed, "It's just so shocking!"

Aunt Gally arrived to see what all the commotion was about. "Oh, my God, Theo! I never would have recognized you!"

"I know," Mom agreed.

"Don't worry," I said quickly, "This isn't my new look…"

"Don't you like it?" Jigger asked.

"Yeah, I actually look cool," I played with one of my pigtails. "And believe me, I am *not* cool!"

Everyone laughed, sharing this happy moment—although it did feel strange to be the center of attention because that was something I definitely wasn't used to.

"Are you guys hungry?" Mom asked.

"Always," Jigger and I said in unison.

It turned out to be a really awesome night, with Mom and Gally telling us funny stories about their experiences as Miss Apple Blossom. Jigger asked them if they'd ever heard of the Miss Apple Blossom Curse.

"That's not real." A flicker of amusement crossed Mom's face.

"Oh, yes it is!" Gally declared. Looking at me, she continued, "The day after grandma was crowned, she had a bad car accident. The day after your mother was crowned, she broke her foot. The day after *I* was crowned, I broke out with poison ivy over every inch of my body!"

"Well," said Mom, "if you'd kept your clothes on, that never would have happened."

We all enjoyed their stories, but at ten o'clock, Jigger had to leave because she had to start work at four in the morning. Reluctantly, we said goodnight.

Before I washed my face, I stared into the mirror one last time. I felt like a little kid on Halloween, excited to take on a different persona. Later in bed, I scrolled through the pictures that Jigger had taken of me earlier. I found the sickest one and sent it to Lexi. Instantly, there was a *ding!*

Lexi

OMG, is that you? You look like some psycho killer. What is going on?

I loved her response. I texted her back, explaining the picture and the whole evening. But once again, she seemed distant—like she couldn't relate to my new life. I told her I'd talk to her later.

Scrolling through the pictures yet again, I got a wicked idea. I'm not saying I'm proud of these ideas, and usually I stop myself before I carry through on them, but sometimes I don't. I was feeling a little reckless, and there was something inside of me that wanted to lash out at my father. I wondered if Dad ever worried about us—or if he even cared anymore.

I unblocked my father's phone number. I went to the "Unknown Senders" Inbox and saw that he'd sent me hundreds of messages. I didn't bother to read them. Instead, I sent him the most deranged photo of myself. I picked one that scared even me.

In the message, I wrote #MovingOnInMinnesota

Next I hit "Send."

And then I blocked his number. *Again.*

❀ 23 ❀

So Dad totally freaked out about my picture. He seemed to agonize about what had happened to the child he'd left behind. Was I into drugs? What exactly was going on? I guess he'd thought we would stay in a time capsule and be exactly the same forever. Maybe it was painful for him to see that our lives had also changed. Or perhaps he was alarmed that his daughter had turned into a psycho killer.

Anyway, he sent Mom a flurry of texts full of concern about my stability. Mom wasn't upset at all—in fact, I think she kind of relished the whole thing. She simply told Dad that, "Theo is growing up," and she left him to ruminate about what kind of person I was growing into. Perhaps she wanted him to feel that his departure had turned me to the dark side.

That's the thing about Mom—I never could predict how the needle on her emotional scale was going to swing. Although it was very apparent where that needle was this afternoon. Because *this* afternoon, she was obviously happy—happier than I'd seen her in months. And it didn't have anything to do with the recent text messages from Dad. No, she was simply delighted to be out on the lake.

Originally, I didn't want to go with Mom and Gally, but they dragged me along. It was the first warm day we'd had since moving to Minnesota, and they were soooo excited to hit the water. I had to shake my head at their enthusiasm. Maybe it was something genetic in all Minnesotans. As soon as the thermometer got one degree above freezing, they'd go out on the water.

Anyway, I was really glad I'd come along. For one thing, I got to see the boathouse, which I hadn't explored before. Since we'd arrived, I'd been through all the cabins and every inch of our big house, but the boathouse was new to me. It was a really cool place.

The building itself jutted out onto the water, held aloft with massive pilings. Large windows on both sides showed awesome vistas of the lake. I wondered if Mom might let me move in there—at least for the summer. The open rafters in the high-pitched roof were a great architectural detail, and the floor was made up of three docks and open lake water.

I filmed the entire interior as Mom and Gally struggled with the boat. Finally, Thing 1 and Thing 2 stepped in, helping them get the massive twenty-foot rowboat into the water.

Mom looked at the bodyguards with her hands on her hips. "I'm not sure it's necessary for you guys to tag along. Do you think we're going to be attacked by walleyes?"

Things 1 and 2 didn't budge.

"Hey, I packed enough food for an army. The more the merrier!" sang Gally. "And besides, it'd be a shame to let all those big muscles go to waste. You guys can do the rowing!"

And with that, we were off.

Poppy stood on her hind legs at the bow of the boat, sniffing the air, very excited. This was the first time she'd ever been in a boat, and I could see she was a true sea dog at heart.

The air was cool on the lake. Even though the temperature was in the seventies, I put up my hoodie. Leaning over the side of the boat, I stuck my finger in the water, and it was freezing! The oars creaked loudly as the bodyguards rowed away from shore. From this vantage, I could see our whole resort, with cabins dotting the forest, each one facing the lake. It was charming.

"It looks pretty quiet up there," I said.

Gally, who was sitting next to me on the wooden seat, said, "The workers are in town for lunch. I think they got word that we were heading out on the lake. When the cat's away, the mice will play," she joshed. She handed me a tuna fish sandwich from the cooler. I bit into it and resumed filming.

Suddenly, she ordered the bodyguards to stop rowing. The boat floated gently in the calm water.

"See that bluff up there?" She pointed to a jagged rock formation that jutted out to a point, looming at least a hundred yards above us. "That's Lover's Leap. Legend has it, if you jump off it with your sweetheart, your love will last forever."

I filmed the dangerous-looking rock. "Did you ever leap off?" I asked.

"Oh, yeah." She smiled.

"No way! Really?" I was totally impressed.

"I jumped off with my boyfriend from high school. But we broke up the very next week, so you can't always believe the legends." She chuckled.

"Did Mom?" I asked curiously.

"Oh, my God no, are you kidding me?" She laughed.

"I heard that," Mom said from the back of the boat.

Gally passed out sandwiches to everyone before she ordered the rowing men to veer right, around a corner of shoreline that opened up into an inlet.

"And that's Butterfly Cove," she pointed out to me. She whispered, "That's where your mom had her first kiss."

"I heard that too," Mom said again.

"How old was she?" I asked.

"Oh, let's see now. About twenty-nine, I think."

One of the stoic bodyguards made a choking noise.

"Gally, stop it," Mom said, but you could tell by her voice that she wasn't bothered.

"Let's row closer," Gally ordered.

We approached the small inlet, which had a horseshoe-shaped beach, encircled by woods. I filmed the beautiful setting.

"We used to have campfires here when we were little," Mom said wistfully.

"Grandma Fay loved this spot," Gally added. "Every fall she'd spread milkweed seeds all along the edge of the forest. And every year, the monarchs would come. Remember how beautiful it was, Ana?"

"Yes," Mom agreed. "I wonder if the butterflies still come around?"

The oarsmen rowed back into the middle of the lake, continuing on with our tour. Gally pointed out how far our property spanned, which seemed to cover the entire west side of the lake—and it was a *big* lake. It made me wonder how much land we owned, and how long it had been in our family. So I asked, and Gally told me.

"Grandma Fay's mother, who was your great-great-grandmother, purchased this land back in the 1920s. I've heard countless stories about her. I guess she was a real character and a huge activist in Women's Suffrage. She got arrested many times."

"She sounds interesting!" I opened a bag of potato chips.

"Oh, she was *very* interesting," Gally continued. "She patented this natural remedy cough syrup with her cousin, and they made a fortune. With that windfall, she bought these 2,000 acres and became a benefactress to the whole town." Gally looked at me with a twinkle in her eye. "You know, she'd make a fascinating subject for a documentary. If you're interested, her name was Esme Dooley."

"That's a cool name," I said, munching on Old Dutch potato chips, only half-listening. "Hey, these chips are awesome! How come I've never had them before?"

"I don't know. We grew up on them." Gally stole one from my bag.

It was an hour into our boat ride, and the bodyguards were starting to show signs of being winded. Reluctantly, Mom said, "I think we should probably head back."

Even though they'd had to *drag* me out on this freezing lake, I now felt sorry to leave. The lake was fabulous! It made me look forward to going out with Jigger, although I didn't really want to try fishing.

We were mostly quiet as we headed back to the boathouse. Poppy was now on my lap, exhausted from all the excitement of the journey. As I stroked her back, I thought about something that Jigger had told me the other night.

She said her brother Josh wanted to hang out again. So then I told her I thought Josh was really cute, and she found that hilarious. I'd begged her not to tell him, and I was trusting her to keep my secret. I'd already told her so many personal things that I'd be devastated if she turned out to be a blabbermouth.

The bottom line was that I *did* trust Jigger. We were planning to meet in a couple of nights. She'd talked me into filming the Miss Apple Blossom practice, and afterwards, we were heading to the library to write down our thoughts about these murders. I hoped she'd have some insights.

Poppy stirred in my lap, breaking my daydream. She lifted her head, smelling the air. She started barking, and I turned to see what she was looking at.

Black smoke twisted into the air. On the ground, orange flames spat angrily.

"Oh, my God!" I screamed. "A cabin's on fire!"

❀ 24 ❀

"Faster!" Gally called. "Can't you go any faster?" She was frantic.

Things 1 and 2 were rowing as fast as was humanly possible, and both of them had beads of sweat running down their foreheads. Everyone was strained. We could see the flames growing larger, but we couldn't get to the shore fast enough.

Mom whipped out her phone and dialed 911. Although as soon as she'd gotten through to the dispatcher, we could hear the fire engine sirens—their wails carrying mournfully out to the lake. They were getting closer. As I watched, I squeezed Poppy, probably too tightly.

"Don't go all the way back to the boathouse," Gally cried. "Just row up to the beach."

The fire engines roared into view, racing past the big house, towards the cabins. We watched as they came to a quick stop. Men disembarked, rushing into action. We lost sight of them, as the boat came ashore on the sandy beach.

Scrambling as quickly as I could, I jumped into the lake. The water was at knee level, and it sent chills through my body. Mom and Gally hopped out too, as Things 1 and 2 pulled the heavy boat partway up on the beach. Carrying Poppy, I followed Mom and Gally up a pathway to the cabins, with the bodyguards close behind.

The air lay heavy with smoke, making me cough. I tried to cover Poppy's snout with my jacket as I ran, but she kept pulling her head back out, as if she didn't want to miss anything.

By the time we made it up the incline, the fire was extinguished. Firemen stood at a distance, assessing the situation. The damaged cabin had been Uncle Dickie's.

A sudden sadness hit me. Everything that was left of my dead uncle was in that little dwelling. At least it hadn't been a complete loss. It looked like only the kitchen had been totaled. But could we save the rest of the structure? And what about the smoke damage? A friend of mine had a fire in her house, and her family had lost more to smoke damage than to the actual fire.

I set Poppy down and began filming. As we stood there, staring at this disaster, Deputy Pete arrived. Mom looked very relieved to see him, which made me uneasy. He actually put his arm around her and gave her a supportive hug. I stood behind them and captured this on film. Then an idea hit me, and I whipped out my phone and snapped a picture. This might come in handy later.

I edged away from Mom and Pete and scooted over by Gally, who was talking to some firemen. She asked if they had any idea how the fire had started. They said they didn't know, and they couldn't speculate because that was the fire inspector's job.

I continued to film the destruction as the firemen wrapped up their hoses. Why had Uncle Dickie's cabin been the one to catch fire? The workmen weren't working or staying in this particular cabin because it was still sealed off as a potential crime scene.

Had someone set the fire to hide evidence? Someone who was guilty of poison? I mean, it did make me wonder. In the other cabins, the electrical wiring was being brought up to code, so maybe an accident could have occurred in one of them. But in this one? It made me suspicious.

Gally moved away from the group of men and headed towards a lone fireman who was standing away from the group. He'd removed his helmet and was drinking a bottle of water. He nodded to my aunt.

Casually, I moved closer with my camera. I slipped behind them, making my way into the pine trees—planning to eavesdrop. But my footsteps were loud on the forest floor, with small branches breaking under each step. I couldn't be very sneaky at this rate!

Suddenly, I heard another set of footsteps—or maybe it was just my imagination. I stood still, trying to separate the noise from the talking voices nearby. Poppy let out a soft, low growl. Setting her down, I let her lead me.

She pulled me towards a wooded knoll behind the cabins. As we climbed the incline, I clearly heard someone moving in the forest.

And then I gasped because a stocky man loomed in front of me.

Poppy and the man's dog sniffed each other curiously. It was Mr. Anderson—the Burl Ives guy I'd met at the vet's office the other day.

"Goodness, you almost gave me a heart attack!" He placed his hand on his chest.

What was he doing, skulking around our woods at this most suspicious time? Could *he* have started the fire? In his large cargo shorts, hiking boots, and Patagonia windbreaker, he certainly didn't *look* like an arsonist. But then again, what did arsonists wear these days? My expression must have shown my wariness, for right away, he explained his presence.

"I heard the commotion and came to see what was going on. Arthur and I walk these woods every day." Sadly he added, "Or we used to, anyway, when your Uncle Dickie was alive. Today was such a nice day I thought it would be good to get out."

Well, he did have a point about the nice weather. And how was I to know his daily routine? Maybe he'd walked these woods every day to keep tabs on my great-uncle and report back to Grandma. I was torn between believing him and mistrusting him.

I felt a presence behind me and turned around quickly. It was only Thing 1. Sighing with relief, I faced Mr. Anderson again.

"So what happened?" he asked innocently. "I take it there was a fire. Is everything alright?" He looked at me strangely for a few seconds, waiting for me to say something. Thing 1 stood silent, as I did. Struggling to come up with a response, I was grappling with the image of the snowman from "Rudolph" setting a fire.

All of a sudden, Doc Vesper came up behind Mr. Anderson. He too was walking a dog. The vet looked surprised to see us on this pathway.

"Good afternoon." He nodded at everyone. "I heard sirens. Is everything okay?"

115

I studied his expression. He *looked* innocent enough, but then again, how did I know? His jeans and pullover were no more incriminating than Mr. Anderson's outfit. Neither man had disheveled hair, and neither had any soot on him. Both of them could have been innocent. Or both of them could have been extremely good actors—and guilty.

I knew they were waiting for an answer. Finally, I said, "Deputy Pete is over there. You can go ask him."

With that, our conversation was over. They lumbered over the knoll and towards the burned cabin. I followed them, watching to see what they would do. They went straight over to the deputy and Mom and started talking.

So I went back to my plan of eavesdropping on Gally and the handsome fireman. As quietly as I could, I inched around the burned cabin—out of their sight, but close enough so I could hear their conversation. Thing 1 stayed annoyingly close by.

Apparently, the fireman was *another* old acquaintance of Gally's because they spoke on familiar terms. I stroked Poppy, hoping to keep her quiet, so I wouldn't be detected.

"Oh, I'll never forget that!" The fireman chuckled. "Not as long as I live! We still talk about your drag race down Main Street, at 120 miles per hour."

"You must be thinking of someone else," Gally joked. "But seriously, how do you think the fire started? And don't tell me you have no idea," she said conspiratorially.

"Gally, we're not supposed to give our opinions. I could get kicked off the department."

"I'm not going to tell anyone." My aunt sounded sincere. I wished I could see their faces. "Hey, I'll take you out to dinner if you just tell me what you think."

"Is this your way of asking me out on a date?" His voice sounded flirty.

She flirted back. "Not a date—more like catching up on old times. Besides, you could be *married*, for all I know."

"Divorced," he told her.

Hmm, I wondered what Grandma would say about all of this. I didn't think Gally needed any matchmaking help. She was doing just fine on her own.

"I get to pick the time and place," he continued to bargain.

"Okay, fine."

"Remember," he paused. "You didn't hear it from me."

"Scout's honor."

I had to smile. I happened to know that Gally had been kicked out of the Girl Scouts. Mom, on the other hand, had earned their Gold Award.

"Okay," he finally conceded, "I think it was set deliberately."

"I knew it!" Disgust filled Gally's voice.

"There was a strong odor of gasoline," he added. "I can still smell it."

I inhaled deeply. Besides the overwhelming smoke, I thought I *might* be able to detect the smell of gas. But maybe that was just the power of suggestion.

"So you're saying…" Aunt Gally hesitated.

"I'm guessing it was arson."

❀ 25 ❀

The gymnasium walls at the high school held banners of their past students' achievements. The Class of 2012 had won the State Baseball title. The girls' Dance Line teams were State Champions three years in a row, from 2016-2019. But neither of these could compare with how many times the football team had won State. Obviously, they took their sports very seriously.

The most prominent thing on the gym walls was a gigantic banner bearing the image of their team mascot—a beaver in a red-and-white jersey, holding his finger (if beavers have fingers) in the "We're #1" position. I thought it looked like the beaver was giving me the finger.

I sat in the bleachers, filming the rehearsal for the Miss Apple Blossom pageant. Thirty girls in workout clothes were being tortured by Miss Honeycutt. Her gray roots still showed in her dyed red hair. Apparently her schedule was so busy she couldn't take care of unimportant matters. Oddly, she held a megaphone in one hand and a roll of paper towels under her arm.

"That was great, girls!" Miss Honeycutt shouted through her megaphone, as the deafening music came to a screeching stop. I should have worn earplugs! Thank goodness I hadn't brought Poppy along. I could have been charged with animal cruelty.

"Take two, and then we'll do it again!" Miss Honeycutt shouted.

I filmed the girls gathering in groups, panting. I watched as the girls congregated around Jigger. You could just tell she was popular. I couldn't understand why she thought she had to lose five more pounds. She looked great—better than anyone else. As the girls recovered, Miss Honeycutt bounded over to a folding table where she conferred with none other than Mrs. Banger.

Mrs. Banger wore tights, covered by shorts, with a baggy tunic that barely covered her generous behind. She had a sweatband around her forehead, although there was no evidence that Mrs. Banger had actually even moved since the practice had begun. The two women chatted, and then Miss Honeycutt resumed her position.

"Okay, girls," she bellowed through her bullhorn. "Let's take it from the top—except this time, I want Crystal to be front and center." She pointed to Mrs. Banger, who hit a button, and the song started over for the bazillionth time.

"If tomorrow all the things were gone I worked for all my life…" The lyrics of "I'm Proud to be an American" filled the gymnasium. I turned down the volume on my video camera to the lowest setting I had ever used.

Each girl carried a flag during the synchronized dance routine, saluting the audience now and then. I zoomed in on Jigger. She was one of the best dancers—if not the best.

I turned my camera on Mrs. Banger. Bobbing her head to the music, she looked fixated on the girls.

Next I turned my camera on Thing 1 who sat several feet away. Thank God the bleachers were full of observers. Otherwise it would have been *sooo* awkward with just the two of us there. As it was, we were drawing enough attention—probably because we were the only outsiders in the place.

I moved my lens back to the crowd and saw Josh, Jigger's brother, sitting with a group of boys. Were they his brothers? Just then, he looked at me and waved. I felt my cheeks grow hot. I waved back and quickly turned away.

I directed my lens back to the dancing contestants, just in time to catch one of them accidentally slamming the end of her flagpole into another girl's face, giving her a bloody nose. The crowd moaned. Maybe there really *was* something about this Miss Apple Blossom Curse.

"Stop the music!" Miss Honeycutt ordered, bustling over to the injured dancer. She unwrapped some paper towels and wadded them on the hurt girl's nose before leading her off to the sidelines. Aha! That's why she had the paper towels. This must have happened more than once. Who knew dancing with flags could be so dangerous?

"Okay. From the top!" Miss Honeycutt cried.

And so the music started—again!

I couldn't take any more of this.

I stepped down the bleachers and slipped into the hallway. Even though I'd eaten two helpings of Mom's sweet-and-sour pork for supper, I was hungry again. They *had* to have a vending machine around here. Didn't all schools?

I heard the sound of footsteps behind me and turned around. Of course—why did I even bother looking? It was Thing 1. Actually, I felt kind of grateful that I wasn't alone. The dimly lit hallways reminded me of something in a slasher movie. Was the school having some kind of budget crisis? I mean, why did they have to keep the hallways so dark?

The school architects must have copied the plans of a rat maze. Numerous turns, leading to dead ends, made no sense to me. Finally, I found the cafeteria. The expansive room was closed off with a massive metal gate. The folding tables and chairs had been pushed to one side of the room, and a janitor was mopping the floor. I could smell the disinfectant.

"Excuse me, where are the vending machines?" I called out to him.

The janitor paused. Slowly, deliberately, he pointed with his skeletal arm to the right. Now, that kind of creeped me out. He could definitely be in a horror movie.

I found the vending machines. I checked my pockets, knowing full well I didn't have any money on me, but I hoped Thing 1 would get the hint. And he did, producing several dollars from his billfold without me even asking.

I got two bags of Doritos, and I gave one of them to him. He accepted it and nodded. I nodded back. Who needed to speak? Who needed sign language? Our form of silent communication was more than adequate.

Then I heard the unmistakable voice of Mrs. Banger booming through the bullhorn. "Alright girls, Miss Honeycutt is taking a break, so *I'll* be taking over for a few minutes. Remember to watch those flag-poles!" The music started again.

I didn't feel like going back to the gym, so I wandered the halls. I came across a lighted cabinet that housed awards for the outstanding students. This was interesting. Old black-and-white photos of boys doing the javelin and shot put were quite artistic. Trophies of past achievements picked up the dim lights of the showcase. I wondered if all these people, who had toiled so valiantly to receive these trophies, were now dead. I admit, it was somewhat depressing.

But then my spirits lifted because I found a picture of Mom giving her valedictorian speech for the Class of 1984. I'd never seen this picture before. It made me feel proud, yet also a little sorry for Mom. She looked so young and nervous. There were plaques with the name "Ana Gillman" for outstanding scholar. She'd been the recipient of several scholarships. It looked like she'd been a big deal.

As hard as I searched, I couldn't find anything with Gally's name.

I'd been standing there for quite some time, lost in my own thoughts. Thing 1 was examining the cases too. We were so quiet, no one would have known we were there. The music from the gymnasium stopped, and I wondered if practice was over.

The sound of voices close by made me jump. Someone around the corner began talking. And I'd bet you all the gin in Bangkok (as Grand-ma liked to say) that they were clueless about our proximity.

"Did you see the price in the stock market today? It almost killed me!" a man's voice whispered angrily. Well, it wasn't exactly a whis-per, but you could tell he was trying to keep his voice down.

"Don't even talk about it," a woman's voice snapped back.

"We're wasting time…" he started.

She sighed. "You have to be patient. We've gone over this how many times?"

"Well, what if we…"

"No more bright ideas," she hissed. "Your last one almost blew the whole thing!"

"But things have changed. We didn't think they'd stick around after they found old Bert hanging in their house. Or Millie's body. Or their cabin burned to the ground."

This made the hairs on the back of my neck stand straight up. They were talking about Mom and Gally and me! I stole a glance at the bodyguard. He raised his eyebrows.

I waited anxiously to hear more, but suddenly, my phone *dinged.* Shit. Scrambling, I pulled it from my pocket and turned it off. Now they knew someone was close by. I froze, listening.

Dead silence.

Neither the bodyguard nor I moved. From the sound of it, no one else did either. Slowly, I tiptoed towards the direction of where the voices had come from. Pasting my body against the wall, I ever so slowly peeked around the corner.

No one was there.

❋ 26 ❋

"How come your phone had to go off at that exact moment?" Jigger whispered. "You might have been able to hear more. Or find out what they were talking about!"

"I know! The timing was terrible," I whispered back.

"I bet you wanted to strangle that person!" she lamented.

"Umm, it was you." I bit my lip to keep from smiling.

She groaned loudly.

"Girls, shhhh!" the librarian warned us for the third time. Although *why* we were supposed to be quiet was a mystery. Jigger and I were the only patrons in the library—except for Thing 1, who was reading a newspaper over in the periodicals section. The grumpy librarian had pursed her lips in disapproval when we entered her hallowed domain. I swear she was a twin for Margaret Rutherford.

The Black Beaver Bay Public Library was an old, elegant building—the nicest in town. The plaque outside said it was built in 1924. Constructed in stone in the neoclassical style, it was complete with Roman columns. It bore an everlasting, timeless quality.

Inside the library, it felt like we'd stepped back in time. The entrance was actually a rotunda with a glass dome overhead, and the floor was composed of black-and-white marble squares. Very classy. And everything felt antiquated. Even the ornate wooden tables looked original to the building.

The library tables held the initials of kids through the ages, scratched in different-colored pens. No doubt I'd find Gally's initials, probably even Grandma's, and perhaps even Grandma Fay's. The only set I knew I'd never find was my mom's.

Jigger picked up her backpack, and we moved as far as possible from the librarian's desk.

"Did you recognize the voices?" Jigger whispered, once we were settled.

"I don't know anyone in town."

"But now you know it has something to do with your land."

"Yeah. We found the remnants of a purchase agreement in Uncle Dickie's fireplace. But is that worth killing someone over?"

"Anyone would want it. It's beautiful," Jigger confided. "Don't you have, like, acres and acres of lakefront property? That's really valuable real estate."

"Okay, so who would have offered to buy it from Uncle Dickie? Who are the richest people in town?"

"Mrs. Banger." Jigger held up her hand, putting up her pointer finger.

"Mr. Chad." She put up her middle finger.

"The Nyes." She put up her ring finger.

"And Archie Green." She put up her little finger. "As far as I know, they're the richest people in town."

I typed the names into my phone. "Who is Mr. Chad?"

"He owns the strip club," Jigger said.

"Okay, who are the Nyes?"

"They own the apple orchard."

"Who is Archie Green?" I asked while I typed.

"He won the lottery a couple of years ago."

Hmm, I looked over this very short list of suspects. "So who do you think is capable of murder?"

Jigger looked at my phone, deliberating. "Mrs. Banger is too much of a bible-banger—no pun intended—so I think you can cross her off."

"I don't know, I think she's like, kind of psycho. I mean I can see her stabbing a knitting needle deep into someone's brain. You gotta watch out for those religious types—Jim Jones and all that purple Kool-Aid."

Jigger starting laughing and quickly clapped her hands over her mouth.

"Girls, *shhhh!*" the unseen librarian reprimanded us from somewhere in the library.

"The Nyes are a really nice, old couple. I can't see them doing anything evil," Jigger continued. "And Archie Green doesn't seem motivated enough to do anything. He's too lazy to even come into the diner. He wants me to deliver his food. So I would count *him* out."

"That leaves Mr. Chad. How can we investigate him?" Mom would ground me forever if I went to his strip club.

"He comes into the cafe every Saturday morning at 9:00, like clockwork. He's the best tipper I have. We could talk to him then."

"And what would I say to a strip club owner? Why would he even want to talk to me?" I had serious reservations about this.

"That's easy. Just tell him you're looking for a job."

"What!" I said, a little too loudly, since I was completely shocked.

"Shhhhh!" the warning came again from the imperious librarian.

Jigger giggled. "Not as a stripper. Just last week he asked me if I would be interested in a cleaning job. We could probably find out a lot just by talking to him. And if you want, I'll pretend like I'm interested in applying too."

"So you definitely see him as a potential suspect?"

"I don't know. Not really. He seems pretty nice, actually. Although out of all the people on your list, he's the one I know the least about."

"Okay, so I'll be at the cafe on Saturday morning." I typed that into my phone's calendar.

"Sounds like a date." She smiled. "But if we're going to be thorough, we'd better talk to everybody on that list."

"You're probably right." I rubbed my head as I looked at the list again. "Deputy Pete said Mrs. Kerkenbush's autopsy revealed she was killed before we even moved to town. And Uncle Dickie was also poisoned before we got here. So I wonder if there will be any more murders. I mean, now that they know we're not leaving, maybe they'll give up on scaring us."

"That would be nice," said Jigger. "But after that conversation you heard tonight, I don't think they're giving up."

"Yeah…you're right," I whispered.

Jigger pulled out a bag of celery and took a loud bite. She looked around, expecting to get a scolding from the librarian. "I'm starving," she whispered.

"You don't need to lose any more weight. You've got the best figure of all the girls. Seriously," I whispered back.

Jigger's smile lit up her face, revealing deep dimples in both cheeks. "I know this is going to sound crazy, but if I don't reach my goal, I don't think I'll win."

I must have looked puzzled because Jigger tried to explain. "Like when you throw something away in the wastebasket, and you tell yourself, 'if I make this shot, then I'll get an A on my test.' I know that sounds stupid, but that's what this whole diet has become to me. I don't think I'm going to win if I don't reach my goal weight."

I understood. I made bets with myself all the time that weren't logical. Months ago, I bet with myself over and over that if I did something right (like make a wastebasket shot), Dad would return. Lately, I'd been betting with myself about someone kissing me. Illogical, I knew—but there it was.

As we sat talking, I kept looking up at a life-sized oil painting that hung on the back wall. It was a portrait of a young woman—a pretty woman, with chestnut hair and stunning eyes. But that's not what caught my attention. No, what made this picture unique was the fact that she was sitting on the front seat of a gypsy wagon, with books stacked up beside her. Was she an old-fashioned, traveling librarian?

Pulling my camera from my backpack, I told Jigger I'd be right back. I went to look more closely at the painting.

Jigger followed me. Standing beneath the portrait, we read the brass plaque attached to the bottom of the picture frame. It read, "Esme Dooley—the benefactress that made this library possible. She believed that books made the world a better place." I filmed the portrait, trying to imagine why this woman was posed on a gypsy wagon.

Where had I heard that name before?

"You look like her," Jigger whispered.

"Really?" I was surprised.

"Yeah, the first time I saw you, I thought you looked like that girl from the movie 'Slumdog Millionaire.' I don't know her name."

"Freida Pinto?" I couldn't believe it. Even if it wasn't true, that was like the biggest compliment I'd ever received. It's funny how people see you so differently than you see yourself.

"The first time I saw *you*, I thought you looked like Kristin Stewart," I confided.

"I like that," Jigger whispered. "She can be so badass!"

I looked back at the painting, thinking about this mystery woman's name. And then it hit me. Gally had talked about her on our boat ride. She was my great-great-grandmother.

I studied her keenly. She wore a tight-waisted dress and a wide-brimmed hat—like the kind they wore in "My Fair Lady." She had such an amusing grin, like she was about to burst out laughing. It looked like she loved books the way I love movies.

"She's my great-great-grandmother," I whispered to Jigger. "She's the one who originally bought the Cove." I wished I knew more about this long-lost relative.

"Really?" blurted Jigger, way too loudly.

"Girls, that's it!" The librarian had had enough. "Please remove yourselves from the premises!"

✻ 27 ✻

Grandma

Have you seen my old nemesis lately?

Theo

Mrs. Banger? what is this feud you have with her? what happened ?

Grandma

We grew up like sisters, very close. But after I won Miss Apple Blossom, she became bitter, spreading malicious rumors about me all over town. She claimed I slept with one of the judges so I'd get the title. She did a real smear campaign, a complete character assassination.

Theo

what did you do ?

Grandma

I succeeded in life, that's what I did. I know it must bug the hell out of her

Theo

well i hate to be the bearer of bad news but mrs. banger is pretty successful - she drives around in a limo

Grandma

oh limo schlimo

Theo

hey - guess what? Tomorrow morning I'm going to pretend that I'm interested in becoming a cleaning lady so I can talk to this guy - mr. chad - who owns the strip club

Grandma

I take it your mother is unaware of this plan

Theo

you are correct - but Gally's going with me so it's cool.

Grandma

Any clues about the arsonist?

Theo

No

Grandma

Who would have something to gain from burning down my brother's cabin? Were they afraid of something being discovered? Or are they simply trying to scare you away?

Theo

we don't know - we searched his cabin pretty well before the police did their search - deputy pete told mom they hadn't found anything suspicious in there. i do think it's strange that mr. anderson and doc vesper were there - do you think they could have done it?

Grandma

What would be their motives? I am still in contact with Anderson. I'll do some fishing around on my end to see if I can find anything out.

Theo

cool - hey, you don't have to worry about finding a matchmaker for gally - i think she has a date with some firefighter

Grandma

so the veterinarian is out?

Theo

idk, she might still be interested in him. she attracts men like flies

Grandma

the apple does not fall far from the tree - ha!

Theo

when it comes to Mom, i think the apple rolled down the hill

Grandma

> the problem with your mother is that she has always been too earnest - men like a little levity

I thought about that as I took another bite of my leftover curried chicken, trying not to drop any on Grandma Fay's quilt. I petted Poppy, thinking back to the fire. Why would Mr. Anderson or Doc Vesper want to burn down the cabin? Or were they simply in the wrong place at the wrong time? Hmm, I turned up a Billie Eilish song, "I had a dream I got everything I wanted. Not what you'd think. And if I'm being honest…" I sang along.

Grandma

> Any news about the grave robbers and Mr. Hendrickson's body?

Theo

> cigarette butts were found by his dug-up grave - they are supposedly being tested for DNA - but since it was raining so hard that night, they don't know if they'll be able to be retrieve anything - and the footprints they left behind were compromised by the storm

Theo

> hey - i was in the library with jigger the other night and i saw a picture of my great great grandmother, Esme. did you know her? did she leave behind any scrapbooks or diaries or anything about her life? I'd like to find out more about her.

Grandma

I recall an old suitcase that was full of her belongings. But I can't imagine where that would be now

Theo

did you ever meet her?

Grandma

I wish I had, but she disappeared before I was born.

Theo

what do you mean, disappeared?

Grandma

Just that. My mother Fay was a teenager when her mother Esme went to explore some unchartered isle off the coast of South America where she had long-lost relatives - and she disappeared off the face of the earth. It was my mother's biggest heartache in life. No detective could ever give her an answer. She waited all her life to hear some news of her mother, but over the years she presumed she was dead.

Theo

OMG - that's so sad

Yes. Tragic. That is why it's so important that you make up with your father and forgive him. How would you feel if he disappeared? Wouldn't you regret the time you wasted with your anger?

I thought about this. I knew Grandma was right. But it also *angered* me that she was right. Why couldn't I stay mad at him for as long as I wanted—if not indefinitely?

Grandma

So have you talked to your father?

Theo

no - i sent him a picture - but it wasn't the nicest one

Grandma

Yes, I heard...But the very fact that you sent him anything is a start

Theo

idk - i have another picture i'm thinking about sending him

Grandma

That's lovely. I encourage you to do so. With that said, I am currently getting a foot massage from Aditya. I must let you go. Keep me posted on your investigation.

Who was this Aditya? Grandma had mentioned him several times in the last month. I imagined some love-smitten dude doting on her. But the thing with Grandma is, you just never knew.

Then I heard that darn goat again. I didn't bother looking for it from my window. I half-believed it was all in my mind. I pretended I didn't hear it.

I flipped through the pictures on my phone until I came to the one of Deputy Pete putting his arm around Mom—the one I took at the fire scene. It was taken from behind. Mom had her head leaning on Deputy Pete's shoulder. It could be misconstrued as something romantic—which was exactly my intention.

Grandma had encouraged me to do this, although she didn't know what I had in mind.

I sent the picture to Dad, with a text #MovingOnInMinnesota.

I wondered if it would bother him. I wanted to make him jealous, but I wasn't sure if he would even care. I guessed I'd find out.

As I hopped out of bed to look in the boxes of clothes I hadn't unpacked yet, I banged my shin on the footboard. *"Ouch!"* I had to figure out what I was going to wear tomorrow morning. Pulling wrinkled T-shirts from a box, I wondered how a prospective cleaning lady would dress.

Probably very neatly.

❀ 28 ❀

"Slow down, slow down," Gally cried, pushing her hands against the dash to brace herself.

"This from the woman who was going 120 down Main Street!" I said smugly.

Gally rolled her eyes.

I was going at least fifteen miles over the speed limit. We were driving into town—to my breakfast date with destiny.

I had made Gally complicit in my plans because how else would I get to the cafe? I seriously doubted if Mom would approve of my fake interview to become a cleaning lady—or my secret investigation in general.

I'd told Mom that Gally was helping me put in some driving time, so I could get my license. Which was the truth. I just didn't tell her the rest of it.

I rounded a corner going too fast, and our tires gave a little squeal. I had a hard time with corners. I wasn't sure why. I either went too slow or too fast. I glanced over at my aunt. She was closing her eyes. Thing 1 let out a grunt from the back seat.

"Hey, you're supposed to be filming this," I told Gally. "How can you, if your eyes are closed?" I thought it'd be fun to film my driving. It would be another snippet of the documentary I was brewing in my imagination.

Suddenly, a gargantuan tractor pulled out in front of me. I slammed on the brakes, making the three of us lurch forward. We proceeded at 20 m.p.h. I waited for him to pull into some field, but he kept going his slow pace down the middle of the highway.

"Don't pass him," Gally pleaded. "We have plenty of time. We won't be late."

I obeyed for a couple of seconds. Then I got impatient and pulled to the left, preparing to pass. I saw an oncoming truck! Quickly, I steered back behind the tractor.

"Oh, my God, Theo!" Gally moaned. "This is terrifying!"

"Well, I'm not used to these farm machinery things. We didn't have them in Oak Park."

"They rule the road here." She sighed. "Just stay behind him."

A song from Sam Smith came on the radio. I turned it up, only to have Gally immediately turn it off.

"No distracted driving," she half-joked, yet her expression looked pretty frazzled.

Finally, the glacially-slow tractor got out of my way and freed me up to drive. We were approaching town. I passed Hank the Beaver, where the speed limit switched to 35. I got it down to forty and thought I was doing pretty well, until another huge farm machinery thing came plowing towards us, forcing me over in my lane.

To avoid hitting him, I had to go dangerously close to a parked car. I accidentally smashed one of my side view mirrors into the other car's side view mirror, shearing off ours and leaving it dangling by its wires. Thing 1 groaned.

"Mom is going to kill me," I wailed.

Gally said under her breath, "Not if you do it first."

I saw the cafe coming up on the right, so I slowed down, putting on my blinker. But I couldn't figure out how to parallel park. I sat motionless trying to remember my driver's training.

"Just pull backwards, real slow," Gally tried to coach. "Okay now, start cranking your wheel...No, the other way!...Okay, now turn it back..."

I bumped into the front fender of the car behind me.

"Um, now pull forward," Gally suggested.

I bumped into the back fender of the car in front of me.

"Back up a foot," Gally suggested.

I rammed back into the car behind me.

136

"Okay," she conceded. "Turn off the car."

I did, and immediately she took the keys.

"Was it that bad?" I asked. I mean, I hadn't killed anybody.

Thing 1 let out another undecipherable grunting noise. We got out of the car and looked at the damage to the other cars' fenders. "They look fine." Aunt Gally sounded surprised.

So we went inside the cafe, which was empty except for a man who sat in the back booth. That had to be Mr. Chad. Stevie Wonder's "Superstition" drifted from the kitchen. I led us to the booth next to his, set down my camera and turned it on. I waited for Jigger. She greeted us immediately with a tray of water glasses, saying she was both the cook and the waitress today. With her parents out of town, she was flying solo. I wondered what kind of cook she was.

Dressed like she was on the first day I'd met her, Jigger winked at me.

She chatted while she took our orders. Then, in a very nonchalant way, acting like it was *such* a coincidence, she introduced me to Mr. Chad. She said I was interested in finding a cleaning job, and then she took our order to the kitchen.

He didn't look at *all* like what I'd thought he would. I had imagined some slimy-looking guy with sunglasses, like a hustler from Las Vegas. Instead, Mr. Chad looked like a meticulously groomed businessman, with not a hair out of place. He was a dapper dresser, complete with a pink silk handkerchief folded elegantly in the breast pocket of his silk suit.

He glanced at me for a second before turning his gaze to my aunt. Slowly a smile spread across his face. "Well, I'll be damned." He chuckled. "If it isn't Gally Gillman."

Gally looked at him, confused. I could see she was trying to remember who he was, probably shuffling through that rolodex of acquaintances from her past.

"Chad?" she asked questioningly. "Chad Peterson?" Her forehead was so furrowed you could have planted seeds in it.

He let out an easygoing laugh. "So you *do* recognize me." He looked pleased. "Say, do you remember when you duct taped Mrs. White to the flagpole on the last day of school?" He laughed again. "I do believe she failed you in Home Ec for that little escapade."

"You must be thinking of someone else." Gally's eyes twinkled.

I'd heard my aunt say this quite a few times now. It made me wonder if everything she had done was slightly naughty. Or downright naughty. Or perhaps totally incorrigible.

Gally slid into Mr. Chad's booth and began talking with this former classmate. I adjusted my camera on the table, aiming it straight at them, hoping to catch their interaction.

So much for my job interview. But I actually felt relieved. Since I'd planned to talk to him under false pretenses, I didn't have to worry about that—not anymore. And knowing my aunt, she'd get more out of him than I ever would.

Jigger brought out our orders. I ate my Trucker's Special while Thing 1 ate scrambled eggs and bacon. It was just as awesome as the first time I'd eaten here. Jigger was an *excellent* cook.

I eavesdropped on my aunt and Mr. Chad, trying not to miss anything.

"So what are you up to these days?" Gally asked, as she sipped her tea.

"I own the strip club in town, but I'm getting out of that. I have something bigger on the horizon," he said smoothly.

Hmm, I wondered if his bigger something was our land. I continued to eat, trying to chew very softly, so I could hear everything they were saying. He bragged about also having a business down in the Twin Cities and some kind of charter boat gig in Florida. Gally told him about her freelance decorating business and what we planned to do with the Cove.

"That's some beautiful land," he said, wiping his mouth.

So beautiful you'd kill for it? I wondered. From the sound of it, this man definitely had the money to buy our property. But then again, maybe he didn't—maybe he was just trying to impress Gally.

As I was shoveling a huge bite of cheesy hash browns into my mouth, Jigger's twin, Josh, came in through the door. He smiled, waved, and walked my way. His arrival startled me. Was he coming over to talk? I turned around to see if there was anyone behind me that he was heading towards—which ended up being a huge mistake.

Because I choked. Literally.

No air was getting into my lungs, no matter how hard I struggled to move the food up or down. I grew more panicked, pointing to my throat. Thing 1 jumped out of his seat and picked me up like a rag doll. I realized he was performing the Heimlich maneuver on me.

As he jerked me up and down, I kept looking at a diorama that had a beaver dressed as a ballerina—pink tutu and all. Please don't let that be the last thing I see before I die, I thought. Going into the hereafter with that image on my mind was just too ridiculous.

Within seconds, a huge glob of hash browns flew out of my mouth, landing right on Josh's very new-looking shoes.

OMG, I was horrified—but alive.

"Hey, are you okay?" Josh asked, looking down at his sneakers.

If I could have snapped my fingers and disappeared, I would have. This was so humiliating.

Gally was rubbing my back, and Jigger was by my side. Everyone was making such a fuss. "I'm fine," I gasped, trying to catch my breath.

I grabbed the bodyguard's hand and gave it my hardest squeeze. "Thank you," I said sincerely.

It's a freaky thing when you come close to death. It makes you appreciate your life so much more. I felt embarrassed that my food had landed on Josh's shoes, but I was even more regretful about something else. That text I had sent to Dad last night was *sooo* immature. Why had I done that? And if I had died just a few seconds ago, I could never have made it right. I remembered Grandma's words and knew I had to stop wasting time.

"I need some fresh air," I announced. Everyone took a couple steps back and let me pass. Gally and Jigger followed me outside.

"Theo, that was so scary." Gally rubbed my back as we stood in front of the cafe.

"Who knew a job interview could be so stressful?" Jigger teased.

We laughed, which actually hurt my diaphragm. While I caught my breath, an ambulance approached us with its sirens on. OMG, I hoped they hadn't called that for me. But it didn't slow down. Instead it flew straight past us, heading out of town towards the Cove.

Gally's phone *dinged.* It was a text from Mom.

Ana

> Please get home - there's been a terrible accident!

❀ 29 ❀

Gally's driving was even worse than mine—if that's possible. As she sped furiously back to the Cove, we were actually on two wheels as she whipped around a corner, almost tipping us over.

I texted Mom while we were en route. I learned there'd been a bad accident that involved one of the workers. A painter had fallen from the scaffolding, which had mysteriously given way. Mom was in a pretty panicked state.

When we roared into the driveway, we saw a group of people huddled around someone lying on the ground. It looked as if the paramedics were still assessing the damage. Mom was in tears.

And of course, Deputy Pete was standing close by.

Gally and I pulled Mom aside, trying to comfort her.

"I heard the most awful scream," she told us, wiping her nose. "I was inside the house when I heard it. Such a terrible, bloodcurdling scream. I ran outside to see what had happened, and he was lying on the ground with his legs at a sickening angle. It was horrible."

"At least he's alive," Gally tried to console her. "Let's just pray he's not paralyzed."

Mom let out a soft wail. While Gally hugged her, I watched the paramedics. Standing a respectful distance from them (and Deputy Pete), I hoped to find out what was going on. I watched the EMT's brace the poor man's neck, preparing him to be moved onto a stretcher. As bad as it was—and it did look bad—at least he wasn't being taken out of here in a body bag. I'd seen more than my share of *those* in the last two weeks.

I plodded over to a group of painters who were gathered by the front porch. They were smoking, looking pensive. When I asked them what had happened, all five of them began talking at once, giving me their versions of the accident.

They were suspicious, due to the fact that the scaffolding had been working fine all morning. Yet when they came back from their coffee break, one of the planks had simply given way. They said someone had removed a crucial clip from the system, but they couldn't imagine who. They seemed leery to return to work—and I couldn't say I blamed them.

I watched the paramedics load up the injured man and slowly make their way out of our drive. Was this just terrible luck, like my near-choking? Or was something more sinister at play?

When I glanced at Mom and Gally, I saw they were talking to Deputy Pete, so I turned and went straight into the house. I found Poppy frantic. Calming her down, I gave her a huge hug. I wasn't fully recovered from my near-death, choking experience.

Hours later, I'd finished reading all of my dad's text messages from the last couple of months. His messages hadn't erased all of my anger, but they had made me feel better. Most of them were apologies.

He said he was so sorry. And that this had nothing to do with me. And that he missed me. And that he wished I would talk to him.

He said he hadn't been happy in his marriage to Mom for a long time.

I was thinking about texting him when my phone *dinged.*

Jigger

how ru? RUOK?

Theo

I'm alright, still feeling sore

Jigger

that was freaky - i'm so glad ur alright

Theo

thnx

Jigger

my brother wanted to talk to you before your near-death experience - i think he has a crush on you

Theo

really?????

Jigger

don't get too excited, once you get to know him you'll find out he's a moron

Theo

you only say that because ur his sister

Jigger

hey - gossip in town is that your painter isn't paralyzed but he did break both of his legs - pretty nasty breaks my cousin told me - could be months before he's walking again

Theo

that's terrible - i'm starting to feel like this place is cursed - how many more things are going to happen - we need to get to the bottom of this before we're all killed - the painters told me that SOMEONE had removed a clip from the scaffolding - that's why the guy fell

> wow - someone really doesn't want you guys fixing up the place - it's just like the fire - oh - gotta go - I'm still at work

I threw my phone down on my bed and lay back to think. I wanted to write to Dad and apologize for being so immature. I wanted to tell him about everything that had happened since we'd moved to Minnesota, yet I just lay there doing nothing. Where would I begin? It would be the world's longest text message.

And then I thought about Josh having a crush on me. That made me smile. But when I recalled what had come out of my mouth and landed on his shoes, I groaned, covering my face with my pillow. That was so totally humiliating.

Enough, I finally told myself, hopping out of bed. Grabbing my camera, I snapped a leash on Poppy and headed outdoors. Thing 1 was on the porch. He followed me as I walked away.

It turned out to be a beautiful afternoon. The morning clouds had passed, leaving a cerulean blue sky with bright sunshine. The wind was brisk, though, making me zip up my vest as I forged down the road towards the cabins. The smell of fresh-cut wood filled the air, and I could hear the carpenters sawing and pounding.

Some of the workers were up on the roof, where the radio was playing "Cupid Shuffle." They didn't see me. I filmed them as they moved to the music, and I had to smile. For a bunch of middle-aged white guys, they could almost groove.

I found Mom and Gally in the third cabin. Quite a transformation had occurred since the last time I'd been here. I pulled out my camera and filmed the new kitchen cabinets and floor. True to Gally's vision, they looked vintage. Different shades of red paint swatches were on the wall, along with samples of wallpaper.

"There you are." Mom smiled. She'd obviously recovered from the painter's accident and looked like she was ready to become Martha Stewart. Gally was trying to sell Mom on a red-checkered motif. "It's very retro, very Fifties," she gushed. I filmed their decision-making process.

"I don't know," said Mom. "What do *you* think, Theo?"

"I like it! It's cheerful." I beamed at both of them.

Poppy was pulling on her leash to go back outside. "I'm going to take her for a little walk. I'll be right back," I told them, heading out the door.

Poppy and I entered the woods. Everything smelled so green and fresh. It made me believe that spring was actually on its way. Thing 1 followed discreetly behind me, giving me space. The roofers' radio began to fade, and after a few minutes, I could hear the sound of the lake. I thought I might have heard a goat, but I didn't even want to entertain that idea.

I was feeling hopeful. Even with the murder, grave robbing, arson and accidents, it was impossible not to feel optimistic on such a beautiful afternoon. Or maybe it was because I was alive and hadn't choked in the cafe. Or maybe it had something to do with my feelings towards Dad. It couldn't possibly be that I was giddy because Jigger had told me her brother liked me. Could it?

I came to a weather-beaten boulder on the edge of the forest and sat there for a minute, petting Poppy. I offered a seat to Thing 1, but he shook his head no. So I pulled out my camera and filmed the view.

I looked at the sky, marveling in its color. The lake took on a pleasant blue hue, instead of its usual gray. I could see how a person could fall in love with this place. It had already put me under its spell. It had been days since I'd felt homesick for Oak Park.

Suddenly, Poppy began her low, guttural growl. I panned my camera to my right, where I detected some bushes moving. Through my lens, I saw a person with binoculars looking straight back at me! I zoomed in the best I could. I saw a baseball cap and sunglasses. Instantly, the person ducked down.

Poppy leaped off the rock, forgetting she was on her leash—almost choking herself in her excitement. I got up and followed her to where the bushes had been moving. I could hear Thing 1 following me.

By the time I got there, we heard a sputtering boat motor. I ran to the edge of the lake and saw a boat speeding away, quite a distance from the shore. I tried to film what I saw, but it was too far away. I couldn't even see who was driving the boat.

I backtracked to the bushes where the "spy" had been hiding. On the ground, I found several footprints in the sand. They were small. They must be from a woman—or from a man with unfortunately small feet. I filmed the prints, zooming in on the pattern that the tread had left behind. Then I placed my foot by one of the prints. They were smaller than mine. That ruled out Mrs. Banger. She had feet the size of Paul Bunyan.

So someone with a size 8 shoe (or smaller) had been spying on us. I wondered if that someone was responsible for the painter's accident—or perhaps even murder.

❀ 30 ❀

"No, you do it like this." Jigger took my hands and placed them on the cow's teats. "Now you squeeze and pull at the same time." She demonstrated.

We were in the milking parlor at her family's farm. They had such a huge herd of cows that they couldn't milk them all by hand. Instead they were hooked up to these machines that did it automatically. But Jigger thought it'd be fun to teach a city girl how to do it the old-fashioned way.

"What if she doesn't want me touching her there?" I asked. Jigger and Josh laughed, making me blush.

"Oh, she wants you to, trust me." Jigger sounded sure.

I concentrated on the job at hand. The cow's udder felt warm and spongy. I gently squeezed and pulled and—bingo! It worked! A stream of milk hit the empty bucket, making a noise I'd never heard before.

"There you go," Josh encouraged me.

"You'll be a pro before you know it," added Jigger.

I kept going. Slowly, I got into a rhythm. This was kind of fun, I thought. Milk gradually covered the bottom of the bucket. Who knew the simple gratifications of country life?

Suddenly the cow, whose name was Darla, turned around and let out a loud *"MOOOOOO!!!!!"* I fell backwards, flat on my butt, accidentally kicking over the bucket and spilling its meager contents.

We all started laughing. Jigger offered a hand and helped me up from the ground. "What did I do wrong?" I asked.

"Nothing. Darla was just checking you out," Jigger reassured me.

She led me to a room off the parlor, where we washed our hands. She offered me a soft drink from the fridge and grabbed herself a water. "Four more pounds to go!" she said, clinking her bottle with my can. "Do you want to film anymore?"

"I think I'm good." Previously, she'd given me an extensive tour of their farm, and I'd filmed everything eagerly. It was all kind of fascinating to me—like a completely different world, but one that she took totally for granted.

She led me to the chicken coop, and we passed my mom's vehicle where Thing 1 sat dutifully waiting for me. I had pleaded with him to stay in the car, and for once, he'd let me have my way. I waved a guilty little wave as we passed him, feeling bad about how long I was making him wait. He waved back.

Jigger grabbed a basket by the chicken coop's door and thrust it in my arms. She took a scoop of grain from a bag and scattered it outside, making the hens do a frenzied dash out of the coop, filling the air with feathers and dust. Meanwhile, Jigger went from nest to nest, taking eggs and placing them in the basket I was holding.

Once again, I was aware of how she knew so much more than I did—about so many things. It made me smile. When I first moved here, I thought my arrival from the big city would make me wiser than the local kids. I couldn't have been more wrong.

"So how long are your parents going to be gone?" I asked.

"Two weeks." Carefully, she placed two pale green eggs in the basket. "They go on a mission with our church every spring. My brothers run the farm, and I'm in charge of the restaurant. It's no big deal. We can do it with our eyes closed." Maybe her accomplishments were no big deal to her, but I was very impressed. She'd been living and working in the real world while I'd just been filming it.

Josh popped his head in the door, and Jigger scolded him, "Get out of here, you dope." He disappeared. "He bugs me all the time about you," she complained. "I think it's, like, the first time he's been in love."

My cheeks burned. I felt hugely flattered yet tongue-tied at the same time. I wondered how this budding romance was ever going to develop if Jigger kept him at arm's length. More importantly, I didn't want her to think I was hanging with her just to get close to her brother.

Because that wasn't true. I really loved hanging out with Jigger. She made everything fun.

"This is a pretty one," Jigger said softly, holding up a pale pink egg in the sunlight. The shell was smeared with chicken poop, which she gently rubbed on the hay.

"It reminds me of an Easter egg." I sighed. I never knew that hens could lay such a variety of beautiful pastel colors. I wondered if Lexi knew this? Or any of my other city friends?

We left the chicken coop and went back to the washroom off the milking parlor. Jigger began to wash the eggs, revealing their true beauty. "You can take these home to your mom," she offered, placing them in a recycled egg carton. "We have more than enough."

As I scrubbed my hands, I listened to the radio, which was playing "Nessun Dorma" from the opera "Turandot."

"Nice music," I joked. "Do you play a lot of this?"

"Actually, my Dad totally believes that playing opera for the cows helps their milk production." She smiled, almost shyly. "I've listened to it all my life. My dad permanently keeps it on NPR. I've probably heard more opera than country-western music."

"You never cease to amaze," I teased.

Jigger seemed lost in her thoughts. After a moment, a shadow crossed her face.

"What's wrong?" I asked.

She shook her head slightly. "Just thinking about Dad," she said softly. "This is the only life he's ever known. I mean, I can't wait to get out of here. But my dad? Well, he's never wanted anything else. He loves farming. This place has been in our family for four generations." She plopped down in a chair at the table by the refrigerator. I sat down beside her.

"It looks like he's done really well," I said soothingly. I didn't know *anything* about farming—zilcho! But what I'd seen during the tour she'd given me was really impressive.

She smiled sadly. "He's the hardest-working dad I know." Tears sprang to her eyes, and she pushed them away angrily. "We're barely hanging on. Industrial farming has made it almost impossible for little family farms to survive. If it wasn't for the money Mom pulls in from the cafe, we would have been forced to sell a long time ago."

Listening, I felt terrible for her.

"That's why this pageant is so important. I mean, I think this whole beauty queen shit is so stupid." She stuck her chin out defiantly. "But I really need that award money. Mom and Dad don't have the money for my college." She sighed heavily.

I reached over and gave her a hug. "I think you're going to win," I said, trying to encourage her.

She smiled, and it was like the sun had just come out. Trying to change the subject, she said, "Hey, can you show me the footage of that shoeprint?"

So I whipped out my camera and rewound it to the footprints. She was more interested in the footage of the boat than the prints. She didn't recognize the boat, which was disappointing. "That's so generic—tons of people have boats like that. Too bad you couldn't get a close up." I tried zooming in, but it grew so blurry it was unrecognizable.

Then I rewound the tape to the beginning, so she could see everything I'd filmed since we'd moved to Minnesota. She shook her head when she saw herself dancing, but when we got to the police questioning, she told me to stop. We tried to zoom in on the map that hung in Deputy Pete's office.

"Hmm." Her fingers drummed the table as she was thinking. "In the courthouse, they have a huge map of the whole town and beyond. I think we should go there and study it."

"You think that would help? I mean we already know who our neighbors are."

"The one in the courthouse is more detailed. What can it hurt?" she asked. "I can meet you Tuesday after school. Sound good?"

We agreed.

As it was getting close to noon, Jigger had to go to work, even though she felt like hitting the lake. Yet she said she couldn't complain. With her parents out of town, at least she'd been able to skip church that morning.

"You're like busy *all* the time," I shook my head.

"Well, you know, idle hands are the devil's workshop." She rolled her eyes. "Mom and Dad think they can keep us out of trouble if they keep us busy. They have *no* clue." She giggled. "We have the hugest party every year when they're gone. It's next weekend, and you are definitely coming!"

I imagined Thing 1 tagging along to a teenage party. Could I possibly ditch him and go alone? Would I have to crawl out my window for a night of freedom? The whole idea raised immediate alarm bells—not the least of which was meeting other kids my age. So far, I'd felt super comfortable with Jigger, and I didn't really want to meet other girls. I thought of that movie "Mean Girls" and it gave me a knot in my stomach.

"I don't know…" I began.

❋ 31 ❋

I was on the internet, Googling causes of audible hallucinations. I had heard the phantom goat bleating just ten minutes ago, and I thought I'd better figure out what was wrong with me. The results I'd found weren't encouraging. Epilepsy, brain tumors, mental illness, or intense stress were just a few things that could be causing this. I was narrowing down my options of what I thought it could be when *ding!*

Grandma

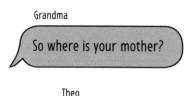

So where is your mother?

Theo

out on a date, with Deputy Pete - GAG!!! and gally is with that cute fireman. i guess you'd call it a double date but both mom and gally claim it's not a date at all. just an adult gathering. old friends getting together, they said. and they've been working so hard they wanted a break.

Grandma

so you're home alone?

Theo

Thing 1 is around here somewhere

I was up in Grandma Fay's room, which I now called my bedroom. Poppy was splayed across the bed, snoozing. I was eating a sizable plate of leftover bean burritos, listening to that old OutKast song "Hey Ya!" and texting Grandma because she seemed to be the one and only person in the entire world who wasn't busy right now.

Grandma

> Have you talked to your father yet?

Theo

> i was going to text him yesterday but i haven't gotten around to it. i'm going to. i almost choked to death and that kind of changed my perspective on life.

Grandma

> Your mother told me about that. I'm glad you're all right. There is nothing like a near-death experience to help clarify what is important in life. One should also remember the value of mastication. Shoveling food in one's mouth is not good for the digestion and can be dangerous.

I had just started to take a huge bite of burrito, but after I saw her advice, I bit off a small chunk instead. I didn't want to repeat what I'd gone through yesterday. Even though I felt like I was starving all the time, I guess I needed to pay closer attention to *how* I was eating.

Grandma

> Well, I'm glad you've decided to reach out to your father. If he ever needed to hear from you, it would be now.

Theo

> did something happen?

My mind raced through all sorts of scenarios. Did he have a close brush with death also? Was he sick? Injured? What did she mean?

153

> I am sorry to be the bearer of bad news, but his young companion and unborn child perished in a car accident yesterday.

OMG! This was horrible! I mean I'd secretly wished a lot of bad things would happen to Alessa, his young mistress from Peru, but I'd never actually meant them. My poor Dad. And my half-brother or sister who I'd so resented—well, now I felt terrible. I turned off my music and pushed my food away.

Theo

> How do you know this? Is Dad okay? Does Mom know this? Tell me everything.

Grandma

> I've been in communication with your father ever since he left your mother. Some may call that disloyal, but I've known him for decades. The dissolution of his marriage was not a reason for me to stop communicating with him.

Hmm, I didn't know that Grandma had been talking to Dad. Or texting him. I wondered if Mom knew this. I wondered if he'd been checking up on me through Grandma. Suddenly, I had a ton of questions.

Grandma

> Your father just texted me. I haven't been able to get hold of your mother to inform her. I think she shut off her phone. Anyway, Alessa was driving on a treacherous mountain road and they don't know if her car experienced mechanical difficulties, or what exactly happened, but she ended up going over the side of the mountain. Horrific, really. Your father is beside himself.

Theo

OMG - that's just so sad. What is Dad going to do now? You don't think Mom and Dad will get back together, do you? I mean, will he come back to the states? What will he do?

Grandma

If I were a betting woman, which I am, I would guess that your parents won't reunite, so please don't get your hopes up. They'd been having problems in their marriage for quite some time. And at this point, I doubt your mother would take him back. This is why I've been encouraging you to develop a relationship with your father that is separate from the one your mother has with him. You're almost an adult now. Don't you want him in your life?

Theo

well, i think so. i mean i've been like crazy mad at him for months now, but things have changed. i've changed - idk - but i do feel sorry for him.

Grandma

Do let him know your sentiments. He lost a child today. It would give him great comfort to feel he's gained one back.

Theo

i'll text him right now

Grandma

Okay darling. I'm off to the market with Adyita. Much love

I set down my phone and thought about Grandma's texts. This was so shocking. I mean dead people have been popping up all around us since we moved here, but I'd never known them—I didn't have any connection with them. This was so different! She was only a few years older than me.

It wasn't like I'd known Alessa that well, but I had been friendly with her until I caught her with Dad. After that, I had terrible thoughts about her, which now made me feel agonizingly wretched.

A person's thoughts couldn't make something bad happen, could they? I mean I didn't have a voodoo doll, and I hadn't put curses on her or anything, so I couldn't be responsible. Or could I? OMG, I wished I'd never had those evil thoughts to begin with.

I wondered how Mom was going to react when she heard this. I wished she'd get home from her date with that stupid Deputy Pete. This was so much more important than what she was doing now. I tried texting her. I waited a couple minutes. She never answered.

I hopped out of bed, stubbing my toe. *"Ouch!"* I paced back and forth, trying to think of what I'd say to Dad. I regretted never responding to his hundreds of texts. Poppy watched me from the bed, tilting her head, trying to figure out what was going on.

Finally, I bit the bullet.

Theo

❀ 32 ❀

The quietness of the courthouse had a somber feel—almost like a funeral home. Although with its marble walls, it reminded me more of a mausoleum. Not that I've ever been inside a mausoleum. I've only seen them in movies. The stillness was so immense that even unzipping my backpack produced an echo. As I waited for Jigger in the foyer area, I couldn't stop thinking about death. Or more precisely, Alessa's death. When I had told Mom the horrible news, she'd grown quiet. She didn't speak much about it, only saying that it was very sad. Did Mom wonder if Dad would try to come back to her? Did she want him to?

I pulled my video camera from my backpack and turned it on. The courthouse foyer was stately—totally constructed of marble. Through the huge glass doors, I filmed the outdoors. It was raining. I recorded a raindrop slowly rolling down the glass pane, intersecting with other droplets before dissipating into nothingness.

A blurry figure raced towards the building. I realized it was Jigger, trying to outrun the storm. She came into focus as she neared the glass doors. When she opened them, a blast of cold wind burst into the foyer, carrying a stinging rain.

She shook her short hair—exactly like a dog would, making droplets fly all over me. Quickly, I wiped my camera lens. "Not much to film here," she said cheerfully.

"I was worried you'd forgotten."

"Forget you? Never," she teased. "Hey, where's Thing 1?"

"He's in the car. I told him nobody was going to do anything to me in the courthouse. Maybe he just didn't want to get wet."

She opened the other set of doors that led inside. There was a massive staircase to the right of a long hallway filled with closed doors. No one was around. It was four o'clock, and the courthouse didn't close till five, so where was everyone? It felt like we were in a post-apocalyptic movie. I wouldn't have been surprised if zombies had popped up.

Jigger's sneakers squeaked on the floor, as she led me to the township map. It was huge—at least six feet long, and it was framed, covered in glass. Filming anything covered in glass was tricky for me because of the glare it created. But I tried anyway.

Jigger pushed a bench underneath the map and stood on it. Pointing, she said, "This is the Cove." I tried to zoom in, but that didn't work with the glare, so I hopped up on the bench beside her to get closer to the map.

"This is Mrs. Kerkenbush's farm." She pointed north of the Cove. "Over here, you have Banger Sausage."

"What's north of the Kerkenbush farm?"

She leaned in closer, almost putting her nose to the glass. "That's Bridge Road," she muttered. "Mr. Anderson owns some acreage out there. Not a farm, but I've heard he has a nice chunk of land."

"Girls! Get off that bench this instant!" The commanding voice made both of us jump.

We turned around and saw a thin, hunchbacked, elderly woman dressed in a gray cardigan and skirt. She looked ancient, and her face was a roadmap of wrinkles. She wore bifocals that were attached to a string of pearls that draped around her neck. Her disapproving expression was enough for us to hop down from the bench immediately, making me accidentally twist my ankle. *"Ouch!"*

"Sorry, Mrs. Drew," Jigger apologized. "We were just trying to get a better look."

"If everyone treated public property that way, there would be no public property left. Look, you've left your footprints all over this antique bench. Wipe them up and mind your manners." Huffing, she spun away. We watched her march down the hallway with a military gait to enter a door on the left.

"Who was that?" I whispered.

"Mrs. Drew, my principal," Jigger rolled her eyes. "She's a real bit…"

Just then, Mrs. Drew came stalking back towards us! Jigger quickly used the arm of her hoodie to wipe up our wet footprints. Mrs. Drew stopped in front of us and looked me up and down.

"Who is your friend, Jessica?" the old biddy demanded. "She's not one of my students."

Well, thank God for that, I thought.

"Um, this is Theo. Theo, this is Mrs. Drew."

Neither I, nor the crusty old principal, extended our hands.

"And where do you hail from?" She pushed her glasses up her nose to get a better look at me.

"I'm from Oak Park, Illinois. But my family recently moved here to reopen the fishing resort—the Cove," I explained self-consciously. This woman made me nervous—like she could see into the deepest recesses of my soul, and somehow I came up lacking.

"Hmph," she snorted. "You're not in any way connected to the Gillman family, are you?" she continued her interrogation.

"Well, actually, my mom is Ana Gillman. And my aunt is Gally."

"Your mother was a decent student, but that aunt of yours…" She shook her head, and then her whole body shuddered with displeasure. "Why, I'm surprised she didn't turn out to be a lifelong criminal, spending years behind bars."

It was all I could do to keep from laughing. I wondered what Gally had done to this woman to deserve such an accolade. I couldn't wait to tell my aunt what her old principal thought of her.

"You find that amusing?" Mrs. Drew snapped, giving me a withering look.

Before I could answer, Miss Honeycutt, the woman who had coached the Apple Blossom girls in their dance routine, came out of nowhere and joined our little group. I noticed she still hadn't had time to get her roots touched up.

Visibly relieved, Jigger smiled at Miss Honeycutt.

"Hi Jigger," Miss Honeycutt said happily. "What's going on here?"

"I am single-handedly preventing the destruction of public property," droned Mrs. Drew. She gave everyone a stern look and then stomped away.

"We were standing on the bench to get a closer look at the map," Jigger explained to Miss Honeycutt. Then Jigger introduced me.

"How nice to meet you," Miss Honeycutt said kindly. "Please tell your mom and aunt I haven't had time to stop out at the Cove yet. I've been a little busier than usual lately."

"Nice to meet you," I said.

"Well, of course you're busy. You do everything in the world," Jigger gushed. Jigger's admiration for Miss Honeycutt was tremendous. Every time she bought up the woman's name, she would rattle off all her talents and accomplishments. Honestly, it got a little old.

I studied Miss Honeycutt. She had a thin face with close-set eyes. When she smiled, her crow's-feet bunched up—as if she'd smiled often in her life. I wanted to say she looked like Molly Shannon, but I'd been told recently that comparing everyone to movie stars was annoying.

"I'm in a hurry, as usual," she said with a laugh. "I have to turn in these permits to the chamber of commerce before five. Please give my best to your mother and Gally!" And with that, she hurried down the hall.

"Maybe we shouldn't get up on the bench again," Jigger admitted. "Jeez, you would have thought we created a global crisis."

"Look!" I pointed to the shiny floor where Miss Honeycutt had just been standing. "That looks like the shoe tread I found on the beach the other day." I filmed the wet print, bending over to get a closer look. "You know—when that person was spying on me and then took off in a boat?"

"It's probably a pretty common tread." Shaking her head, Jigger added, "There's no way it could be Miss Honeycutt."

"I can compare the two treads," I said cautiously because I knew how much she admired her tremendously busy idol.

A flock of people came through the front door. I saw Mrs. Banger enter. She had her back turned to us, talking to someone I didn't know.

"Well, yes, I hope I can expand before next year," Mrs. Banger's voice carried loud and clear through the marbled hallway. "It's just a matter of acquiring more land and permits!" she told the person, who probably wanted to get away from her as much as I did. I whispered to Jigger, "Let's get out of here—before Mrs. Banger sees us."

She led me down the hall to a side door. A bulletin board hung by the exit, crowded with public notices. There was a committee sign-up sheet looking for volunteers to clean up Hank the Beaver. He needed a new paint job because his pelt was looking dull. They wanted Hank in his best form for the upcoming Apple Blossom Days.

So far, just one person had signed up for the committee. Gretchen Honeycutt's signature stood alone, bold and proud. From what I knew of Miss Honeycutt, nobody else would need to sign up. She was more than capable of doing the job all on her own.

An auction bill caught my attention, so I turned on my camera to film it.

It was a notice for a public auction of Mrs. Kerkenbush's farm. "This might be important," I told Jigger. "The person who ends up buying it might be the person who wants our land."

"Brilliant deduction." Jigger smiled. "But you don't have to film it." Without any hesitation whatsoever, she yanked the bill from the board and handed it to me.

"Won't we get in trouble for that?" I looked behind me to see if anyone had witnessed what she'd just done.

"Not if Mrs. Drew doesn't see," she joked.

Stuffing my camera and the auction bill quickly into my backpack, we ran outside, laughing and slipping in the rain.

❀ 33 ❀

"Oh, my God, are you frikin' kidding me?" Gally cried. "How can she still be alive? She was a cadaver when I was in high school!"

Gally was referring to Mrs. Drew. I was recounting my run-in with her old principal. My aunt thought it was hilarious that Mrs. Drew had predicted she'd be a felon—although Gally admitted that back in the day, she had lured a wild raccoon into her old principal's car, which had startled the woman so terribly that she drove straight through the wall of the farm implement dealership.

"I didn't always make the best choices back then." She gave me an angelic smile. "But what do you think about this choice?" She held up a bolt of fabric that had cheerful red-and-cream stripes. She said she was planning to use it for curtains.

"I like it!" I said. "I like everything you've done." My aunt had transformed this tired, gloomy cabin into a delightfully cozy bungalow—while somehow keeping its vintage feel. She had a knack for decorating, which was a good thing because she's been a professional decorator for the past twenty years.

"Oh, and look at these!" she gushed while holding up a pair of lamps that had fishing reels for their bases. "I found loads of fun stuff at that shop down in the Cities. I'm definitely going back there."

I loved her creative changes. They made me feel hopeful and excited about reopening this place. Her enthusiasm was so infectious that I almost volunteered to help her paint. Almost.

"Oh, and come here." She dragged me into the remodeled bathroom. It was no longer that scary kind of bathroom full of unfortunate rust stains and black mold. Instead, it now had a shiny, red-tiled floor, a new toilet, a new sink, and a really cool shower.

I knew she was particularly proud of the shower because she'd designed it herself. The bottom came from a recycled wooden cask, and she'd splurged on one of those huge, copper showerheads. The whole room was nice enough to be in a decorating magazine.

"And I just whipped these up today," she said happily, showing me the free gift baskets for our future guests. "I found organically-made soap, shampoo, and bath gel—all made in Minnesota!" She had tucked these items into a handwoven basket, along with washcloths and a small bottle of mouthwash. "Isn't that cute?"

"This is really going to happen, isn't it?" I said eagerly.

"I never doubted it!" She hugged me. "Your mother can be a bit of an Eeyore." A flash of humor crossed her face. "But I have to say, her mood has definitely improved lately."

"I'm a little worried, though. She's been pretty quiet the last few days—ever since she heard Dad's news."

We stepped back to the cabin's living room, where I tripped on the area rug and fell onto the new couch. *"Ouch!"* Gally sat down next to me. The checkered couch was super comfortable. If I hadn't grown so attached to Grandma Fay's bedroom, I'd be asking to move into one of these cabins.

"Has she talked to you about Dad's girlfriend dying?"

Gally shook her head. "She's been pretty tight-lipped about all that. Has she said anything to *you?"*

"No," I admitted. "Grandma thinks they won't get back together."

"Do you want them to?"

"If you had asked me that a couple of months ago, I would have said yes. But now, I honestly don't know. Everything has changed. I've learned that I can be okay with them being split up. Does that make sense?"

Gally smiled at me. "Oh, Theo, I think that makes perfect sense. You've adapted and grown through this whole experience. And it sounds like you're reaching closure. I'm happy for you."

"But I still don't have my driver's license," I joked.

"Baby steps," she teased. "We'll keep working on that one!"

163

We heard car tires crunching on gravel, so we went to the window and saw the strip club owner, Chad Peterson, behind the wheel of a snazzy foreign car. He turned off the engine and started reading something on his phone.

"Shit," Gally said under her breath. "Of all the days for him to show up. Look at me!"

She was wearing a pair of baggy overalls, and she'd tied a red bandanna around her head, pulling back her dark hair.

"You always look fine," I reassured her. "So does this mean you like him? What about your date with that cute fireman?"

"It wasn't a date." She sounded adamant. Then she paused. "But it sure was fun." She smiled, making her green eyes twinkle.

Chad Peterson got out of his car while my aunt ran back to the bathroom. I followed her and watched her take a swig of mouthwash before she pinched her cheeks to give them some color.

"OMG, you do like him," I teased.

"Shhh!" she whispered.

There was a knock on the screen door. We hurried out to the living room, and Gally opened the door. Expecting to see only Chad Peterson, she jumped when she found the veterinarian, Doc Vesper, standing shoulder-to-shoulder with Mr. Chad. Doc Vesper had a black labrador on a leash, and from the looks of it, they'd been walking. Thing 1 stood behind all of them—alert.

"Oh, hi!" Gally said cheerfully, recovering herself. "Come on in! It's a beautiful day to be out and about." She stepped back from the door, waving her hand to welcome them in. Turning to me, she made a funny face that neither man would be able to see. Her discomfort was palpable.

After saying hello, I told them I had to get going. I said I'd promised to help Mom at the big house.

Leaving the cabin, I walked towards home, with Thing 1 following behind. After a bit, I paused, waving for him to come closer. It was silly we couldn't walk side by side. Over the past few weeks, he'd become like an extra appendage, and I felt totally comfortable around him.

I tried engaging him in conversation. I was curious to hear his voice. "Isn't it a beautiful day?" I asked.

He looked at me and smiled.

Okay, so I couldn't get him to talk. I focused on other matters—like Gally and the two men who were with her at the cabin. My aunt had absolutely no suspicions about either Doc Vesper or Chad Peterson. I thought Gally was altogether too trusting—because *I* didn't trust either one of them.

The far-off bleating of that goat caught my attention. I stopped and glanced around. I saw nothing. I almost asked Thing 1 if he had heard anything, but I didn't. He probably wouldn't have said much anyway.

I noticed a bright chartreuse clump of moss by the side of the road. It was the first real sign of spring that I had seen since moving to Minnesota. Maybe, just maybe, I wouldn't be living in a frozen tundra forever! I began searching the ground for other clues of spring, so I didn't notice Deputy Pete standing ahead of us.

I jumped when I saw him. His presence had startled me. Pete looked grave, although I couldn't see his eyes behind his shiny sunglasses. This was the first time I'd been face-to-face with the deputy since my interview—which hadn't gone so well.

"Good afternoon," the deputy said. "Say, you haven't seen Gus Anderson, have you?"

I thought about the last time I'd seen the Burl Ives guy. It was right after the fire, and I couldn't recall seeing him since.

"No," I answered.

"Well, let me know if you do see him or hear anything about him. He seems to have gone missing."

Lexi

you've forgotten all about me!

Theo

ur the one who lost her phone - but thank God you found it

Lexi

tell me how the boating goes tomorrow !!!!!!! - ttyl

Oh, yes, the boating date. Technically, it wasn't really a date—but it could be looked at that way. Jigger and her brother Josh were taking me out on the lake tomorrow afternoon. Mabel's closes at 2:00, and Jigger said we'd be out on the lake by 2:15. Her brother Josh was going along because he wanted to hang out with me—which in my world, was the closest thing I've ever had to a date.

Every time I thought about it I had to smile.

Anyway, I'd just finished a texting marathon with Lexi. She'd accidentally left her phone in her dad's car, and he'd inconveniently driven off to Texas for a work convention. It was nice to "talk" with her again. She was pretty freaked out about Alessa's death. After all, they'd been sisters-in-law.

I took another bite of Mom's mushroom-and-barley soup. I was self-quarantined in my bedroom. Mom and Gally were having dinner downstairs with Deputy Pete and Doc Vesper. I didn't feel like joining them, and Mom was cool with that. Poppy lay at my feet in Grandma Fay's bed while I snuggled down in the quilt. I went through my playlist and chose Patsy Cline. Grandma had told me that when she was my age, that's who she listened to. I got halfway through a song and turned it off. Poor Grandma! I found an old Jane's Addiction song, "Jane Says" and played that instead. *Ding!*

Grandma

Greetings Darling!

She sent a picture of herself on a festively painted boat, holding what looked like a cut-crystal glass of wine in the air. She looked happy. Studying the photo closely, I could make out a man in the background, peering over the rail to the water below. I wondered if he was the mysterious Aditya.

Grandma

> I've been living on this shikara boat on beautiful Lake Dal. We attended the Tulip Festival in Kashmir and have been staying aboard this dreamboat for the last fortnight. Taking a break from the daily hectic frenzy of filming. How are you ? What's going on?

Theo

> looks like ur having fun - that boat is really cool. my only news is that Mr. Anderson is missing

Grandma

> how long has he been missing? because I haven't been able to get hold of him for days

Theo

i guess the last time anyone saw him was seven days ago. he had a doctor's appointment and never showed up. that was the first tip-off. but he's missed all sorts of things and no one can get hold of him and he was known to never leave town - so they are starting to look for him

Grandma

Hmmm

Theo

Oh - and the shoeprint i found on the beach matched the shoeprint of miss honeycutt in city hall - i compared them on film. why was she down on the beach, hiding behind a bush, spying on us with binoculars? and don't tell me she could have been birdwatching - that's what gally said - mom said she went to school with gretchen honeycutt and she is a nice person incapable of murder - so why was she spying on us?

Grandma

The Gretchen I recall was pretty timid. I don't think she's the murdering type. Did Gally ever learn anything about that strip club owner? I hope to God she doesn't pursue a relationship with that Mr. Chad. I remember him from his youth - he was a shifty teenager - not to be trusted. And why on earth does he use his christian name as his surname? Mr. Chad? That's ridiculous.

Theo

i can see that it bothers you!

Grandma

Thank you for forwarding that auction bill to me. I am very curious to know who purchases the old Kerkenbush farm. That could answer many questions.

Theo

no problem. hey - i sent dad a text message and we've been texting back and forth the last couple days

Grandma

Yes! So I've heard. That's wonderful, darling. I've been in contact with him myself. He is so very happy that you are talking to him again.

Theo

i still can't believe Alessa is dead. do you know if they were having a girl or a boy?

Grandma

It was a boy.

I thought about what it would have been like to have a stepbrother. When I was little, I had wanted a sibling so badly! I bugged my mom over and over. What I hadn't known back then was that Mom couldn't have any more children. I only found out about her hysterectomy two years ago from Grandma. I must have unknowingly tortured my mom every time I asked her for a baby brother or sister. Poor Mom!

And I know that Dad had always wanted more children. The fact that his brother Eddie had five kids became somehow a competition. Dad always told me that it wasn't the quantity of the children but the quality that mattered. Thus, he set out to make me a child prodigy, pouring all of his knowledge into my young brain.

Grandma

I don't know if you're aware of this, but your father has asked your mother if she'd like a lodger for the summer.

Theo

WHAT?

Grandma

Your mother told me she turned him down. She feels it's too soon. But she also said she could have a change of heart tomorrow. She feels terrible about the sudden death of that poor girl. She says your father needs time to grieve, and she was astute enough to know that she couldn't be the shoulder to share that grief. I am proud of her for seeing that.

Theo

so does that mean he's coming? what did mom mean when she said she could have a change of heart?

Grandma

I think that means she doesn't really know what she wants. She's thinking it over. Have you gotten anything out of her lately?

no - not really - she's been pretty quiet the last few days.

Grandma

With the situation as it is, your father does not have a home to go home to. The fact that he would want to be around his only offspring is natural. Shouldn't he be allowed to visit you?

I thought about this. Not so long ago, I too had the feeling of not having a home. Funny how quickly I'd become comfortable in this new place. Grandma Fay's bedroom was now my favorite hangout, and I hadn't even changed a thing in her room. Yet it felt like home.

But this whole Dad thing—I never imagined this, not in a million different scenarios. What would my father think of Black Beaver Bay? He was such a city dweller! I couldn't see him in the country. This was so strange, I just couldn't envision it.

Yet, he truly didn't have a place to go. We had sold our house in Oak Park. And I knew Uncle Eddie would not take him in because he'd disowned Dad after what he'd done. So where would he go?

Grandma

Just so you know, your father is planning a surprise visit this summer. I'm sure he was expecting me to be confidential about that tidbit of news, but I'm not in the mood for secrets. One should be prepared for a visit like that. Being caught off guard can be most irritating. Don't you agree?

OMG! Dad was coming!

❋ 35 ❋

Tying a lure onto my fishing pole, Josh knelt on the floor of the boat. He squinted up at me, peering above the top of his sunglasses. His eyes were the most piercing blue.

I was filming him, asking questions. "So what's this you're tying on?" I pretended I was interviewing him for a documentary.

"It's a rapala original floating lure. You'll skim the surface with this, going no more than five feet deep," he explained cheerfully. I thought he was flirting with me, but I wasn't completely sure.

An old Cars song was playing from Josh's playlist. The boat rocked gently in the waves (but not in time to the music), somehow making me a little dizzy. Or maybe I was feeling dizzy because of Josh. I could feel that he liked me. It was a good feeling.

Jigger sat in the back of the old metal fishing boat, running the motor—another accomplishment I could add to her list. I'd already decided that if I had to be on a deserted island with anyone, it would be her. She would figure out a way to save the day. She was like a real Jessica Jones. Well, actually, she was.

"Let's head over to Lover's Leap," Jigger yelled from the back, trying to be heard above the motor and the music. Josh sat down, and we were off. This boating experience was the opposite of the last time I was on the lake. Instead of the leisurely pace of rowing, we were zipping from one side of the lake to the other, tracking down good biting spots. It felt exhilarating.

Although I doubted Thing 1 felt that way. He was in our old rowboat, diligently rowing after us, no matter how fast Jigger took off. I think she was making a game out of it.

The wind blew my hair wildly around my face. I felt such joy that I laughed out loud. The warm afternoon's sunshine put a halcyon glow on everything, as if I were looking back at an old photograph that had turned yellow with age. The vintage music only added to my future memory. Just then, Josh turned to me and smiled.

Jigger cut the motor, and I lurched forward but managed to catch myself. So far today, I had not done one klutzy thing in front of Josh—and I wanted to keep it that way. There would be time enough for him to find out that I couldn't walk two feet without tripping.

"It might be better here," murmured Jigger. I recognized the looming cliff above us as the place Aunt Gally had pointed out, on my first time on the lake. Jigger snapped into action, casting her line expertly into the water.

"Here, give it a try." Josh held out my pole to me.

"Can you film it while I try?" I handed him my camera. My uncomfortableness around him was fading away.

After showing him the basics of my camera, I took the fishing pole in my hands. Josh encouraged me, as I threw my first line into the lake. "Not bad," Jigger called out.

"Now what do I do?" I asked.

"Just give it a second," he said, "then slowly reel it in."

"Are you getting this?" I wondered what Lexi would say when she saw a video of me fishing.

"Nothing has happened yet," Josh teased. "You've only been holding the pole for, like, twenty seconds." Jigger and Josh exchanged an amused look.

"Well, if something *does* happen, be sure to film it. Maybe I'll land something! Beginner's luck and all that!" I said enthusiastically.

"Fishing is all about patience," Jigger said sagely over her shoulder. "Stop thinking about it, and something will happen."

I handed my pole to Josh, so I could pull a sub sandwich from the cooler. If I wasn't supposed to think about fishing, then I had to eat something while not thinking. Thoughtless eating was my specialty. Jigger looked at my sandwich longingly. "Hey, could you throw me my carrots?"

I tossed the baggie to her. She caught it and nodded. "Only three more pounds to go!"

Josh whispered to me, "I'll sure be glad when this diet is over."

I took back my pole and ate my sandwich. Josh's playlist had moved on to an old Led Zeppelin song. The sun felt warm on the top of my scalp. I was starting to perspire a little, but I didn't want to take off my hoodie in front of Josh. My arms were way too skinny—it would freak him out. God, please don't let me sweat so much that I get rings underneath my armpits.

Suddenly, I thought I heard that goat. But as it bleated, a shimmery fish picked that untimely moment to leap out of the water and splash back down.

"Hey, did you hear that?" I asked Josh and Jigger.

"Hear what?" they said at the same time.

I shook my head gloomily. Maybe I should ask Mom to make an appointment for me to get my hearing tested. Or to get a CAT scan.

Jigger distracted me from my worries by asking, "What do you think about Mr. Anderson?"

The three of us were quiet for a second. Then Josh said, "He must have had an accident. He never would have missed his great-nephew's birthday. All his mail is backed up. Something is up."

"How would you know…" I started but then remembered the highly oiled gossip machine in Black Beaver Bay. I wondered what they knew.

As if reading my mind, Jigger offered, "I heard that the last time he was seen, he was driving into town. Howie Mack passed him early last Friday. Gus was heading into our cafe, like he always does for his breakfast. He hasn't missed a meal there since Mom bought the cafe—so that's like twelve years. He never showed up on Friday, so I know something's up."

"Alien abduction," Josh joked.

"Not funny, Josh, I'm worried about him. He was always one of my best tippers."

"I can see your deep concern," Josh teased her again. I realized he was pretty witty. I liked that about him. He switched his playlist to John Prine and played "Lake Marie." As he began to sing along, I watched him, not paying any attention to my fishing line.

"Try reeling it in," said Josh.

I turned my reel, but it wouldn't budge. "Um, I can't."

Jigger hurried towards me while Josh kept filming.

"This is epic," he said into the recorder. "We might be witnessing the very first fish caught by Theo—I can't pronounce her last name."

"What do I do?" I asked, holding tightly to my pole.

Jigger was by my side, coaching me. "Very slowly turn your reel. Okay, lot of tension there. Maybe you're hooked onto something."

We were right below Lover's Leap. Even though there was no beach here—the bluff rose straight out of the lake—I realized there still must be some kind of vegetation under the water.

"So it's not a fish?" I couldn't hide my disappointment. I guess I'd gotten my hopes up. It would have been cool if I could have snagged a real fish on my first time out. A wriggly whopper! Instead I'd caught my hook on some weeds. Not very impressive and certainly not film-worthy.

"We don't know what it is yet," said Jigger. "Patience, remember."

"Give it a good tug," Josh suggested, while he kept the lens on me.

I gave my strongest tug, and suddenly my line came free of whatever it had been stuck on.

"Now reel it in," said Jigger.

I was excited to see what it was. Even if it was just a weed, I was still excited! And that's when it hit me—this was why some people loved to fish. It's because you never know what you're going to get. It reminded me of Forrest Gump and his box of chocolates.

"Hold up." Jigger sounded concerned. I peered into the water where she was looking. Josh moved to our side and was filming the same area.

"That's no fish," Jigger said slowly. "But keep reeling it in."

I watched my snagged prize come closer to the boat. No, I had not caught a fish. It looked, for all the world, like a human hand. I reeled it into the boat and dropped my pole when the hand swung my way, slapping down on the floor of the boat with a sick, smacking sound. It was definitely a man's hand. All the skin was super wrinkly, and it seemed like you could peel it back like a glove. The hand still carried a ring on its finger.

"I know that ring," said Jigger. It was a man's class ring, with the words "St. Olaf" curved around a red stone.

Jigger's sun-kissed cheeks grew greenish, and she looked like she was going to vomit. Quickly, she spun away, getting sick over the side of the boat. She wiped her mouth and then turned back to us.

Softly, she said, "We've found Mr. Anderson."

❀ 36 ❀

Okay, so this was the third body (or partial body) I've discovered since I've been in Minnesota. We've been here twenty-three days. My father, who not only taught statistics but was also fanatical about them, would say there's a good chance it would happen again.

Or maybe it wouldn't. I was trying to remember what we'd been talking about the last time he'd pontificated about this. Dad was totally unaware that he was giving me a passionate lecture, as we drove to the grocery store. He just couldn't stop himself.

I recall him saying, "Coincidences happen constantly in statistics. Correlation, causation, and coincidence......" he droned on. I should have paid closer attention. Instead, I had fiddled with my face mask, looking in the mirror. Why hadn't I listened? Because right now, I would really like to know what my chances were of finding another dead body. Because I really didn't *want* to find another one.

These thoughts flashed through my mind as we stood there, struck dumb. Finally, Josh handed me my camera and pulled out his phone. He called the police department, reporting our find. As we rode across the lake, I could hear the sirens wailing, coming close. By the time we made it back to the Cove's knotty dock, Deputy Pete was waiting for us—along with other policemen. Men in white suits and a sheriff's boat were also there. I saw Mom and Gally far off in the background, running from the house to the dock.

As soon as we got out of the boat, the men in white suits fumbled on board, almost tipping it over. They used long tongs to pick up the hand and place it in a ziplock freezer bag. Getting out of the boat, one of the men fell into the water and dropped the bag into the lake. A flurry of curses went back and forth before the bag was successfully retrieved.

Josh agreed to take Deputy Pete back to where we had found the hand. Rescue divers had been called in. They were going to try to locate the rest of Mr. Anderson's body.

Mom and Gally reached Jigger and me. Out of breath and panting, they asked a million questions at once.

"Girls, are you alright?"

"Are you okay?"

"What happened?"

Jigger spoke, trying to ease their tension. She told them about our discovery, which put Mom and Gally in a somber mood.

"Poor Mr. Anderson," Gally said softly. "How horrible."

Mom hugged me and held on for a second too long before I pulled away. Suddenly, I felt exhausted. I wondered if Jigger would freak out if I didn't go to her party that night. She and Josh had talked about it while we were fishing earlier, obviously excited. Going to my first high school party was the last thing I wanted to do right now.

Then, making things worse, a familiar, "Yoo-hoo!" came calling out from the big house. We all turned to see Mrs. Banger, waving.

"Oh, no!" Aunt Gally whispered. "What is *she* doing here?"

"How can we get rid of her?" Mom groaned.

We watched Mrs. Banger advance upon us, striding down the incline, as if it were her enemy. We were trapped. But I couldn't stand the idea of talking to her again.

"We need to get ready!" I announced with fake enthusiasm.

Grabbing Jigger's hand, I hurried towards the cabins. I said over my shoulder, "We have to get ready for the party!"

Jigger and I had talked to Mom earlier about the party. Jigger had told Mom that it was at her parents' farm (true), and it was a birthday party for her brother (true), and it was also a May Day party (true). *However,* she had failed to tell Mom that her parents were out of town, and every teenager in the county was going to be there. Not to celebrate her brother's birthday. And not to celebrate May Day. Just to celebrate in general—to party.

Mom had agreed to let me go, but she didn't want me staying overnight. So Jigger and I talked her into having a sleepover at our house—

well, actually, in the cabin that Gally had just redecorated. That's where we headed, as Mrs. Banger came closer to our group.

Jigger and I ran.

"Girls, wait," we heard Mrs. Banger call after us. We turned around, waving, but still running. Mom and Gally stood there, resigned.

Two hours later, we were almost ready. My mood had picked up. Thoughts of Mr. Anderson's gnawed hand weren't flashing through my brain as frequently. That was probably due to Jigger. She *totally* got my mind off the afternoon's horrors.

"Getting ready is the best part," she said, as she put eye makeup on me.

"What?" I said softly.

"Don't talk," she scolded me. "Stay still. My mom says getting ready for a party or for a special date is always the best part of the evening. The dressing-up part is what she likes best."

I smiled, even though I hoped Jigger's mom would be wrong. I was going to my first high school party (albeit with Thing 1 tagging along), and I *wanted* it be memorable—in a good sort of way. Really, I didn't know what to expect. Loud music? Excessive drinking? Drugs? Illicit sex? Who knew what I'd find? If it was anything like the movies, there was bound to be some drama.

We were in the bathroom that Gally had just redone. Jigger adored the new look, and she raved about the pressure in the wooden casket shower. She really loved it all. She was playing "Saturday Night," an ancient song by the Bay City Rollers, to get her in the mood, she said.

"There." She finally stepped back from me, inspecting her makeup job. I jumped up and looked in the mirror.

"I love it!" I cried. I was trying to act excited, but really, I was more scared. I had grave doubts about this party.

I'd voiced all my worries to Jigger over the past few days. She kept telling me everything would be fine, and that her friends weren't scary.

She had lent me a casual spring dress with embroidery around its peasant neck—kind of boho chic. It was super cute. I was also wearing her old jean jacket and rubber boots because the party was in a field, and she said it would be suicide to wear any other kind of footwear.

I heard the sound of that goat again. And it was loud this time, like right-outside-the-cabin sort of loud.

"Did you hear that?" I asked Jigger, totally expecting her to say she hadn't heard anything.

"Sounds like a goat," she said.

Oh, thank God! I hadn't been losing my mind. I wasn't having audible hallucinations. I didn't have a brain tumor. I didn't have epilepsy. I didn't need a CAT scan. My relief must have been noticeable, for Jigger gave me a strange look. She watched me curiously, as I ran from window to window.

"Hey, it's just a goat. Millie Kerkenbush had one old goat left, and it's gone missing since she was killed. There have been sightings of it everywhere."

"Well, I wish I'd had a sighting of it. I've been hearing this phantom goat for weeks!"

Jigger laughed. "Hey, I'll be ready in five. I just want to remove this first." She was scrubbing her fingernail polish off with a cotton ball and remover. The green polish smeared underneath the acetone. "I don't have time to paint on a new color," she mumbled. "There." She held out her hands to look them over.

"Ready?" I asked anxiously, checking my appearance in the mirror.

"Hey, is it cool if I use some of this?" She held up the mini mouthwash bottle. "I forgot to pack my toothbrush."

"Yeah." I waved my hand, as if to say she didn't need to ask.

Jigger swished the mouthwash around in her mouth, making funny faces at herself in the mirror, pretending to be a fish. But even her goofy faces couldn't disguise how pretty she was. Her dress was a little clingier (and shorter) than mine, but it was still in the boho chic genre.

Her mud galoshes were way cooler than mine, though—designed to look like cowboy boots.

"Oh, I almost forgot…" She hurried out of the bathroom and ran to the bedroom. She opened a bag from her bed, pulling out a flower wreath. Vibrant ribbons hung from its back. It looked like it was made from fresh flowers, but I wouldn't be able to tell until I touched it.

"Come here," she beckoned, pulling me in front of a mirror. Carefully, she set the wreath on my head.

"Are you serious?" I scoffed.

A May Day wreath? I knew there were people who still celebrated May Day and wore flower wreaths. Were any of these kids practicing Wiccans? Because I knew Wiccans were big into celebrating Beltane, or May Day. Would there be a bunch of witches there? Just what kind of party was I going to? Suddenly, all my worst anxieties about this evening became real.

"Very serious," Jigger said somberly.

"Do the other girls wear these?" I asked, watching her face.

"Only *you* will be wearing it tonight," she said, in the most solemn tone I had ever heard from her.

"Why only me?" I was puzzled.

Jigger looked at me earnestly before speaking. "Only *you* will be wearing the wreath tonight, for you are the chosen one. Every year, we sacrifice a person to the planting gods. We always pick people who are outsiders—not true Minnesotans."

WTF??

❀ 37 ❀

"You should have seen your face!" Jigger was laughing so hard she snorted.

"Well, you *did* make me think all my fears about this party were coming true," I admitted sheepishly.

I guess I deserved it. I'm sure I had been super-annoying, even if I hadn't intended to be. The whole past week, I'd constantly expressed my anxieties to Jigger about this party. I'd worried I wouldn't fit in, worried the other kids would make fun of me, worried I'd be the only outsider. Finally, Jigger had bribed me by saying she'd make a ton of traditional Minnesotan food. She'd called all her girlfriends and asked them to cook something too. Ultimately, my love of food won over my fears—so here I was.

Jigger now wore the wreath she had previously given me. It lay slightly crooked on her head. She'd spiked her diet Mountain Dew with vodka, but she'd only allowed herself two shots. She said alcohol was a huge waste of calories. She only had two-and-a-half pounds 'til goal weight. She said she wasn't going to blow it now.

I, on the other hand, totally overindulged. On food! Everyone had brought a dish to pass—that's what they called it. It was fabulous, a smorgasbord of Midwestern specialties. The stuffed mushrooms were my favorite. I had seventeen. But the meatballs in gravy were a close second. I had twelve. Then again, the "pigs in a blanket" weren't bad either. I had eleven. And then there was this divine thing called a "tater tot hot dish"…

I'd taken two plates of food to Thing 1, who sat in Mom's car, at a distance. It was the least I could do. He must have been bored out of his mind. Although he seemed content enough listening to some ball game on the radio.

The kids at the party seemed nice. No one really talked to me except to say "hi" when Jigger introduced me. But on the other hand, no one seemed mean or hostile. They were almost welcoming.

There was, however, one person who struck up a conversation with me. While I was getting my seventh plate of food, a boy came up and introduced himself. He said he was a classmate of Jigger's. He told me he had moved to Black Beaver Bay last year, from California. He said he could imagine how I was feeling, having come from Chicago. He predicted I was experiencing severe culture shock.

The whole time he talked, I kept eating and nodding my head. He was a little guy, not even five feet tall. I was a skyscraper next to him! It dawned on me that as awkward as I felt with my growth spurt, it must have been just as hard for him because he *hadn't* gone through *his* yet. Suddenly, I could really identify with him.

His name was Adam Adams, and he turned out to be sooo funny. He was a super good impersonator—like he could imitate the Queen of England dead on. He said he'd learned to use his mimicking skill as a way to get people to overlook his shortness.

There were moments when I wondered if he was flirting with me. I wasn't nuanced in the art of flirting, so I honestly couldn't tell. I hoped for his sake he didn't like me. Because it would be so awkward if he tried to kiss me. He'd have to use a ladder!

We ended up standing on the edge of a tilled pasture, around a glowing bonfire. I threw my empty paper plate into the flames. It was nearing sunset, and I was thankful for the fire because it kept my bare legs warm. An old Pixies' song, "Here Comes Your Man" was blaring in the background. I looked around the party for Josh but couldn't see him. There were gobs of kids here—well over a hundred.

A maypole had been erected in the distance. Two drunk girls were goofing around, dancing with the ribbons in an erratic fashion. I bet they had no idea that the winding and unwinding of the ribbons symbolized the days growing longer, and it was a very precise pagan dance.

It wasn't like the horsing around that these girls were doing. I knew this because Dad had taught me about these rituals just last year.

I also knew that bonfires were an essential tradition in May Day celebrations. The fire was thought to have protective powers—even the ashes from the fire were considered sacred. All I knew now was that the fire was protecting me from freezing.

I looked around for Josh again. I couldn't see him anywhere. I thought back to this afternoon on the boat. There had been a brief second when I thought he was going to kiss me. I'd been showing him how to work my camera, and our faces had been close—close enough for him to steal a kiss if he'd wanted to. But he hadn't done it.

I remembered him in the sunlight. He had the same color blond hair as Jigger had. But that was about all they had in common, even though they were twins. Although I'd definitely witnessed some twin connections—like when they would finish each other's stories. And they could be quiet for like ten minutes and then blurt out the exact same thing at the exact same time. Spooky. I wondered if the Swallow Sisters had shared things like that too.

I glimpsed Jigger by the food table. She looked like a May Day Queen—an ultramodern, hip one. I thought it was good practice for when she'd be crowned Miss Apple Blossom. Because I really believed she would win! She was the prettiest contestant, in my estimation. The only way she could lose was if she had a terrible talent act. She wouldn't tell me what she was planning to do, no matter how many times I asked her. She wanted it to be a surprise.

I noticed that some of the other girls had made makeshift wreaths of their own, copying Jigger's look. This wasn't the first time someone had copycatted Jigger. I'd observed this during the pageant practices. I'd been to five of the rehearsals, and I'd noticed that some of the girls had gotten their hair cut exactly like Jigger's. She was what Grandma would call a bellwether. I'd call her an influencer. But the funny thing was, she wasn't aware of it. She was just being herself. There was something about her confidence that was very attractive, and I'd seen how people tended to congregate around her. And she was *so* positive. And funny. I felt grateful that we had become friends.

Loud cheering made me look over towards the barn, where kids were doing keg stands. Things were starting to get pretty wild.

Scanning the crowd again, I saw Josh coming my way. I told Adam it had been wonderful to meet him, and we shook hands. As I turned to walk to Josh, one of my galoshes got sucked in the mud, and before you knew it, I lost my balance.

Adam tried to catch me, but I ended up knocking him over. As I tried to brace myself, I fell flat into a mud puddle!

I heard laughter before my face even hit the muddy water. My humiliation was complete. I wished I could snap my fingers and just disappear. Instead, I pulled myself out of the mud. But I wasn't very graceful, because the mud was like suctioning me to the ground.

I extended my hand to Adam, to help him up. Quickly, Josh was helping both of us, and then he put his jacket around me. Adam laughed, saying it had been great to meet me. He was such a good sport about it.

I kept wiping the dirty water from my face and hair. More than anything, I just wanted to get out of there and go home.

Josh led me away from the crowd, heading towards the mess of cars and pickup trucks.

"How embarrassing," I moaned. He opened the door to his truck, fished around inside, and handed me a tub of hand sanitizers.

"Left over from the corona," he explained. He had the funniest smile on his face, as if he didn't think he should laugh. Now that I was away from the other kids, I was starting to see the humor in the situation, and I covered my face with my hands, half-moaning and half-laughing. Then he started laughing too, and we couldn't stop.

"I can run you back to your cabin, so you can change," he offered.

"I'm supposed to go with Thing 1," I told him. I'd explained all about *that* earlier in the day, when we were on the lake. I mean, it was pretty obvious that Thing 1 was following us everywhere in the row-boat, so I'd felt like I had no choice but to tell Josh the truth.

"I know a backroad that's half the time. He won't even know you're gone." Josh's eyes looked mischievous in the sunset. Why not, I thought. It could be fun. I hopped in his truck, and we left.

By "backroad," Josh meant "gravel road." I thought he was a good driver. He didn't go too fast, and he handled his corners beautifully. If *I'd* been driving, no doubt I would have skidded on the gravel. That was one of my biggest fears about driving—not being able to handle the curves on gravel.

He turned up the heat. "Are you cold?"

"No, I'm okay," I said shyly. This was the first time we'd been alone together. My brain was working overtime, trying to think of something to talk about, but I couldn't think of *anything!* We rode along silently, listening to "S.O.S" by The Glorious Sons.

Before I knew it, Josh was pulling up to the long row of cabins at the Cove. He hadn't gone by the big house. This was another entrance onto our property that I hadn't known about. Why, *anyone* could have quick access to these cabins, and nobody at the big house would ever know about it.

He followed me into the red cabin. I turned on a table lamp, telling him I'd be right back, before I went to the bathroom and peeled off the sopping-wet dress. I took a fast shower and threw on my hoodie all within five minutes. When I went back to the couch, he was standing there, looking at me.

Then he turned off the light.

He stepped closer to me. The illuminating moonlight poured through the big picture window, giving the whole room a surreal feel. We stood there silently, looking at each other. "Hey, do you have any gum?" he whispered shyly.

OMG. He was going to kiss me. This exact same thing had happened to Lexi when *she* had her first kiss. The boy had asked her if she kept any gum in her purse—which made sense. I mean, who wanted to kiss someone with halitosis? Then I was hit with the self-realization that my own breath reeked of garlic from all those stuffed mushrooms I'd devoured. Maybe he was giving me a hint!

"There's mouthwash in the bathroom," I murmured.

He followed me into the dark bathroom. I felt for the switch, but before I could turn on the light, he gently grabbed my hand. He held it softly, caressing it. Very slowly, he ran his finger up my wrist, giving me goosebumps.

This was going to happen. I shuddered in anticipation. And I was happy it was going to happen in this newly refurbished bathroom, which was my favorite room, in my favorite cabin.

But was there ever a bad place to have your first kiss?

I began freaking out about my garlic breath. With my free hand, I grabbed for the bottle of mouthwash that Jigger had left by the sink. Being courteous, I offered it to him first.

Josh opened the bottle and took a large chug. Instantly, he spat the fluid out of his mouth and—accidentally—straight into my face. I let out a muffled cry. My eyes burned as if they were on fire.

"Water!" he gasped.

I turned on the bathroom light and the tap. While I splashed water into my eyes, he drank handfuls from the faucet.

"What was that?" he croaked.

I looked at the bottle he'd dropped. Liquid was creeping across the newly tiled floor. OMG! I'd accidentally given him Jigger's fingernail polish remover!

❀ 38 ❀

They found Mr. Anderson's car the following morning. It was submerged in the water right below Lover's Leap, where I'd found his hand. A crowd had gathered on top of Lover's Leap, waiting for his car to be winched up and out of the lake. Jigger had taken her fishing boat out on the lake and convinced me to come along. She wanted to see what they'd find. She even suggested I film it.

So I went along, even though my heart wasn't in it. All I could think about was my tragic accident of giving Josh the fingernail polish remover instead of the mouthwash. I kept trying to make things better in my mind by telling myself that it was dark. And that the bottles were the same size. I mean, *anybody* could have made the same mistake. But for me, my mistake had robbed me of my first kiss.

Of course Jigger thought it was hilarious. Josh had told her about it, claiming that I had tried to poison him. His absence today was palpable. I found myself sighing over and over again.

"Knock it off," Jigger teased. "If you keep sighing like that, you'll hyperventilate."

"Really?" I'd never heard that before. I petted Poppy's head, thinking about that theory.

"Just kidding, but seriously, it's no big deal. You should be laughing about it. After all, it's just Josh. He's a moron," she scoffed.

Strangely, none of this made me feel any better. I didn't think Josh was a moron. I thought he'd been really nice last night. He and Adam were the only ones at the party who had helped me during the mud puddle fiasco. Jigger said she hadn't seen me fall, but she'd heard about it later.

I ended up not going back to the party last night. After my debacle in the bathroom, my eyes had been so swollen and red from the polish remover that I'd told Josh I just wanted to stay at the cabin. So Josh left, super awkwardly, like he couldn't get out of there fast enough—like romance was the furthest thing from his mind.

Anyway, he went back to his farm and told Thing 1 that I was already home. Later, around midnight, Josh dropped Jigger off at the cabin, but he didn't come in. By that time, I was fairly convinced he hated me.

That was all last night, yet I kept replaying the scenes in my head over and over again. I wished I could turn them off and stop torturing myself. Sighing, I unwrapped a cucumber-and-potted-meat sandwich. Grandma had taught me how to make these when I was four. Thinking of Grandma, I realized I hadn't heard from her in a couple of days. I wondered what she was up to—because Grandma was always up to something. I tore off a piece of my bread and gave it to Poppy.

I watched Jigger cast her line perfectly into the lake. She wore wraparound sunglasses and a backwards baseball cap. Since we were waiting for Mr. Anderson's car to be yanked out of the water, Jigger said we shouldn't waste this chance to get in some fishing. But the last thing I felt like doing was fishing. God only knew what I'd pull out of the water this time. And besides, I was busy eating my fourth sandwich.

"You make that sandwich look *so* good," she moaned.

"Sorry!" I quickly popped the last bite in my mouth. What kind of person was I? I was torturing the only friend I had here with my gluttonous eating, while she was trying to lose weight.

"Hey, want to hear a funny story?" she asked. She was no doubt trying to cheer me up. I wasn't sure I wanted to be.

"Well, it's not really funny. It's actually kinda sad," she quickly added. Suddenly, I really wanted to hear that story.

"What is it?" I asked, petting Poppy's head.

"I heard that Cyrus—he's an eccentric, old farmer that lives past Millie's place—found Millie's missing goat. You know, the goat you kept hearing? Well, actually, the goat found Cyrus. It had been bleating all night long outside his door. Cyrus was convinced that the creature was looking for Millie, so he took the goat into the coroner's office, so the goat could understand that Millie was dead. Cyrus said that even goats need closure." She paused, breaking into a smile. "The coroner kicked the goat and Cyrus out of his examination room."

I could appreciate the humorous way Jigger told the story, but it was really kind of tragic. I wondered if I would ever meet this goat. Would he mourn for the rest of his life? Did animals go through the seven stages of grief, like humans?

I thought back to a conversation I'd had with my Aunt Penelope. After Mom filed for the divorce, Auntie Pen took me aside to have one of those "talks." She said divorce was really the death of a family. I would need to grieve. She explained the seven stages. And she said that until I allowed myself to feel those seven stages, I would never have closure.

I remember looking up the definition of closure. I knew what the word meant, but I wanted to see the different ways the dictionary described it. My favorite was "letting go of what once was." Speaking from experience, sometimes that's painfully hard to do.

But maybe—just maybe—I was nearing the last stage of grief, which was acceptance.

I thought of Millie's goat and wondered if he was going through stages too. Which stage was he at? Suddenly, I felt a great empathy towards this unseen goat. I hoped he was healing.

Eventually, I turned my view to the horizon. The leaves on the trees hadn't unfurled yet, and the millions of buds created a green haze against the dark branches and rocky bluffs. It was beautiful! When we were out on the lake yesterday, I'd been so wrapped up in Josh that I hadn't even noticed how cool it looked. Could it be that spring was finally here?

"Hey, look," Jigger said, pointing towards the rescue boats. I turned on my camera and began filming. She moved the boat a little closer to the scene, where police boats were scattered around the emerging wreck.

When she came abreast of the other boats, someone called out to her, "Jigger, you shouldn't be here. You don't want to see this."

"Oh, yes I do," she responded, not budging her boat.

I turned and saw Thing 1 rowing up. At least he hadn't needed to chase us all over the lake like he had to yesterday. Perhaps I wasn't the easiest person to protect, if you looked at it from a bodyguard's point of view.

Slowly, we saw the car's back fender rise from the lake. It was being winched into the air by the tow truck parked way overhead on Lover's Leap. I panned my camera to the tow truck and boom that extended over the edge. The cable that held the car looked so tenuous! I felt a foreboding that something was bound to go wrong. But what other choice did the rescue mission have? There was no beach below Lover's Leap—the rocky bluff rose straight out of the lake.

As the back doors of the car emerged from the lake, water began to pour out. The windows had been down. Well, that made sense. How else could his hand have gotten out? As the car inched out of the lake, the front doors of the vehicle were exposed.

"Oh, my God, I think he's still in there!" Jigger cried. I zoomed in. Yes, he was *definitely* still inside his old Crown Victoria. Suddenly, his arm unceremoniously swung out the window with a gush of water, making all of us let out a collective gasp. Poppy growled. I wondered why the rescue divers hadn't removed him from the car first. Maybe they had tried but hadn't been successful.

Mr. Anderson's arm was missing a hand. In some gruesomely optimistic way, I felt glad I'd found it, so now it could be reunited with its owner. But then a horrible thought came into my head. What if I'd been the one who had yanked his hand off?

This morning, I'd looked up drowned corpses on this forensic website I'd found. I was wondering if everyone's skin wrinkled like Mr. Anderson's hand. There was actually a term they used for this condition. It was called "washerwoman hands"—I guess because women who used to do laundry for a living had water-soaked, wrinkly hands—

191

but anyway, I hoped his face wouldn't look like that. I debated turning off my camera.

As the car rose higher, we could see his body through the windshield. He was definitely strapped into his car seat with his seat belt, although it looked like there was a whole lot more going on than that. His neck appeared to be tied to his headrest with some plastic jump ropes—like the kind a five-year-old would use—those ones with the plastic handles. He definitely couldn't have tied himself into *that* position.

His head was tipped slightly back, resting at an odd angle. There must have been several jump ropes used because I could see various colors. It was sooo bizarre that it didn't look real. If I were seeing this in a movie, I'd think it was fake.

As we watched poor Mr. Anderson wrenched from his watery grave, the scene became somber. Everyone stood respectfully quiet.

Then Jigger's cell phone went off. "Knock, knock, knockin' on heaven's door…" rang loudly, echoing over the previously silent lake. She quickly turned it off.

Suddenly, the cable yanked hard, making the car jerk up and down. Instantly, Mr. Anderson's head flew off his body, tumbled out the window, and fell straight into the lake. Jigger and I screamed!

I turned off my camera, feeling like I would be sick. Well, what did I expect? It was another holiday—and holidays were now following an awful trend where I either discovered something deeply troubling or experienced something morbidly sad. Happy May Day, I told myself.

❋ 39 ❋

Before mouth-to-mouth resuscitation was discovered, other methods were used in the attempt to revive a drowned person. One of the most interesting methods was the one where they'd take smoke-filled bellows and stick the pointy end into a person's rectum, blowing smoke inside their body. Crazy at it sounds, this had actually worked on a drowned sailor—or so it was documented.

I wondered how the sailor felt when he was brought back to life. Was he thankful? Or was he mortified to be lying on the deck of the ship (with his crewmates gathered around), stripped nude of his trousers, with a bellows hanging out of his behind?

That's the thing about death—it can catch you off guard and be quite undignified. I came to that conclusion when I watched the footage that I'd filmed since I'd moved to Minnesota. Studying the dead bodies, I didn't think any of them would have appreciated the states in which they were found.

But then again, how do you know when you're about to be murdered? I'm sure that if Mrs. Kerkenbush had been forewarned, she would have had her hair done and worn her Sunday best. Although in her case, all her efforts would have been in vain because even if she'd gussied up, no one would have really noticed, since they'd all be staring at that knitting needle sticking out of her eye. And because she was found in the water, getting her hair done for her death would have been a complete and utter waste of time.

And poor Mr. Anderson sure wouldn't have been happy with the way in which *he* was discovered. His autopsy revealed that he had been killed before his body and car were pushed into the lake. His neck had been almost completely severed and then strangely wrapped up with jump ropes, as if to attach his head again. It was just so bizarre!

I'd been reviewing all my film, trying to piece together a narrative of the events that had happened. As I watched, I was plowing my way through a jumbo bag of Starbursts, listening to an old Spacehog song.

Mom barged into my room. Well, not really barged, because I could only see the top of her hair above my barricade of boxes.

"Theo, I think this might be it!" She raised her arm above the boxes, brandishing a key.

I hopped off the bed and grabbed it from her. "Thanks Mom!"

"Let me know if that works. A plumber is waiting for me. I have to go!" She ran down the stairs.

For weeks, I'd been trying to find the key to Grandma Fay's closet. Yes, I had to unpack my boxes of clothes and put them somewhere, but more importantly to me, I wanted to know if there were any other family treasures tucked away—like the scrapbooks I'd devoured. It had become my nightly ritual to read through Grandma Fay's memoirs while I ate some bedtime snacks. I looked forward to it.

Ever since Grandma had told me she recalled a suitcase full of her grandmother Esme's belongings, I'd searched the attic, basement, boathouse, garage, and every closet—looking for that very suitcase. I hadn't found it. But it had to be here.

Anxiously, eagerly, I placed the key in the locked door to the closet. It opened!

A knotted string was attached to an overhead light. Well, this will never work, I thought. I mean, how old was this light bulb? I pulled the string, and the light bulb illuminated the entire little closet. It gave me a hopeful feeling.

Grandma Fay's clothes hung at the back. There weren't very many of them. I held one of her dresses up to my body. She had been tiny.

I looked over the lined shelves that covered one side of the closet. Dainty shoes, boots, and hatboxes filled the shelves, and underneath, I saw suitcases! I lifted the first one and could tell it was empty. But when I went to lift the second one, it was obvious that something was inside.

Hauling it out to my bedroom, I set the dusty suitcase on top of the bed and fiddled with the latches. When I got it open, I found that the whole case was filled with yellowing newspapers, photos, and letters. Bingo! Instantly, I knew I would not be doing the unpacking Mom so urgently wanted me to do. I was looking at an entire afternoon's worth of reading.

On the very top lay an old-fashioned photograph, the kind mounted on heavy stock board, of my great-great-grandmother, Esme. I could tell it was her because she looked so much like the oil painting in the library. She was a very pretty woman, with a slightly turned-up nose, light eyes, and a full mouth. Actually, I could see a lot of Gally in her.

Next, I unfolded a fragile newspaper from 1904. It was *The Wabasha Gazette*. A picture of a woman in long braids and a kerchief around her neck, standing next to a wrecked vehicle, took up the entire front page. Who was she?

Later, I found a grainy photograph of two children and that same black-braided woman. On the back of the photo, written in pencil and very faded, I read, "Esme, her grandmother Papuza, and her cousin Tommy Dooley." I pieced together that this Papuza was my great-great-great-great-grandmother! She looked like such an interesting character. I wondered what her story was.

Looking at Papuza's photograph, I felt it was nothing short of astonishing that I carried this woman's DNA. Before Dad left, we'd been studying research about memory and whether it could be passed down through DNA. Not only memories, but knowledge too. I peered closer at her picture. I wondered if I held some of her memories inside my head.

Then I came across a charming old advertisement for Dooleys' Doses, a medicine which Esme and Tommy had patented together. Their pictures were in ovals on either side of the text, which read:

Is your throat sore and burning? Are you sniffling, sneezing, and coughing? Do you find yourself so close to death that you are ponder-

ing life insurance companies? Take a drop of Dooleys' Doses, and soon you will be the very picture of health. From our family to yours, stock up on our secret remedy today!

Then I discovered a group of photographs that had been taken at a circus. Esme was wearing a fancy headdress, sitting on top of an elephant. "Esme and Buttercup" was scrawled across the bottom. A picture of Esme and Tommy posing with clowns and acrobats was my favorite, with Esme sitting on top of some giant's shoulders. I wondered if they had traveled with a circus.

The more I searched through the suitcase, the more grateful I felt for finding this treasure trove of family history. I had nothing like this on my dad's side. My dad couldn't even remember his life before he came to the United States.

The orphanage in India where he'd been dropped off with his newborn brother had no idea who had left them there. The only clue was that my father had a strip of paper with the name "Chandalavada" written on it and pinned to his clothing. "Chandalavada" is a common surname in India—maybe like "Smith" in America. The couple that had adopted the brothers felt it was wrong to strip them of their birth name.

Yet my father had no interest in his birth name or his birth country. And even though he didn't care, I did. I wished I knew more about his side of the family.

Towards the bottom of the suitcase, I uncovered a bundle of letters that were tied together with a faded, orange ribbon. I slid the letters free from their restraint and looked at the addresses on the outside of the envelopes. Many had been postmarked from Bristol, England in 1918. They were sent from a Private Thomas Dooley and were addressed to Esme Dooley of Zumbro Falls, Minnesota. Gently, I unfolded the letters and read.

The letters were about Tommy's WWI experience. His writings to his first cousin Esme were full of humor, mixed with horror. He must have felt very close to her to confide such personal stories. I knew they were first cousins, but it sounded like they were best friends too.

When I came to the last letter, I felt disappointed. I wished there had been more. Sighing, I opened it up and read:

Dear Esme,

*I'm coming home! I've managed to survive the Great War **and** the Spanish Flu, and I'm shipping out tomorrow from Bristol. I reckon I will reach Zumbro Falls by the end of the summer. I can't wait to see you, and Pa, and my brothers who have already made it home. I hope and pray my other brothers are on their way back too.*

I'll tell you right now, Esme, I expect you to meet me at the train station. Gosh-almighty, I'll groan if you ain't there because you got thrown in jail again. I know it's hard to be the only suffragette in Zumbro Falls, but maybe—just maybe—you could take a break from protesting on the day that I come home?

By the way, I think we should start to produce Papuza's cold remedy right away. Those bottles you sent over here were a huge hit with the boys in the trenches, and some of them even swore it plumb saved their lives. I figure we could finally start our medicinal business.

I feel mighty fortunate to come home with only a leg full of shrapnel. Shucks, my days of traveling with you were actually more hazardous than the front line in France. I have to admit, Esme, you trained me well for war.

As for that land up north, could you wait until I get back before you jump into something headfirst (as usual)? We could drive your new motorcar up there because I'd really love to see those acres with my own two eyes before I go in with you and plop down a chunk of cash. I know you got excited when White Crow said the land holds great riches, but how do you know that ain't just an old legend? We need to be smart about this and have some mineral studies done...

I set the letter down without finishing it. So there it was. I now knew the motivation behind these crimes—or at least I thought I did. Maybe the perpetrators didn't want the land because it was so beautiful. Maybe they wanted it because of what was buried underneath.

❃ 40 ❃

"Ten, ten, ten, ten, ten, ten, ten, ten, do I have ten dollars?" the auctioneer, whose name was Major Jack, rattled on, scanning the crowd for any bidders.

"Oh, what the hell," Gally mumbled before raising her bidding number in the air. "Who doesn't need vintage jigsaw puzzles? They'll look cute on a cabin shelf."

"Sold!" Major Jack yelled, pointing at Gally. She had quickly become his newest best friend because she was literally buying everything.

We were at Mrs. Kerkenbush's auction. Mrs. K's personal belongings had been spread about her farmyard. Boxes of her smaller items were stacked on haywagons, where people dug through everything, searching for treasures.

I had no idea there would be so many people here. I'd never been to a farm auction. There was a bit of a festival air to the whole thing, with children running around, streaming red balloons that came free with every purchase of Mrs. Banger's world-famous sausages, which she was selling out of her circus-like lunch wagon.

I hated to admit it, but her sausages were pretty good. I'd already eaten five. I actually wanted another one, but I didn't want to talk to Mrs. Banger, and Jigger wouldn't buy any more for me. Mrs. Banger had made a snide comment to Jigger when she was buying me my fifth sausage, reminding Jigger that the pageant was less than a week away, and there was no time for costume alterations at this late date. *Now* was not the time to start pigging out, Mrs. Banger had warned.

Of course Jigger hadn't told Mrs. Banger that all the sausages had been for me. Nor was Mrs. Banger aware that Jigger was still valiantly working on her goal weight—with just one-and-a-half pounds to go!

So now I stood sausage-less, scanning the crowd and farm with my camera. It was a beautiful setting, with apple trees and lilacs ready to burst open. The barn, where she'd kept all her goats for the last seventy years, sat empty. There was no sign of her roaming goat that Cyrus had taken to the coroner's. I wondered if Cyrus still had him.

I turned my camera on Poppy, who lay panting by her water bowl in the shade of a tree. Thing 1 held onto her leash. I wondered if Poppy would lament my death—like Millie's goat lamented Millie.

Turning back to the crowd, I spotted Deputy Pete by one of the haywagons, talking to Mrs. Drew—that crabby, old principal who had yelled at us in City Hall. I filmed them because it looked like Mrs. Drew was scolding the deputy.

Right next to them, I noticed Miss Honeycutt snooping through junk. I zoomed in on her. I couldn't help but notice she'd dyed her hair, covering up her roots. Her new shade of red was pretty vibrant—sort of along the lines of Rudolph's nose. I imagined she'd be easy to spot in a Minnesota blizzard.

I continued to film her as she hurried over to the veterinarian, Doc Vesper, who was examining a rustic rocking chair. They appeared to be well acquainted. I wished I were closer, so I could hear what they were talking about.

I panned my camera over to Mr. Chad, who stood aside from the active bidders, taking pictures of the house with his cell phone. I wondered if he would be bidding during the real estate part of the auction, which would start at 3:00. We were all curious to see who would be bidding on this place. Grandma was convinced that the high bidder would turn out to be the murderer. I wasn't totally onboard with her theory, but I wasn't totally against it either.

I stood away from the crowd, next to Thing 1 and the growing pile of Aunt Gally's purchases. Jigger was searching through Gally's boxes, having a grand old time.

"Hey, look at this," she said from the ground, where she was squatting above a box. She lifted a ceramic figurine of a white-haired lady who had the words "Chopper Hopper" on the front of her apron. The figurine opened up at the waistline, revealing an empty space.

"This was for her dentures," Jigger told me, raising an eyebrow in amusement. I thought back to finding Mrs. K's body. Her mouth had been open, but I didn't recall seeing any teeth. I wondered if her dentures had fallen out when she was in the lake. The thought of it made me sad. I was once again struck with the feeling of how undignified death can be.

I looked over the crowd. Mom was now talking with Deputy Pete, and they seemed to be having a super serious discussion. I hoped to God she wasn't breaking her promise to keep quiet about our land possibly having valuable minerals. Because we had all agreed to keep that on the down-low for the time being.

Last night, Mom, Gally, Grandma, and I had a powwow on Skype, trying to decide what to do with the information I'd found in that surprising letter from my great-great-uncle Tommy.

Mom did not think it was worth going to the police, and she thought we were all making a mountain out of a molehill. It was just speculation. And if the land did hold valuable minerals, why hadn't Esme and Tommy mined them? So maybe there was only dirt under our dirt. That was her take on it, anyway.

Gally, on the other hand, was convinced that there were valuable deposits of *something* beneath our feet. She said she could feel it in her bones.

Grandma thought that, more than likely, we were sitting on top of iron ore. After all, we weren't far from the Iron Range. Although from what I'd read on the internet, iron ore wasn't the only mineral found in northern Minnesota. Zinc, lead, platinum, diamonds, gold, and titanium were still under exploration.

Grandma persuaded us all to wait a bit with this information. She wanted to check with her personal attorney and have him do some digging—literally. I totally agreed with Grandma. However, I did tell Jigger everything.

"Sold!" Major Jack cried, pointing to Gally once again. My aunt clapped her hands excitedly. "I really wanted that!" she sang happily.

One of the runners for the auction came our way, carrying Gally's latest purchase. It was an antique dressmaker's dummy, and I could see why Gally wanted it. It would make a cool piece in one of the cabins. Lately, she'd been throwing around the idea of hosting quilters' retreats at the Cove.

After Gally accepted her purchase, Miss Honeycutt came up to us. I watched her and my aunt talk, laughing occasionally about childhood memories. Just a few days ago, I was convinced that Gretchen Honeycutt was the guilty one—although my belief had not been well received by Jigger, Mom, Gally, or Grandma. No one thought she was capable of murder.

Yet the problem was that they didn't think *anyone* who lived in Black Beaver Bay was capable. When I'd suspected Mrs. Banger, Doc Vesper, Chad Peterson, or Miss Honeycutt, I was met with excuses and justifications for why I was wrong. My family's past connections with my list of suspects gave them a different outlook than I had.

But if I looked at it in another way, maybe I was the only one who had a clear eye because I *didn't* have a shared history with any of these people. Maybe I was the only one who could be totally unbiased.

Hmm, but then again I had been wrong about Mr. Anderson. I had suspected him until I fished up his hand…

"Ladies and gentlemen, if I could have your attention, please…" The auctioneer pounded his gavel before mopping his brow with a crumpled bandanna. The afternoon had turned warm, and everyone was shedding layers.

Even though I was growing uncomfortable, I was too embarrassed to take off my hoodie. My arms were so freakin' skinny, I looked ridiculous. And just in case Josh would happen to show up (which Jigger had said was possible), I had to keep my arms covered up. I mean, it's bad enough that I had vomited all over his new pair of sneakers *and* he thought I could be a potential poisoner *and* I kept finding dead bodies. My skeletal-like appendages didn't have to be another dissuading factor.

No one ever said love was easy, I thought, as I pushed back my damp bangs.

Major Jack cleared his throat into the microphone. "Say, I want to thank each and every one of you for coming out today. If Millie were here with us, I know she'd appreciate this turnout." I zoomed in on the auctioneer's face. He looked just like Mr. Lahey on "Trailer Park Boys"—a show Mom had forbidden me to watch, but somehow, I'd never missed an episode.

"As I said at the beginning of the auction, we would take a break from selling Millie's personal effects at three o'clock, so we can take care of selling the house and land…" As he droned on about the legal details of the real estate transaction, I looked over the gathering, wondering who would be bidding. I was growing more and more curious.

"So with that said, I just want to remind you that we are also taking online bids, as we stated on the auction bill. Okay now, who wants to open the bid at $500,000?"

A slight murmur rose from the crowd, as if the auctioneer was starting out too high.

"Can I get five, five, five, five hundred thousand?"

There were no takers.

"Can I get four fifty, four fifty, four fifty, anyone four fifty?"

Gally and I glanced at each other. She raised her eyebrows.

"Well, let's start in the basement then." Major Jack sounded disgusted. "Four hundred thousand, and that's a real steal folks. Four, four, four, four, anyone four?"

His clerk hurried up, and we watched as she whispered something in his ear. Major Jack's face lit up like he'd just seen Lady Godiva. He hooted, "We have an internet bid of $400,000!"

The crowd clapped for the opening bid.

"Can I get $450,000?" he asked hopefully.

A hand shot up. I turned my camera. It was Doc Vesper!

"Do I have $500,000?" the auctioneer begged.

His clerk dashed to his side again, whispering.

"Yes!" Major Jack crowed. "Do I have $550,000?" he pleaded.

Doc Vesper raised his hand. An audible murmur came from the crowd. Gally grabbed my arm and squeezed it.

"$600,000?" Major Jack threw out there, gleefully.

The clerk nodded, confirming the bid.

"Yes!" Major Jack bellowed. "$650,000?"

A commotion in the crowd was created when Mrs. Banger raised her arm.

"Yes!" Major Jack crowed. "Do I have $700,000?"

Mr. Chad raised his arm.

"Yes!" the auctioneer cried frantically. "$750,000?"

Mrs. Banger nodded.

"Yes!" the auctioneer accepted her bid.

Then the clerk ran up and whispered in Major Jack's ear one last time.

"Folks, we have a million dollar bid online. Can I get $1,050,000?"

But he couldn't.

And so some unknown buyer on the internet was the winner. Hmm. How was I going to find out who that was? Little did I know, I'd have my answer within hours.

❀ 41 ❀

Shocks to your constitution are something to be avoided. Such stress wreaks havoc on the human body. And it is my theory that shocks to your constitution should—at all costs—be *especially* avoided first thing in the morning. I believe it's bad on your heart. It can't be a coincidence that most heart attacks happen before noon.

As I innocently ate a bowl of cereal the morning after the auction, doing research on my phone, I was clueless about the unbeknownst shock I was about to receive.

I was prowling the internet, looking up prices for minerals on the stock market because I'd recalled the voices I'd overheard in the high school hallway. I was deep in thought when Gally shuffled into the kitchen in her slippers, with a serious case of bedhead.

"Hey," she said sleepily. "I was up 'til three, fixing our website." She yawned. "But I got it working. At least I *think* I did."

My phone rang. It was Grandma.

"Oh, God, put her on speakerphone, but don't tell her I'm here," Gally moaned, reaching for a cup from the cupboard.

"Hello," I answered.

"Darling, I got married!"

Crash!!! Gally dropped her coffee cup on the floor, smashing it to pieces.

"Wow, Grandma!" I managed to say. "That's great!" I wanted to ask who the groom was, but I couldn't think of a polite way to inquire. She had been mentioning some guy, though. What was his name? Addy?

"It was so beautiful," she continued. Gally hurried to the table, stepping over her mess. She plopped down beside me and stared at the phone.

"Aditya and I tied the knot in an incredibly romantic ceremony on a beautiful shikara boat, strewn with flowers…" I heard the distinct

205

sound of ice cubes clinking together. It must be cocktail time in Kashmir.

"But that's not why I'm calling. I have some other news." Gally and I shot each other a glance. "I wanted to let you know that I am the one who purchased Millie's land at the auction. I just couldn't let Marcella Banger outbid me."

"What?" I couldn't hide my surprise. "But you said whoever bought Mrs. Kerkenbush's place was the murderer! What are you telling me, Grandma?"

Grandma laughed, obviously amused. "Of course I'm not the murderer! The highest bidder—besides me—was Marcella. I bet she is the murderess! Once a sour apple, always a sour apple!" We heard her take a sip.

"My reasons for buying that place were truly altruistic. I want to give Ana and Gally the honor of waiting on me and Aditya in our declining years."

"What?" Gally whispered. My aunt's face held a look of complete horror. I worried about her heart.

"And please tell your mom that the first house guest I'm going to have at Millie's old place will be your dad!"

"Grandma…" but I was interrupted by a deep baritone voice mumbling something indistinguishable.

"I must go, darling. My husband is calling…"

"No, Grandma, wait…" I begged.

But she had hung up.

"Oh, my God." Gally shook her head. "I need coffee. Where's your mom?"

"She ran to the grocery store with Thing 2 to get a sympathy card. She said we'll need to be ready to go by 10:30."

"Oh, no!" Gally groaned. "I forgot all about Millie's wake." She pulled herself up from the table and stood there, catatonic. I wondered what she was thinking. Finally, she said, "Let's not tell your mom all this news until after the service. I think that's the kindest thing we can

206

do." She shuffled away to take a shower, oblivious to the mess on the floor.

Maybe it's the kindest thing to do this morning, I thought, as I cleaned up the broken cup. But if you think about it, would there *ever* be a good time to tell this to Mom?

Later, as we stood in line to view Mrs. Kerkenbush's body at the First Lutheran Church, I was wondering about this very question. Well, actually, I was worried about telling Mom this news but also freaked out about seeing Mrs. K's body—*again*. I was hoping the undertaker had done a good job on her, so I could replace the image I had in my mind of how she'd looked when I'd found her.

I scanned the crowd, looking for Jigger. The church was almost full, with mourners standing in quiet groups, talking amongst themselves. I couldn't see her.

Then I looked for Josh. It had been over a week since I'd seen or heard from him. It wasn't like I was in love with him—or anything even *close* to that. It's just that he represented a hundred percent of all the boys who have ever shown any interest in me. I've hardly been around teenage boys. Being homeschooled put a kibosh on that. And of course the coronavirus hadn't helped much with the whole socializing aspect.

Suddenly, I realized that Mom, Gally, and I were the next people to view the casket. My stomach knotted. I kept my focus on the shiny gold coffin until I forced myself to glance at Millie's face.

She looked totally different. She looked at peace. They had placed a white silky eyepatch over her wound, which helped a lot. And they'd done a really lifelike makeup job on her face. Her cheeks were blushed, and her mouth had the tiniest smile. I let out a huge breath, relieved.

We moved past the casket and mingled with the other mourners. I felt awkward and shy, listening to Mom and Gally chatter with old acquaintances. No one talked to me, but then again, why would they? I'm just a kid.

I thought about taking my camera from my backpack. It would probably be considered impolite. The nice thing about having a camera in front of your face is that it kind of makes you invisible—at least in my head it does.

Thing 1 stood by my side. I thought about striking up a conversation with him but knew better than to expect much. Just joking, I asked him, "Are you having fun yet?"

He peered down at me with a subtle look of amusement.

I eavesdropped on a conversation that Gally was having with a group of old acquaintances. "Do you remember when you pulled the fire alarm during your sister's valedictorian speech?" a dowdy-looking, middle-aged woman asked Gally.

Poking fun at Gally, Mom asked, "Yes, do you remember that?"

"Hey, they never proved it was me," Gally said, a little too innocently.

Just then, a commotion broke out at the front doors of the church. I heard a very familiar bleating. Oh, my God, could it be? Was I finally going to see the goat that had been tormenting me for the last month? Instantly, I got my camera out of my backpack and started shooting.

"He's paying his last respects!" a voice shouted, followed by another loud bleat. Growing quiet, the crowd parted way for an ancient-looking man, clad in overalls. This must be Cyrus, I thought. His curved spine and cane did not prevent him from charging down the aisle—probably because he was being pulled by a big, white goat.

I zoomed in on the goat. His long, matted hair almost touched the ground. His horns were larger than I had thought goat horns could get. His eyes were wise, but maybe all goats have that knowing look. His most striking characteristic was his long, flowing beard.

I filmed the goat making his way to the casket, but before he could reach it, Mrs. Banger stepped up. "Cyrus," she boomed, "you can *not* bring that filthy animal into a house of worship!"

"Listen here, you old blabbermouth." Cyrus whistled as he pronounced his S's, which reminded me of Gopher from Winnie-the-Pooh.

"If I recall the Good Book, Jesus was born in a stable with animals. And they have animals in here every year for the children's Nativity show. This goat is a creature of God. So it seems to me, he has just as much right to be here as you do."

He continued, "Billy has been bleating at my farm for days now, looking for Millie. Why, he was with her for over twenty years. He's got every right to say his last goodbyes. Now get *out* of my way, you old biddy!" The feisty man shook his cane at Mrs. Banger, while he struggled to rein in the goat.

I decided I liked Cyrus—a lot.

Mrs. Banger's sturdy body grew even bigger as she threw her shoulders back, blocking Billy's way. Suddenly, the goat broke free of the old man's grasp and charged ahead, straight into Mrs. Banger's crotch. The crowd gasped, as Mrs. Banger toppled backwards, and Billy trampled her. Before anyone could rush to her aid, the goat had succeeded in getting to the casket. I feared he'd knock it over! But I hadn't needed to worry. Billy respectfully rested his two front hooves on the coffin's rim.

He peered down at his late owner.

Billy threw back his head, and the most melancholy sound came out of his mouth. It was heartbreaking.

It was the sound of anguish—of acute loss. I felt my eyes grow moist. Somehow, the goat had shown much more remorse than any of the mourners had managed to muster.

Shortly, the goat jumped down and sat, hanging his head. As he grieved, a ray of sunshine burst through the stained glass windows, falling directly upon him. The sunlight reflecting off the shiny, gold coffin gave Billy a golden aura, transforming him into a celestial goat—or something else divine. I wondered if I were witnessing a true-life miracle. It looked like he had some holy glow all around him.

"In the name of the Father, the Son, and the Holy Goat," Thing 1 said softly. The sound of his voice made me jump, and I almost dropped my camera. I'd been with this guy for weeks, and he'd never said one word. Maybe more miracles were unfolding before me.

But he never said anything to me after that—ever again—so if it was a miracle, it was a really short-lived one.

The shaft of light shifted, and Billy looked like a normal goat once more. And just like that, he trotted around the five men who were failing to lift Mrs. Banger, and he went straight down the aisle and out the front door of the First Lutheran Church.

He was never seen again.

Later, the gossips in town claimed that Billy was touched with the divine, for anyone who had witnessed that beam of light would never forget it. They said he left town and became a recluse in an abandoned cave where he attained some kind of goat guru status and wore flowered wreaths around his neck.

Others say he wandered forlornly into the wild—until abject grief overtook him.

Of course, the gossips couldn't leave it at that. Oh, no. Soon there were sightings of a ghostly goat that guarded Mrs. Kerkenbush's grave. People claimed this goat was draped in a holy robe and served as a sentinel for his beloved Mrs. K.

And there were even those who swore they saw the same ghostly goat peeing on the Banger family cemetery plot. When all the grass on that cemetery plot died, people insisted it was due to the golden urine from that ghostly apparition. And *that* proved the story was true.

Or so they said.

✤ 42 ✤

Mrs. Banger suffered from deep-tissue bruising in her groin area, due to her altercation with Billy the goat, and for the time being, she was unable to walk or stand. Even so, her injury would not keep her from her role as Chairwoman of the Miss Apple Blossom Pageant. She said she could fulfill her duties from a prone position. Yes, reclining in her Lazy Boy recliner, which she'd had moved from her house, she lay immediately offstage in the high school auditorium, running the show.

I knew this because I was one of the people she bossed around. And it was all because of Jigger, who had texted me hours before the pageant. She was in a complete and total panic—like really freaked.

Jigger

> i didn't make my goal weight! our old scale at home this morning said i'd made it - but i just weighed myself in the locker room, and i still have half a pound to go!! i'm not going to win this - then i won't get the scholarship - so i'll never get out of this town - i'll be stuck working in my mom's cafe until i'm wearing diapers for old people!! 😥

This was not the confident friend I had grown to know and love. I read the text over twice, wondering if she was suffering from stage fright. I tried to think of something I could say to help her. Before I could answer her, she texted again.

Jigger

> i'm going to sneak away and hide - i mean WTF - i'm not going to win - why bother

you won't win if you don't participate - and the wager you made with yourself about your goal weight isn't logical - you know that. Don't jinx yourself! You're ready for this. This is yours for the taking.

thanx theo. but i'm already freaked - everything went wrong at the rehearsal - a light dropped and smashed on stage - almost hitting katie - remember the girl who does the magic act? she totally freaked out and couldn't stop screaming - then the sound system broke - and now the man who was gonna film the pageant can't cuz his wife went into labor - all the girls are sayin it's the apple blossom curse !!!!!

I can film the pageant for you. I mean, i was planning to do it anyway

OMG you're a lifesaver Theo. i'll tell Banger you can do it. Can you be here in an hour?

So before the Miss Apple Blossom Pageant started, Jigger met Thing 1 and me at the back door of the high school. Still noticeably nervous, she ushered us to Mrs. Banger.

"Oh, there you are," a cry of relief broke from Mrs. Banger's lips. "You are doing us a huge favor, young lady." Gratefully, she grabbed my free hand, which grossed me out. Something about her seemed off.

Her speech was ever so slightly slurred. I was unaware that she'd already consumed her weekly allotted dose of pain medication.

Trying to avoid eye contact, I looked at the floor. I noticed a white electrical cord coming from underneath Mrs. Banger's lap blanket. She must have put a heating pad on her injury. I'm sure she was in pain. I would almost feel sorry for her, but I still didn't trust her. Maybe she *had* poisoned my great-uncle. Did murderesses deserve sympathy? And even though she was injured now, it didn't mean she wouldn't strike again.

Jigger dashed away, needing to finish her makeup and leaving me alone in Mrs. Banger's clutches. Mrs. Banger noticed Thing 1 looming behind me. "Is this your father?" she snooped.

I shook my head no. Since I wouldn't give her any clue as to the identity of Thing 1, she gave up prying and got straight down to business.

She told me where she wanted me positioned for filming. She asked if I was familiar with filming in dim light, and did I have enough battery to last at least two hours, and when did I expect my father to come to town?

Her last sneaky question threw me off guard. Before I could think of an answer, one of the contestants rushed up to Mrs. Banger with a broken sash, needing it to be pinned, or taped, or sewn, or *something!* Welcoming the interruption, I hurried away to my designated filming spot.

I bumped into Miss Honeycutt, who wore a sparkly evening gown. Her hair was swept up in some fancy do, and her makeup was so thick she must have applied it with a trowel.

"Oh, Theo, I heard you're doing the filming. Thank you so much!" She squeezed my arm to show her appreciation before rushing off on another last-minute errand.

I'd been instructed to film from the back of the gymnasium, where a temporary filming deck had been erected. It was just big enough to fit two chairs for Thing 1 and me. I got my camera set up on its tripod, turned it on, and checked everything to make sure I was ready to go. And then I scanned the crowd.

It was a full house. I looked for Mom and Gally, but I couldn't find them. Nor could I see Josh, but I knew he was here. I did spot two people I recognized, though. It was those meth heads I'd seen at the bowling alley, weeks ago. What were their names? Dale and Dudey? They were the only people in the whole place who were wearing stocking caps.

The overhead lights grew dark.

A man wearing a tuxedo and bow tie strode onto the stage and stepped to the microphone. "Ladies and gentlemen, I'd like to welcome you to the seventy-fifth Miss Apple Blossom Pageant!"

Applause broke out from the audience. The bow-tied host went on to thank all the fine sponsors for making this possible, and on and on.

Then the curtains parted, revealing the participants dressed in patriotic cowgirl outfits, toting cowboy hats and flags. The crowd clapped, as the orchestra began the first notes of "I'm Proud To Be An American." The girls began their routine. Some improvement could be noted in their dancing from the last time I had seen them. No one smacked anyone in the face with a flagpole.

Jigger was doing a perfect job. It was hard not to focus only on her. I could imagine Mrs. Banger's wrath if I only filmed Jigger and no one else. The thought of it made me smile.

The number was coming to an end when one of the girls swung her flag and knocked off another girl's hat, which tripped up *another* girl and caused countless others to tumble down by the time the curtains had closed. I wondered if the curse of Miss Apple Blossom was crossing anyone's mind at the moment—or was it just me?

The next part of the show was the Talent section. Jigger *still* hadn't told me what she was planning to do. I had to admit, I was pretty curious.

The first talent act was performed by a very nervous girl in a purple cape and top hat. She did magic tricks. I felt sorry for her. Her jitters were so apparent that when she pulled the rabbit from her hat, it looked like the poor animal's brain would be scrambled on account of her nervous shaking.

The next act was a piano recital of some Bach piece. She was pretty good. She did mess up a little in the middle.

The third act was a baton-twirling dervish. She dropped her baton twice but still got a hearty applause.

I waited impatiently for Jigger's performance, as I filmed two more pianists, a mime, a tumbler (who fell into the orchestra pit, but she was unharmed), and a ventriloquist. Finally, the announcer cried, "Please give a warm welcome for Miss Jessica Jones!"

Jigger walked onstage in a pair of old jeans and cowboy boots. She was carrying a guitar. She was dressed so simply that I got an uneasy feeling. Everyone else had gone overboard on their costumes for the Talent section. Maybe this was why she hadn't told me what she was going to do. Maybe she wasn't prepared.

A knot formed in my stomach. I knew how much she had riding on this competition. If by chance she did lose, I decided I'd talk to Grandma to see if she could help Jigger with her college tuition.

At this point, I think I was as nervous as Jigger was. I filmed her as she sat down on a stool next to the microphone and adjusted her strap. She smiled at the audience, and then she closed her eyes. She began to strum and sing.

"If I should stay, I would only be in your way. And so I'll go, but I know, I'll think of you each step of the way. And I will always love you..."

Tears sprang to my eyes. Her voice was beautiful—so pure and clear, it gave me goosebumps. Why hadn't she told me she could sing like this? She was absolutely killing it. I was so moved by the way she sang the old Dolly Parton song, I found it hard to fight back tears. And I wasn't the only one. From my view at the back of the gym, I saw half the audience wiping their faces. By the time she'd sung her final note, she had a standing ovation. I felt *so* proud of her.

But before she could even take a bow, the lights went on in the auditorium. A murmur rose in the crowd. I turned and saw Deputy Pete and two of his underling cops marching over to the bleacher area, where the two meth heads sat. The two younger cops pounced on the meth heads, handcuffing them roughly in front of the stunned audience.

"Hey, man, what's going on?" one of them cried.

It seemed to me that Deputy Pete was soaking up the attention. And why had he felt the need to come in and interrupt the whole pageant? Couldn't he have waited until it was over? What was their supposed offense anyway? Robbing parking meters? I suspected the deputy wanted to showboat his authority.

"We didn't do anything, mannnn," the other handcuffed youth yelled.

The auditorium was now in complete silence. You could have heard a snowflake melt. Every eye was glued on Deputy Pete, wondering what he would say—if anything.

"Dale Johnson and Doogie Portham," Pete said, in what I thought was a very fake baritone voice, "you are under arrest for the desecration of a grave and tampering with a corpse. You have the right to remain silent…"

❋ 43 ❋

The Black Beaver Bay band uniforms were made of a thick nylon material that would not breathe, which made the band members miserable. To make matters worse, they topped off their uniforms with tall, black, furry helmets—like what the witch's guardsmen wore in the "Wizard of Oz." They all looked like they were going to croak of heatstroke. The boy playing the tuba worried me. He was so tiny!—the tiniest little tuba player I have ever seen. His eyes were obscured by his helmet, which had slid down his forehead. I worried he wouldn't last until the end of the block.

The tuba player pushed his helmet back from his eyes, and that's when I realized it was Adam, the boy who had talked to me at the party! He caught my eye and gave me a grin. I waved back enthusiastically.

The band trudged on, plodding out of step, clutching their instruments tightly to their chests. I turned my camera to the *next* thing in the parade. Finally, I thought. This was what I'd been waiting for—the Miss Apple Blossom float.

"Be sure to film *all* the girls," Mrs. Banger boomed at me, from a wheelchair by my side. "Don't just focus on Jigger. I watched your film from last night, you know," she said pointedly.

I didn't know why I was taking orders from her. She'd called Mom this morning and had asked to meet me at the parade, so she could pay me for filming the pageant last night. I was cool with that. But once she paid me, I couldn't get rid of her! She kept sticking by my side, directing me on how to film the parade. Since when had I become her minion?

Well, the heck with it. I aimed my lens directly at Jigger. She stood under an archway of freshly cut apple blossom boughs. She'd abandoned the traditional beauty queen gown. Instead, Jigger wore a white netted tutu (which barely covered her butt, but it looked great!) paired with a white jean jacket that she'd hand-accessorized with white se-

217

quins. The jacket was open, exposing her bra—which she'd glittered—and her fishnet stockings were iridescent. She'd also hot-glued white rhinestones all over her Doc Marten boots. With her bad-girl makeup, Billy Idol hair, and shiny tiara, she looked absolutely fabulous.

Mrs. Banger gasped—which was followed by a groan. "What is she wearing?" The old battle-axe sounded horrified. "I never approved that goddamned outfit!"

Jigger had also abandoned the traditional beauty queen wave. Pumping her arms in the air, she held a bouquet of flowers in one hand, while her other hand was clenched in a fist with her pinkie and thumb extended.

The Sour Apples, or the girls who hadn't won, sat behind her on the float, whipping candy into the crowd. One of the pieces struck the side of my head. *"Ouch!"* I wondered if that was on purpose. I noticed other people were getting assailed by malicious throws also. Geez Louise, they really *were* sour apples.

The P.A. system on the float blared out an old-time melody, "I'll be with you in apple blossom time…" which repeated itself on a loop. I could only imagine how tired Jigger must be of that tune by now. I saw Miss Honeycutt marching behind the float, scrolling through a phone, not paying much attention. Once in a while, she'd wave her hand, but her face was glued to the screen.

Mrs. Banger sat incapacitated, fuming over Jigger's wardrobe choices. But what could she do? Stop the parade? Insist that the queen change into something more queenly? For Jigger had won the pageant last night. She was the new, reigning Miss Apple Blossom.

Although it hadn't been easy for her to win last night, because it hadn't been easy for the pageant to continue—after the shocking arrests we had all witnessed.

Before the lights had even dimmed again in the auditorium, I'd gotten a text from Jigger backstage.

Jigger

Whoa! I just heard that the cigarette butts they found by Mr. Hendrickson's grave came back with DNA that matched Dale and Doogie! people are saying they dug him up because he was buried with his gold pocket watch - they wanted to pawn it for drugs

Theo

but why would they take his body to our house? and remember those voices i heard in the school hallway - it was definitely a man's voice AND a woman's - Dale and Doogie can't be responsible for all these crimes - some woman is involved too

Jigger

banger is yelling at us to line up

The show had gone on, moving into the interview section of the pageant. I thought most of the questions weren't worth asking. Although things got more interesting when Miss Honeycutt got to the trembling girl, who had performed the magic act. Miss Honeycutt asked her, "Recently, we've had more violence in schools. How do you think we can better promote safety and harmony in our hallways?"

The poor girl looked terrified. Before she could answer, loud and piercing screams filled the auditorium.

At first I wasn't sure if this was somehow part of the question. Maybe it was an on-the-spot test. It was clear from the contestant's expression that she didn't know what to think either.

But when shouts of "Fire! Help! Fire!" came from backstage, accompanied by smoke wafting from behind the curtains, Miss Honeycutt rushed off, leaving the timid contestant alone at the microphone—alone and very silent. Her inability to aid in the current situation suggested that she would be pretty worthless in promoting safety within the school system.

Some members of the audience hurried backstage to see if they could be of any assistance. Soon, everyone knew that the heavily dosed Mrs. Banger had passed out, unaware until too late that her defective heating pad had sparked a fire on her blanket and recliner.

After the fire was successfully doused, the show went on, only to be interrupted a little later when the paramedics carted Mrs. Banger through the audience. Once again, the lights were turned on. Everyone watched, as Mrs. Banger was borne away to the emergency room.

Later, people would say it was the most exciting pageant they'd ever seen. They predicted that next year's show would never be able to live up to this one.

So the pageant finally concluded, but like I say, it hadn't been easy. Or pretty. Well, it *was* pretty when Jigger was crowned with the tiara. I'd been jumping up and down, clapping. Even Thing 1 was smiling. I was so excited that I almost toppled over the railing of the filming platform, but Thing 1 grabbed the back of my overall straps just in time, saving me from a super-embarrassing accident, and maybe even death!

But all of that was last night, and now *no one* was smiling, because the sun was melting us to the sidewalk. It was 95 degrees! A freak hot front had descended into the valley, making people retreat to the shade. I panned the parade crowd with my camera, as farmers rolled cheerfully by on tractors, and crazy clowns rode tiny motorcycles in circles.

Suddenly, I stopped filming.

I'd spotted Josh, looking very friendly with some big-busted blonde. I felt a pang in my heart. It wasn't a huge pang, like someone had stabbed me with a butcher knife. Instead, it was more like a miniature dollhouse knife had slashed into me. So it was small, but it still hurt. Suddenly I felt very thankful that I had never kissed him.

Mrs. Banger began to gripe—well, she'd never really *quit* griping, but her griping became more insistent. Mom, Gally, and Things 1 and

2 stood by silently, as if they couldn't hear her, watching the end of the parade.

"Please, someone—anyone—get me to the shade. I am dying!" Mrs. Banger lamented. No one rushed to move her.

Finally, Mom's guilt overtook her, and she tried to move the wheelchair but found it was too heavy. Thing 1 stepped in and successfully moved Mrs. Banger under a tree. Although by that time, the parade was over.

Mom and Aunt Gally had volunteered at the Lioness stand to sell apple pies, so they left for the festival grounds with Thing 2. I had planned to meet Jigger at the high school after the parade. Since Mrs. Banger was also headed to the school, I received the unfortunate job of accompanying her. She demanded that Thing 1 push her.

Mrs. Banger griped the whole way. Her bruises were killing her. Her burns were killing her. The heat was killing her. I asked myself, if everything was killing her, why was she still alive?

As I thought these uncharitable thoughts, my phone *dinged.*

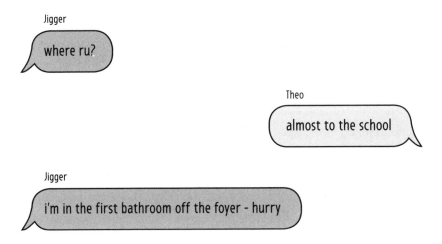

Jigger

where ru?

Theo

almost to the school

Jigger

i'm in the first bathroom off the foyer - hurry

A minute later, we entered the cool, dark, deserted foyer of the school. We sighed in relief. Mrs. Banger actually became silent. I thought there might be a God after all.

"I have to go to the bathroom," I told Thing 1 right away, nodding my head towards the bathroom door. I didn't wait to get permission. "Theo, wait!" Mrs. Banger called behind me. "I need you to..." Her voice was cut off, as the door swept shut behind me.

Jigger stood at the end of the very long bathroom, looking totally deflated—like the saddest, badass beauty queen you've ever seen. I immediately knew something was wrong. She motioned me to the last stall, and then pulled me inside, securing the door behind us.

"It's Miss Honeycutt," she whispered. She didn't have to say any more. Of course I knew exactly what she was talking about.

"Are you sure?" I whispered back.

Just then, we heard the bathroom door open. We froze, listening. We heard the sink turn on, and then the hand dryer. Then we heard the door open again. We waited until it had closed, and everything was silent.

"Look." She pulled folders from inside her buttoned-up jean jacket and handed them to me. She began to explain, as I looked over the contents.

"Before the parade this morning, I was at Honeycutt's, finishing the float. I had to help her wire all these apple blossoms to the archway, and it was—well, anyway, I had to change my clothes and get ready for the parade, so I went into her house to use her bathroom. I happened to pass her home office, and I couldn't help but notice this folder on her desk." Jigger pointed to the one I was holding.

"When I saw 'Final Score Sheets' written on the tab, I was instantly curious because I'd heard some of the girls complaining that the whole pageant was rigged. So I thought, why not find out? And I know it's wrong, but I took it. I threw it in my gym bag because I heard Honeycutt coming into the house. I didn't realize there was another folder beneath it. I grabbed this one without even knowing." She pulled out a second folder. "Look!"

The second folder had notes, receipts, letters, and newspaper clippings. There was a letter from a geological survey company that said the samples they had received were high in titanium. There were newspaper clippings of stock prices, with titanium's value circled in ink. There was a receipt for six plastic jump ropes, a bill from a survey company, a receipt for a pair of cable snippers, and a receipt for hazmat suits and tarps. There was a receipt from "The Eager Beaver" for six drinks, and on the back, she'd written "Dale and Doogie." I also found a receipt for zip ties, and I wondered what she'd done with them.

The most damning evidence was a cheap, pocket calendar. In tiny, meticulous writing, she'd mapped out her every strategy and expense—and written snarky comments on the side. Like on the day she'd poisoned Uncle Dickie, she wrote, "The master wood chucker chucks no more. Time of death 1:47 P.M." On that page, she'd used a receipt for cyanide as a bookmark.

Starting back in January, her first note said she'd learned of possible treasure out at the Cove from Gus Anderson. Her actions grew more sinister as the months went on. Every action or purchase was recorded. It was like a book of her bad deeds—and also a balance sheet. She'd kept track of the price of murder.

"We need to show this to my mom. I mean, like right now," I said urgently.

Jigger nodded. "Just give me a second. I've gotta pee."

Still holding the folders, I left the bathroom stall, and Jigger closed its door behind me. I walked over to the sinks, and there stood Miss Honeycutt, pointing a gun straight at me.

❀ 44 ❀

The fight-or-flight response was described by Walter Cannon, an American physiologist. Basically, when a human faces a threatening situation, their body will physiologically prepare for either fighting the situation or running away from it.

But I think old Walter got it wrong. He should have named his theory "Fight-or-Flight-or-Freeze." Because when I saw the gun that Miss Honeycutt pointed at me, I neither fought nor fled. I just stood there, frozen.

She snatched the folders from my hands and shoved them into her satchel bag. After slapping a piece of duct tape over my mouth, she whipped me around and placed zip ties on my wrists.

This was it, I thought. I started trembling, like, uncontrollably. I was sure she was going to shoot me in the back of the head. I thought of Mom, Gally, Grandma, Poppy, Jigger, Lexi, and Dad. So maybe your life really does flash before your eyes when you're about to die.

But she didn't shoot me. Instead, Miss Honeycutt patted my body down, found my phone and placed it on the edge of the sink. I could still hear Jigger peeing. But I couldn't warn her.

The toilet flushed. Miss Honeycutt waited for Jigger to join us.

The stall opened. I had to warn Jigger of her impending ambush, but how? I screamed as loud as I could, but the duct tape smothered my voice, making it a muted moan. Would she hear it?

Jigger walked right into Miss Honeycutt and her gun.

"Put your hands behind your back," Miss Honeycutt said in a low, steely voice.

Instead, Jigger's fight mode kicked in. She swung her fist at Honeycutt, trying to knock the gun from her hand. But Honeycutt jumped to the side and pistol-whipped Jigger with the butt of her gun. Jigger staggered backwards, smashing into a bathroom stall, and her tiara fell off her head as she crumpled to the ground.

I cried out again, but I only managed to sound like a muffled chipmunk. Had she just killed Jigger? My friend was so very still. Blood began oozing from the wound on her temple. I kept willing Jigger to give me some kind of sign that she was okay.

I watched in horror as Miss Honeycutt turned Jigger over on her stomach and zip tied her hands behind her back. She rolled her back over and put duct tape on her mouth. After patting her body down, she found Jigger's phone and removed it. Then she took both of our phones and set them on top of the hand dryers.

I knelt by Jigger's side, nudging her. Her eyelids fluttered, and she started to stir. Thank God, she was alive.

Miss Honeycutt emptied our backpacks, strewing the contents around the bathroom. My camera hit the floor with a sickening thud. She tossed Jigger's work clothes around, pausing to use a T-shirt to wipe Jigger's bloody head. Then she took that T-shirt and smeared the blood on the wall. Finally, she took our cell phones and smashed them with her heel.

"This looks like quite a fight went on in here." She nodded at the scene with approval. "I'll tell everyone that when I left you in the bathroom, everything was fine. You two must have had some horrible fight! And who knows? Maybe you ended up going off and killing each other." A satanic smile spread across her face.

She stood in front of the mirror, straightening her blouse. "You two thought you were quite the teenage detectives," she said snidely. "Regular Nancy Drews." She ran her fingers through her hair, to tidy it up. "I read through Jigger's text messages while she rode on the float. If she had bothered to read the rules of the pageant, she would have known that phones are *not* allowed on the Miss Apple Blossom float." She sighed as if she were weary. "I had to write that into the rules five years ago, after the Sour Apples were glued to their phones instead of throwing candy and waving to the crowd. Even the queen was busy texting and taking selfies. It was a disaster. Teenagers and their phones," she spat out contemptuously.

She removed a makeup bag from her satchel and found her lipstick. She began to apply it, then stopped. "It was really quite touching to read how valiantly Jigger defended my honor. She didn't believe it could be me!" She finished with her lipstick, smiling at herself. "I can only imagine her shock when she discovered the truth." Gloating, she beamed.

"But can you imagine *my* shock when I realized that my folder had been stolen? Thank goodness I had to rush home after the parade because I'd forgotten the tickets for the beer tent. If not for that, I wouldn't have been home until way after midnight." She was now applying eye makeup. "And then I might not have noticed that the folder was missing until tomorrow. And *that* would have been too late. Because I'm sure you *were* planning on going to the authorities with this information."

The way she said "*were* planning" made my stomach drop.

"So you see how close I came to getting caught. It was a matter of luck, really, that I had forgotten those tickets. And it had to be Jigger who had stolen my files because she was the only one in my house this morning. How fortunate that I was able to read her texts! I knew she was meeting you at the high school, and when I got here, Mrs. Banger told me exactly where you were."

She finally turned away from the mirror and looked directly at me. "If I had been only *minutes* later, I would have missed you!" Miss Honeycutt sighed deeply. "But since I caught you just in time, I feel I was meant to see this project through." Then she smiled sweetly—which really creeped me out.

She bent over and picked up Jigger's tiara. For a second, I thought she was going to set it back on Jigger. Instead, she went again to the mirror and gently lowered the crown onto her own head.

She stared sadly at her reflection.

Then angrily, she snatched off the tiara, snapped it in two, and whipped the halves at Jigger and me. I ducked to avoid the sharp edges.

Miss Honeycutt stepped around a partition and opened the bathroom door. I couldn't see her from where I was, but I could hear her clearly. "I'm sorry to ask this of you, but we seem to have a problem," she said cheerfully to someone in the hallway.

Who was she talking to? Could it be Thing 1? Could Mrs. Banger still be out there? I didn't hear any complaining, so I figured the injured sausage tyrant was gone.

"Theo has gotten her period, and this bathroom is all out of sanitary supplies. Could you go the janitor's room? It's at the very end of this hallway and then you take a left. First door on the right. I know the janitor is there. He'll give you what we need. I would do it myself, but I'm helping poor Theo wash out some clothing."

OMG! She was lying to Thing 1. She just wanted to get rid of him. I contemplated running out in the hallway and alerting him. What would Honeycutt do? Shoot me in the back? Shoot Thing 1? What was she capable of? Well, I guess I knew the answer to that.

Jigger opened her eyes! Her pupils were huge, and I wondered if she had a concussion. A trickle of blood ran down the side of her face from the nasty gash right above her temple.

Miss Honeycutt came back to us, ordering us to stand and hurry. Jigger was so groggy that she stood uncertainly, weaving and bobbing. I worried she'd collapse.

Our torturer led us over to the door and peeked out, checking the hallway in both directions. Turning her mad eyes on me, she snarled, "Go. Hurry. Don't let her fall down." She shoved us in front of her, pressing the gun right between my shoulder blades. How was I supposed to keep Jigger from falling when my hands were tied behind my back? Jigger's body leaned into mine, and her steps faltered.

Quickly, Honeycutt led us through the darkened corridors and out a back door that led to a parking lot. Hot air blasted my face as we left the school. She marched us over to her SUV and opened the tailgate. The back of her vehicle was filled with supplies for making a float. Scraps of crepe paper, ribbon, cardboard tubing, and a roll of chicken wire were strewn all over. Cut apple blossoms, which had wilted in the heat, made the whole vehicle smell sweet.

She shoved Jigger inside. Collapsing on a pile of apple boughs, Jigger closed her eyes again, looking for all the world like a slain beauty queen. I looked around the empty parking lot, hoping to spot someone. *Anyone!* I mean this was pretty brazen to kidnap us in broad daylight. Yet the place was deserted.

"Get in," Miss Honeycutt hissed behind me. She jabbed her gun—hard!—into my back. I crawled into the rear of her vehicle, on top of all the supplies.

She threw a tarp over us, got behind the wheel, and drove away.

The SUV was hot, and with the blue, plastic tarp over us, I felt like I would suffocate. I nudged Jigger. She moaned but didn't open her eyes. Where was Honeycutt taking us?

I tried to pay attention to the directions she was turning. But then I realized, did it even matter? Because wherever we were going, she was going to flat out murder us.

We needed to get free during this ride, or it would be the last ride we ever took. But how could I break free? The zip ties dug into my wrists. How could I get this duct tape off?

I was lying next to a roll of chicken wire. Its cut edge was close to my face. I squirmed closer and placed my cheek next to the tip of the wire, trying to lodge the wire under the edge of the tape. I was hoping to use the wire to catch the tape and peel it off.

I thought it was working. I could feel the edge of the tape beginning to pull away from my cheek.

Suddenly, Honeycutt put on her brakes, and the wire gouged my cheek! The unexpected pain seared through me.

I heard her say, "Hey, Pete." Oh, my God, was she talking to Deputy Pete? Her phone hadn't rung, so she must be talking to him in person. I could faintly hear the sound of another engine running. He was so close! I started screaming at the top of my lungs, trying to kick the tarp off, so I could sit up.

But I couldn't get the tarp off! So I started kicking the sides of her vehicle with my feet.

"No, that's just my engine. It's been knocking something terrible in this heat, and my air conditioner has gone haywire." She sighed ruefully. "I'll be at the grounds in just a bit. I have to run some things home first."

I kept kicking. And I nudged Jigger, hoping to rouse her, so she could kick too—but no such luck.

Then Honeycutt said, "She left the high school a bit ago. There were some girl problems, so I helped her with them in the restroom. She's just running a little late. Okay, thanks Pete!"

I felt the car move again.

Jigger was supposed to be down at the town's festival grounds, along with the Sour Apples, to do some queenly traditions, like taking pictures with kids and giving out awards. So this was good news that they'd noticed her absence. Maybe they would start looking for her. Or for both of us. But when I thought about my life depending on Deputy Pete, I had some serious doubts.

"Nice try," Miss Honeycutt called back. I assumed she was talking to me. "You're going to have to do better than *that* if you want to be rescued by our charming Deputy Hicks. He's not the brightest bulb on the Christmas tree." I really wished I didn't agree with her snarky comment.

By this time, I was drenched with sweat. My attempts to pry off the duct tape and to get Pete's attention had made me sweat even more. It was so hot under this tarp! Jigger and I would probably perish from the heat before Honeycutt could kill us.

I felt the SUV slow down and turn to the left. It paused before roaring forward. Where was she taking us?

Her phone rang, and I could hear her saying she was running a little behind, but she would be there with the tickets within the hour. This made my stomach drop again. If she would be back in less than an hour, that meant we had less than an hour to live.

I renewed my struggle to pull the duct tape off my mouth, using the end of the chicken wire. I made progress in infinitesimal increments.

The tricky part was to be quiet. I didn't want her to know what I was doing. I had gotten the tape an inch off my cheek when she spoke.

"I suppose this is the moment when I confess all my crimes—right before I kill you, just like in Scooby Doo." She laughed mockingly. "Only this is no cartoon, girls. You're not going to escape like Daphne and Velma. No, unfortunately you have to be eliminated."

❀ 45 ❀

She went on to say, "I mean, *someone* should appreciate all the clever things I've done—too bad it won't be you two. You won't live long enough to revel in my genius."

I continued to work on the duct tape. Now my head was pressed into the car carpet, trying to roll the tape away. Once again, it was working, but slowly. My cheek began to feel raw with carpet burn. I had half of my lips free. I just needed a couple more inches.

"It all started in the winter, when Gus came back from one of Dickie's poker parties talking about treasure. By the way, Theo, you might not know that Gus Anderson and I are—I mean *were*—first cousins. His claims were easy enough for me to verify. I didn't even have to pay for the mineral survey. I was able to siphon off some money from the town to pay for that. That's one of the perks of being the town treasurer," she chirped happily.

At last, my mouth was free!

I shimmied my way closer to Jigger and tried to get hold of *her* duct tape with my teeth.

Honeycutt talked on. "Gus approached Dickie Gillman with a purchase agreement, but Dickie told him he would never sell the Cove. He said he planned to leave it to his nieces. But then Gus talked to your grandmother, and *she* thought your mother and Gally wouldn't want to move back. So it seemed pretty simple. Kill Dickie Gillman, wait for Ana and Gally to sell the Cove, and I would buy it." She gave a derisive snort.

Finally, I had a good hold on the tape covering Jigger's mouth. With my teeth clamped on for dear life, I slowly pulled it away from Jigger's face. Her eyes were now open. I didn't know how long she'd been awake. We both remained silent, listening to Honeycutt.

"It didn't turn out that way, but what I've found is that I'm highly capable of changing plans in midstream." She sounded quite self-congratulatory. "I did think my murder of Dickie Gillman was rather brilliant. Spiking his hot cocoa with cyanide right before he threw his log in the chucking competition—why, it made everyone think he had a heart attack. Of course I never told Gus what I'd done. He would never have gone along with murder."

We'd slowed down. "Get out of my way," we heard Honeycutt hiss. I could hear the sound of a loud tractor or some farm machinery. Whatever she was hissing at wasn't obeying her. She drove on at a slow speed.

Jigger leaned right next to my ear and whispered the softest whisper in history. "I left some wire clippers in here. They would cut these ties."

I nodded. As Jigger felt behind her back, the murderess continued. "Imagine my frustration when your grandmother told Gus that the Gillman Girls were moving back to restore the Cove." Her voice dripped with sarcasm. "Happy, happy, joy, joy!"

"The Gillman girls were *not* going to thwart my plans again. You know, I too tried out for Miss Apple Blossom—two years in a row. The first year, Ana got to be Queen. Then I lost to Gally the following year, and I had to be a Sour Apple—twice! Well, I wasn't going to let history repeat itself. I began planning how I would scare you away."

Jigger was groping behind her back, shifting, moving—obviously looking for the wire clippers. She wriggled quietly, so as not to arouse suspicion.

"It worked out quite nicely that Albert Hendrickson died in a car crash right before you arrived. Of course, no one ever checked to see if his brake line had been cut." She snorted again. "Bert had to be eliminated. I'm pretty sure he saw me spike Dickie's drink. After he made some insinuating comments, I decided he had to go. And you know, Bert and Dickie Gillman were old flames. I don't want that kind of thing going on in *my* town," she sneered.

Aha! I just realized that the love letters we had found in Uncle Dickie's cabin had been from Bert (Albert) Hendrickson!

"I had to convince Gus to help me move Bert's body. That wasn't easy. Nor was making him wear a hazmat suit, so we wouldn't leave behind any evidence. Gus sure complained about that. But he wasn't opposed to scaring you away. He too had dreams of being rich."

The SUV gathered speed.

"And Mr. Hendrickson was Gally Gillman's first love. She raved about him every day at lunch. The whole school knew how she felt." She paused. "I was kind of surprised she didn't run away with her tail between her legs when you found old Bert. I'd expected his decaying body to have more of an impact."

"My most ingenious idea was placing Dale and Doogie's cigarette butts by the dug-up grave. All *that* took was paying for a few drinks at the strip club. As soon as they left, I gathered their butts from the ashtray."

We slowed down and turned left. I could feel that we were now on a gravel road.

"Millie Kerkenbush's accident worked out nicely too—although at the time, I wasn't sure. When I approached her about buying her farm, you would have thought I'd tried to kill her beloved goat. She came after me, just like a demon from hell, swinging and stabbing a knitting needle at me like a sword. She had really become unhinged. I'd heard she had dementia but *that* was an understatement."

Jigger still hadn't found the clippers. I started searching for some-thing else that might work.

"Millie told me to get off her land, and she actually chased me to my car—well, as fast as someone who is hobbling can chase. Before she got to my vehicle, she toppled over. Just like that," Honeycutt snapped her fingers. "It must have been a massive coronary. Unfortunately, she fell right on her knitting needle, and it went straight into her eye."

I felt the SUV turn again. Another gravel road. Wherever she was taking us, it was going to be in the boonies—where nobody would ever find us.

"I thought I might as well make the most of it, so I left her corpse on your shoreline. Maybe I jabbed the knitting needle a little deeper into her brain—like all the way." Her laugh was sickening. "I mean, I didn't want the needle to wash away. It made such a good optic."

"Anyway, I thought another dead body would scare you. And then Gus burned down your cabin. He thought that would convince you to leave. And then I pulled the pin on your painters' scaffolding—I mean, we really couldn't have tried any harder," she reflected bitterly.

"But after Millie's accident, I could sense a change in Gus. He didn't believe that the old bat had a coronary. He got suspicious, and I couldn't trust him anymore to keep his mouth shut. It became very clear that I had to get rid of Gus."

I realized it was Gus and Honeycutt that I had overheard in the school hallway that night.

"So I met him at Lover's Leap, early in the morning, under the guise of making plans. Instead, I slit his throat—slit it a bit too much." Her hideous laugh made me shiver.

"I had to roll the windows down, so the car would sink quickly. It just wouldn't do to have some early morning fisherman find the car sinking slowly. I was worried his head would float away, once it hit the water, so I bound what was left of his head and neck to the headrest with plastic jump ropes. They were all I could find in my car—leftovers from when I'd made Easter baskets for my nieces. Then I pushed his car over the edge." She paused. "Yes, it made the nicest splash."

This woman was a stark raving lunatic. Jigger and I kept looking at each other, while we desperately searched for anything to free our hands.

Suddenly, the vehicle stopped. She turned off the engine. Everything was eerily quiet. "So now I have to get rid of you two, and then Ana and Gally, and finally I'll be home free. Let's get this over with." She left the van and shut the door.

Jigger whispered, "I found the clippers, but there's no time to cut the ties." I heard footsteps coming around to the back of the van. "Kick

234

her when she opens the door," Jigger whispered, as the rear hatch opened.

Honeycutt pulled off the tarp, and both Jigger and I struck out at her with our legs. She fell, but she was back on her feet by the time we were out of the vehicle. It wasn't so easy to maneuver when your hands were bound behind your back.

"Nice try, girls." She sneered, pointing her gun at us. "I see you got your duct tape off. Well, you can scream all you want, because no one is going to hear you."

I looked around. I actually recognized where we were. We were at the skin bin—the corn crib where Jigger had brought me on the day we went snowmobiling.

"Get inside the building," Honeycutt ordered.

Neither one of us moved.

"I am supposed to be serving beer at the Lion's tent right now. I have a tight schedule, so please don't be inconsiderate. Move!"

Honeycutt stepped closer, threatening us with her gun.

She really *was* going to kill us. I couldn't make any sense out of this. I'd survived the coronavirus *and* my parents' divorce *and* moving to Minnesota, just to die in the skin bin?

Jigger stepped closer to her, begging, "Please, Miss Honeycutt. I've always admired you. You know that." To my shock, Jigger head-butted Honeycutt in the face. *CRACK!*

Honeycutt passed out flat on her back, dropping her gun.

Jigger hopped on top of her, pinning Honeycutt to the ground. "Theo, hurry, before she comes to!" she cried. "Sit on her legs, with your back to me. I'll cut your ties off."

Quickly, I sat on Honeycutt's legs, with my back to Jigger. After a few seconds of struggling, she freed my wrists. Then I turned around, grabbed the clippers, and released her.

As soon as her hands were free, Jigger hauled off and punched Miss Honeycutt right in her nose. "Let's get out of here," she said, jumping up from the unconscious-looking Miss Honeycutt. Jigger peered down at her a second time before she grabbed my arm and pulled me towards the SUV.

Jigger hopped in on the driver's side, and I ran to the passenger side. Immediately, I rolled down the windows because it was like an oven inside. Jigger started the vehicle, revved the engine, and did a donut to turn around.

That's when I heard the shot.

❊ 46 ❊

Everything happened in slow motion. I've read there's a reason for that. It's some trick our ancestors developed to be able to handle danger—to slow down their perceptions, so they would have more time to survive. They considerately, though unknowingly, passed this down to us. But it's not like you can call on this helpful bit of DNA at any time. It only pops up when you're in a real crisis—like the one we were in now.

Everything looked like I was watching one of my films in slow motion. I heard the shot. It passed straight in front of me—for at that moment I'd been playing with the seat adjustment, and I accidentally dropped my seat into a horizontal position. The bullet flew right past me and struck Jigger in her shoulder.

I heard the thud. She cried out sharply, with a stunned expression on her face. Swearing, she slammed on the brakes, making me bang into the dash. She grabbed her shoulder, but I already saw the bloom of blood seeping through her jean jacket.

"Oh, my God, Jigger!" I cried. Her face had turned completely white. Frantically, I looked around for anything to absorb the blood. All I could find was a bunch of napkins from fast food restaurants, tucked in the side pocket of the door. I grabbed them and slipped them under her jacket, pressing hard on the wound. Even as I did so, I realized they weren't helping.

She drew a sharp breath. "It burns."

"Maybe I should…" but I didn't get to finish—because suddenly Miss Honeycutt threw herself onto the hood of the SUV!

I screamed!!!!!

She was like some sort of vampire succubus, clinging onto the vehicle with her evil kind of super-strength.

Jigger floored the accelerator, steering with her one good arm, back and forth in a zigzag pattern, trying to throw Honeycutt off. But Honeycutt kept a firm grip on the hood's cowl with one hand, while hanging onto the gun with the other.

"Why didn't I take the gun?" Jigger cried. "How stupid of me!"

Miss Honeycutt looked totally delusional, as she scowled at us through the windshield. I'm pretty sure Jigger had broken her former idol's nose because now it was twisted and bloody. Her lipstick was smeared, and her swollen eyes—where Jigger had planted that ferocious head-butt—were murderous!

Holding on with one hand, she kept trying to take aim at us, screaming that she would kill us. Desperately, I reached behind me for the roll of chicken wire. Leaning out the window, I shoved it towards her face.

"No, Theo! Get back in here," Jigger yelled, but I didn't stop. After a couple of jabs, I finally got a good poke to Honeycutt's left eye. Howling in pain, she reached for her eye and dropped the gun in the space between the windshield and the hood.

I ducked back in the SUV and started fiddling with the knobs, trying to figure out where the windshield wipers were. I turned on the window spray.

"Those are new wipers!" Honeycutt roared.

The idea that she would be worried about her windshield wipers at a time like this seemed so ludicrous that I almost started laughing. But my humor faded when I saw Honeycutt struggling to reach the gun. I leaned out the window and started ramming her again with the chicken wire.

Just then, Jigger turned off the gravel road and onto the highway. "A tractor is heading our way. Scream at him!" she cried.

I waved the roll of chicken wire in the air and cried, "HELP" to the passing tractor. The farmer stared at us like he'd seen an alien. "HELP!" I screamed at the top of my lungs, but we had passed him.

And in the meantime, Honeycutt had grabbed the gun!

I shoved the roll of wire into her face. Then I began whipping her over the head with it, but that wasn't as effective, so I went back to jabbing. I could feel that Jigger had picked up speed. Glancing at her,

I worried she was going to pass out. The blood had spread through her jacket at an alarming rate. I started hitting Honeycutt with a fury.

We were approaching town, and Hank the Beaver was coming into view.

"Down!" Jigger screamed. I slithered back inside the SUV, barely missing a bullet from Honeycutt. In a feverish attempt not to die, I grabbed her satchel from the floor and edged back out the window. Stretching—with one leg inside, and one leg out—I swung the satchel with all my might, bringing it straight down on her head.

She dropped the gun!

It hit the passing road with a sharp, metallic thud. Even though Honeycutt was still clinging to the hood, she didn't have the power to hurt us anymore. I glanced at Jigger with exhilaration, only to see her go limp over the wheel. I slid back in the vehicle, in hopes of grabbing the steering wheel.

But it was too late.

By the time I got to Jigger's side, I turned my head just in time to see us speeding straight into the newly refurbished Hank the Beaver, who was decked out in a lei of apple blossoms.

❈ 47 ❈

In the days that followed, the fine people of Black Beaver Bay spun many different versions of what had actually happened on that fateful spring afternoon. And of course, everyone felt their version was the honest-to-God's truth because they'd heard it from a very reliable source.

Some believed that the Sour Apples had kidnapped Jigger. For all the Sour Apples had turned into literal sour apples after not being crowned. There was much griping (just as there was every year) that the pageant had been rigged. The losers had wanted their revenge, the gossips said.

But there were those who held onto the belief that all the chaos was caused by the Miss Apple Blossom Curse. They claimed that the apple orchard outside of town was planted on top of an abandoned cemetery. The restless ghosts were angry that their plot had been disturbed, and that's why they wreaked havoc on the festival each year.

There was even one really elaborate conspiracy theory involving the Mafia! But all of these falsehoods came about because no one could believe Miss Honeycutt was guilty. Not until Deputy Pete went to arrest Honeycutt in her hospital room could the townsfolk accept the fact that their star citizen, their Episcopalian minister, their own town treasurer (and so much more) was really a split personality serial killer, who suffered from a grandiose delusional disorder. That last part was Grandma's armchair diagnosis.

But I believe that only Jigger and I *really* knew what had happened that afternoon. And Jigger had been half out of it when Honeycutt was driving us to the skin bin to be executed. Jigger hadn't heard the entirety of the confession and how very deranged the woman had sounded.

Yes, we were the only ones who realized how close we came to death. And I *had* believed I was going to die. I was fighting for my life when I attacked Honeycutt with that chicken wire. I worried it might be the end. And moments later, I was convinced it *was* the end, as we sped towards Hank the Beaver.

Again, everything went into slow motion. I grabbed the steering wheel and cranked it to the left, trying to avoid a head-on collision.

I'll never forget the look in Honeycutt's eyes as she stared at me through the windshield, screaming something indiscernible, looking like the craziest woman in the history of time.

I closed my eyes, waiting for impact. But it didn't come when I expected it.

No, I missed hitting Hank with the *front* of the SUV because I had turned it just enough to avoid him. But unfortunately, the *back* end of the SUV totally smashed into the solid wood statue and knocked it over.

Smashing into Hank lifted Honeycutt off the hood, but somehow, (maybe through her extra evil strength) she managed to hang on.

The force of the rear impact made the SUV swerve in the opposite direction. I tried countersteering, but the vehicle was out of control.

That's when Deputy Pete rounded the corner, and I accidentally T-boned his squad car, jolting the SUV to a shuddering stop. The last thing I saw, before I smashed my head into the dash and blacked out, was Honeycutt flying off the hood and sailing over the squad car.

When I came to, I was in the emergency room. Mom, Gally and Things 1 and 2 were standing by my bedside. It was such a relief to be alive and to see everyone that I started crying. And when I heard Jigger would be fine and had made it out of surgery, I couldn't stop crying— even though I rolled my eyeballs back in my head and squeezed my butt-cheeks together.

And I didn't kill Deputy Pete, but I will always think that *he* thinks I smashed into his squad car on purpose. And Honeycutt had landed on the roof of a porta potty that was set up for the festival. They say the flexible plastic of the portable bathroom roof was what saved her from being paralyzed. Although the person inside the porta potty had a horrendous shock when Honeycutt's body slammed down on the structure. That unfortunate person happened to be none other than Cyrus, the old man who had helped Billy the goat. He said it was a good thing he was in a restroom because it had scared the crap right out of him.

The night of the accident, I was kept in the hospital for observation. Josh came in to see how I was doing. He said Jigger and I had caused quite a stir, and we were now celebrities in town. People were claiming that national news outlets were picking up our story, and any day now, they'd see Jigger and me on CNN with Anderson Cooper.

Or so he said.

We joked around a bit before I came right out and asked him about the girl—the one I'd seen him with during the parade. I felt super foolish when I found out she was his cousin.

I was released from the hospital the following morning. Jigger was let out that night. Josh picked her up from the hospital, and then they swung by the Cove and picked me up. They said they had something they wanted to show me, so I crammed into the pickup cab with them while Thing 1 rode in the bed. I didn't know it at the time, but it would be my final outing with Thing 1.

Josh and Jigger drove us out to Nyes' apple orchard. It was after sunset, so I couldn't imagine what they were going to show us in the dark. They parked on the edge of the orchard, and we waited for at least twenty minutes before a rumbling semi pulled up. Jigger and Josh left their pickup. Thing 1 and I followed. I was getting very curious about what they wanted me to see.

They led us over a barbed wire fence and into the orchard. We watched from a distance as the door on the back end of the semi-trailer rose, and a stream of bees flew from their hives into the evening moonlight.

The bees were pollinating the orchard. It was a one-night nature show that was wonderful to watch. Jigger rolled out sleeping bags on the ground and played Mazzy Star's "Fade Into You." Because the moon was bright, we could clearly see the bees swarm and dive in delight, as they went from flower to flower. The scent of apple blossoms lay heavy in the air, and the whole orchard was alive with the sound of millions of buzzing bees. It was a magical evening—in more than one way.

About a week after the festival, a guy from the local newspaper interviewed Jigger and me. He took our picture and wrote up an article about the whole thing. We ended up being the top story on the front page. I bought three copies. I sent one to Lexi, and one to Grandma, and I pasted the last one in the new scrapbook I'd bought. I thought it would be good to carry on Grandma Fay's tradition, so I've taken it upon myself to be the new chronicler of Gillman's Cove. Because life here is definitely worth chronicling.

And I'm happy to say my camera was not broken when Honeycutt threw it on the floor. I've been working on compiling all my footage from Minnesota and making a mini-documentary. So far, my favorite part was doing the voice-overs for the beaver dioramas in Mabel's. Jigger and I kept cracking up and had a hard time getting through it.

We haven't done anything yet with the information about the titanium that we're supposedly sitting upon. Gally said we need to focus on opening up the Cove, and then afterwards, we can decide what to do. When I was looking up titanium, I was surprised it was used in so many products—from paint to powdered donuts. Lotion to lip balm. It's crazy.

Yes, the last couple of weeks have been a whirlwind. It feels like so much has changed—and a lot has. One of the hugest changes was in Mom.

After Honeycutt was arrested, Mom bloomed into a completely different person. I guess I hadn't realized how much stress she'd been under since we'd arrived and found Mr. Hendrickson's body. She told me that now that it was all over, she could finally feel I was safe. And that she and Gally were safe. She could relax. And she could deal with my father coming to visit. Even though she wasn't going to get back together with him, she was at peace with that. She hoped I would be too. I'm no expert, but I think Mom has reached closure.

Since our imminent danger was now over, Thing 1 and Thing 2 were no longer needed, and they moved on to their next assignment. I hugged Thing 1 when we said goodbye, and I apologized for not always being the easiest person to guard. He ruffled the top of my head, and gave me a wink, but true to form, he never said a word.

Right after the Things left, Gally started getting bookings for our upcoming Grand Reopening of the Cove. It has been really exciting to see the cabin reservations fill up. We're booked to capacity for our first weekend—which is tomorrow!!

Gally wondered if the newspaper story had made people curious about the Cove. Even if the Cove was now linked to grave robbing, arson, and murder, she said she'd take any publicity she could get. She has everything ready for tomorrow's incoming horde of fishermen. She has kept us soooo busy—right up until this afternoon.

Now was the calm before the proverbial storm.

So during this calm, Jigger and I were hanging out on the lake, lounging on extra large inflatable flotation mattresses. Jigger was lying back, totally chill. She still sported a gauze bandage over her shoulder wound. The gash on her head from Honeycutt had healed nicely. She wore oversized sunglasses.

"Why are you wearing sunglasses?" I asked. Although it was warm, the sky was overcast.

"Because it's going to be sunny," she answered. Hmm, even though this girl could do pretty much everything, I had some serious doubts about her ability to predict the weather.

Junk food wrappers and empty containers from her mom's cafe surrounded her. We'd both devoured double orders of the Trucker's Special. "I'm never dieting again." She sighed blissfully. "Never, ever." She had a fishing line tied to her big toe, which was attached to a bobber several feet away. I had to shake my head at her. She really loved fishing.

I was busy eating fried parmesan crisps, sharing them with Poppy, who rested on the float beside me. I was lapping up my idyllic setting, and I was in a bikini, with my skinny arms bare to God and all.

And I didn't care.

I wanted to focus on the right here and now. Thoughts of Memorial Day, which was just a couple of days away, and the impending doom that another holiday could bring, weren't welcome in my current state of tranquility. I mean, wasn't it enough that Jigger (and I) had survived the Miss Apple Blossom Curse?

My phone rang. It was Grandma.

"Hey, Grandma," I answered. Jigger lifted her sunglasses, obviously listening.

"Darling, I've got my tickets. Expect to see Aditya and me next Friday!" she said breathlessly. I could hear ice cubes clinking together from halfway around the world. She made me smile.

"I know your mom and Gally will be too busy to pick me up, so I've already gone ahead and reserved a limo to drive me from the airport."

I honestly didn't think Grandma had even talked to Mom or Gally about picking her up at the airport. I thought she reserved that limo so she could make a showy entrance for her homecoming to Black Beaver Bay. *I thought* she just wanted to impress a certain someone with whom she's had a long-standing feud.

(Speaking of Mrs. Banger, everyone was shocked at the speed of her recovery. The day after the parade, she was out of her wheelchair, and her bandages were off. One could barely see where she'd been burned. Mrs. Banger gave all the credit to the good Lord, and she repeated the story of her miracle to anyone who would listen.)

"Hey, Grandma," I hurried, because you never knew when she'd hang up, or we'd be disconnected. "I found some old journals in that suitcase of great-great-grandma Esme. I was wondering if you've ever seen them. One is green with a tree on the cover, and one is yellow with daises on the cover, and one is purple. Do they sound familiar to you?"

"I can't say as I recall." Grandma sounded thoughtful.

"I just started reading the green one today. Anyway, it's super interesting. I'll show them to you when you get here."

There was a crackle on the line.

"And tell your mother to finalize those funeral plans or…"

I never heard her "or else." The line dropped.

"I can't wait to meet her," said Jigger.

"I can't wait to see her again! I haven't seen her in—like, forever!" I lay flat on my back, trying to soak up the nonexistent rays.

And there was someone else I was growing anxious to see again—Dad. He'd be arriving in a month or so.

I really missed him.

I wondered what he would think of my new life. I was just happy that I *wanted* him in my life, because for a long time, I hadn't. And that hadn't been a good feeling.

Thinking of good feelings, I once again turned my thoughts to an incredibly good-feeling moment, which I'd recently experienced. If you can't guess, I'm happy to inform you that I finally had my first kiss!

And I've been drifting along on a cloud ever since. It wasn't like anything I had imagined. It was sooo unexpected, and yet it turned out to be fantastic—an absolutely fireworks-worthy moment. My heart actually turned over, and I had a tingling in the pit of my stomach. I felt such a rush through me that…

Jigger interrupted my lovely memory.

"Hey, Sleeping Beauty, wake up." She splashed water on me. Just then, the sun broke through the stubborn cloud mass, beating down on us. Jigger played an old Beatles song, "Here Comes the Sun," singing along in her perfect, crystal voice.

When the song ended, Jigger said, "Oh, I forgot to tell you something."

"Oh yeah, what's that?"

"The enrollment form for next year's Miss Apple Blossom pageant came out this morning. I signed you up."